ABOUT THE AUTHOR

Brought up in Lincolnshire, Judith Thomson studied Art in
Leicester before moving to Sussex where she still lives. She is
passionate about the seventeenth century and has gained much
inspiration from visits to Paris and Versailles. In her spare time
she enjoys painting, scuba diving and boating. She is the author
of four previous Philip Devalle novels:- 'Designs of a Gentleman:
The Early Years', 'Designs of Gentleman: The Darker Years',
'High Heatherton' and 'The Orange Autumn'.

Follow her on:-
Judiththomsonsite.wordpress.com
Judiththomsonblog.wordpress.com
and on Twitter @JudithThomson14

The Distant Hills

Judith Thomson

Matador
9 Priory Business Park,
Wistow Road, Kibworth Beauchamp,
Leicestershire. LE8 0RX
Tel: (+44) 116 279 2299
Fax: (+44) 116 279 2277
Email: books@troubador.co.uk
Web: www.troubador.co.uk/matador

ISBN 978 1788034 562

British Library Cataloguing in Publication Data.
A catalogue record for this book is available from the British Library.

Printed and bound by CPI Group (UK) Ltd, Croydon, CR0 4YY
Typeset in 11pt Bembo by Troubador Publishing Ltd, Leicester, UK

Matador is an imprint of Troubador Publishing Ltd

PROLOGUE

King Louis smiled as his cousin James, the former King of England, took his leave of him at Saint-Germain.

Louis had given him sanctuary after James had lost his throne to William of Orange. He had also given him the palace of Saint-Germain, but it had never been Louis' intention to allow James to become too settled there. Waiting for James at Brest would be ten ships loaded with everything he needed to equip the army that the Earl of Tyrconnel had raised on his behalf in Ireland, along with a hundred French officers and the promise of a thousand livres a month to pay his men.

James' flight from England, and the events which led up to it, had caused him to be overcome with a great lethargy. Left to his own devices, James Stuart would have been content to stay in France and divide his time between hunting and attending mass, but Louis had very different plans for him. Far better for James to be at the head of his troops in Ireland harassing King William, who had been Louis' own enemy for so many years!

James thanked him dutifully, but Louis had two more gifts for him. He first summoned the attendant who carried his own cuirass and presented this to James and then unbuckled the sword he was wearing and gave that to him as well.

It was a magnificent gesture, theatrical yet meaningful too, for it demonstrated that with his own arms, as well his money, Louis was protecting James' interests.

He watched him out of sight then turned to his brother, who stood beside him.

"Well, Monsieur, I believe I have supplied our cousin with sufficient means to annoy King William for a while!"

1689

ONE

༄

Philip Devalle, the Duke of Southwick, looked about him at the glittering gathering assembled to celebrate the Coronation of England's new King and Queen.

He thought King William looked weary. It had been a long day, for the royal couple had left Whitehall palace at 7 o'clock in the morning. It was also obvious, from William's expression, that this banquet in Westminster Hall was as distasteful to him as the long ceremony had been in the draughty Abbey, with the weight of the crown upon his head.

Another reason for his lack of enthusiasm, Philip suspected, was that today, of all days, word had reached London of James Stuart's arrival in Ireland!

That news had been quite a blow to Philip also, and on a purely personal level. As an army officer, he feared that he was almost certain to be dispatched there to fight him and, from what he had heard, Ireland was a barbaric place.

There was a further dilemma for him too. He was no supporter of James but he was half-French and he had once fought in the French army himself against the Dutch. To refuse to go to Ireland would cast doubts upon his loyalties now that England had a Dutch King, whilst to fight against his mother's countrymen was unthinkable. It was all very difficult.

His brother in law, Giles, appeared by his side and Philip was concerned to see how pale he was.

"You look dead upon your feet," Philip said frankly.

Giles was auburn-haired and had a naturally fair skin, but

there was almost a transparency about his features now and there were dark shadows beneath his eyes. He would have been handsome but for the jagged scar which ran down the length of his left cheek. Those who knew him well scarcely saw that anymore, which was not to say that Giles himself had ever become reconciled to it.

"I've had a difficult week preparing William for this day." Giles was one of the King's aides. "You don't know how he's dreaded it."

"I can guess, and from the look upon his face he hates every minute. I have never heard of a monarch who was so averse to displaying himself to his subjects, or," he added, "of one who was so uninteresting when he did!"

"He is no showman," Giles was forced to agree, "and that is where he fails in your eyes."

"Not only in mine, Giles." Philip himself was very much a showman and perfectly aware of the impact he was making on the others present. His outfit for the day was one of white brocade, trimmed with gold lace, and there were no others to rival it. "There is more to kingship that raising taxation and ordering the clergy to preach against the profanation of the Lords' day," he said. "He even refused to perform the customary ceremony of touching for scrofula."

The touch of a king upon the ulcerated swellings on a sufferer's face and neck was traditionally thought to cure Scrofula, or King's Evil, as it was sometimes known.

"I tried to persuade him to that but he regards it as superstitious nonsense."

"Which it may be, but it was expected of him on Coronation Day," Philip said. "Would it have killed him to have put on a show just this once? He never even entertains or dines in public. If he wants to make the people love him he must show himself to them a little more often."

"But he can't," Giles said. "This foul London air is affecting him badly. His asthma grows much worse when he is forced to talk. Even Doctor Radcliffe cannot cure him. Some nights, after he has been forced to meet a great many people, he will cough and bring up so much phlegm that sometimes I fear he will not draw his next breath."

"And I suppose it is you who sits up half the night to minister to him. You are not his servant, Giles. I don't like to see you looking so ill."

Giles smiled faintly. "Are you worrying over me? You never have before."

"I have never needed to before. You used to be such a selfish little rat when you were with me!" Philip had once been Giles' patron and had introduced him to society, for which Giles owed him a great deal.

"What else can I do?" Giles said. "He has come to depend on me."

"The Duke of Monmouth depended on you too," Philip reminded him. "Your loyalty to him was nearly the death of you."

Giles had supported Monmouth's ill-fated rebellion a few years before, and had narrowly escaped perishing on the scaffold alongside him.

"But surely my loyalty to William can only bring me glory," Giles argued.

Indeed, it already had. William had made Giles, who did not come from a noble family, the Earl of Wimborne.

"Perhaps," Philip allowed, "but I already hear rumblings of discontent in the city. Some even say they would welcome James back, if only he would turn Protestant."

"Surely not!" Giles looked angry. "It's so unfair. What more can the poor man give them but his health and strength? He has rescued them from oppression and now he governs well, and wisely. How can they be so ungrateful?"

Philip shrugged. "You know the 'Mobile Vulgus', Giles." Philip, who had been a rebel through two Stuart reigns, knew them well enough, for that was the name by which the Whigs referred to the Londoners, who they had incited to riot in the streets in more turbulent times. "You should never underestimate them, or the power they can wield."

"What of you, are you still loyal to him?" Giles said.

"Of course I am. There's no advantage to me whatsoever in the return of James Stuart, but I wish William did not cast such an air of gloom over everything. If it were not for the fact that Betty Villiers has followed him from Holland I would sometimes doubt the man was even human!"

"Oh, you would approve of his having a mistress!"

Since his own good looks had been spoiled Giles was no longer the womaniser he had once been, although he had taken a wife, a pretty Frenchwoman, who adored him, and to whom he was most solicitous, particularly now that she was carrying their first child. He sought her out in the crowd and frowned. "Marianne looks tired, don't you think? The banquet is not due to finish until 10 o'clock so I believe I ought to ask the King's permission for us to retire early."

"If you say so." Philip knew it made little difference what he thought. If Giles had decided that Marianne should withdraw from the company then Marianne would withdraw!

Left to himself again, Philip glanced around for his own wife, Theresa, and spotted her conversing with Queen Mary.

Theresa was small and slim, like her brother. She had vivid red hair, much brighter than his, but she had the same slightly slanting grey eyes, although hers usually sparkled with humour. She could not truly be called a beauty, but her elfin features were appealing and there was a freshness about her which Philip always found contrasted wonderfully with some of the painted ladies of the Court. She was dressed to match Philip for this grand occasion, all in white brocade with gold lace about her dainty shoulders and a gold silk cord around her tiny waist, Philip smiled despairingly to see her bending down, in all her finery, to stroke one of Queen

Mary's little pug dogs, who were scampering everywhere amongst the people, orange bows adorning their collars.

His attentions were soon taken up elsewhere. Philip was rarely left alone at social functions, as he was considered a person it was good to be seen talking with, but his years at Court had taught him to observe what went on around him at all times and he could not help but notice that the Marquis d'Arsay was watching as Giles escorted Marianne from the Hall. He was intrigued to see that d'Arsay himself left a few minutes later.

Philip had been introduced to the Marquis and knew him as a French Huguenot who had refused to convert to the Catholic faith and who had escaped from France at the time when King Louis was purging the country of Protestants. There were many others like him, seeking sanctuary in Protestant countries, and Philip had never paid him any particular attention. Until now.

Giles had never paid him much attention either, although Marianne occasionally spoke with him, so he was surprised, and not all that pleased when d'Arsay visited them shortly after he and Marianne arrived back at Whitehall.

"The Marquis claims to be here upon a matter of great importance to you, master," Ahmed, Giles' Negro servant, explained.

"A matter so important it cannot possibly wait until the morning?" Giles was quite exhausted and not at all in the mood for visitors.

"He says he will be returning to France tomorrow."

"Will he indeed?" That in itself was enough to pique Giles' curiosity. "Then, perhaps, the Marquis is not quite what he pretends to be, though I cannot imagine what he wants with me. You'd better show him in, I suppose."

Ahmed did so and then remained in the room, for he rarely left Giles' side.

D'Arsay bowed. "Your pardon, my Lord Wimborne, for calling at such a late hour. In view of the news concerning King

James and the awkwardness it may soon cause between our two countries I have decided to leave England in the morning, which means that my business with you must be discussed tonight."

"I was not aware that we had any business," Giles said coldly.

"Nor was I until I received a letter from the Marquis de Louvois."

Giles eyes narrowed. Louvois was the French Minister of War. "You are in communication with Louvois? I understood you fled from France to escape his cruelties."

Louvois was responsible for the infamous dragonnades that had killed and tortured the Huguenots who refused to convert.

"Everyone thinks that," d'Arsay said, "but it is not the truth."

"The truth, I suppose, is that you are French spy," Giles said angrily. "I ought to kill you here and now."

"That would not be wise," d'Arsay warned, on his guard all the same for Ahmed had advanced a step, his hand upon the handle of the knife he wore at his belt. "You see Louvois has a service he would have you perform for him."

Giles frowned. He had never had any dealings with Louvois. He had only met him whilst he had been visiting King Louis' brother, Monsieur, who, in common with most people, disliked the man and had as little to do with him as possible.

Giles moved closer to Marianne, who was watching them with frightened eyes. He knew what was going through her mind, for Marianne herself had been a Catholic convert, although she had reverted back to her Protestant faith when she left France to be with Giles. The very mention of Louvois' name was enough to fill her with dread, for his soldiers had marched her and the other Huguenots of her village into a Catholic church and forced them at musket point to convert. Those who had refused had been taken away, never to be seen again.

Giles pressed her hand reassuringly. "Are you certain you want me and not my brother-in-law, d'Arsay? He is better known to Louvois than I."

"No, no, it is you I want, and you must not be so modest, my Lord. Louvois knows a great deal about you," d'Arsay said with a smile, "Firstly let me say that the fates have been kind to you, El Oued."

Giles stiffened. It had been a long while since anyone had called him by that name.

"Oh, I know a great many things about you, Lord Wimborne," d'Arsay assured him. "For instance, I know that after the Duke of Monmouth lost the battle at Sedgemoor you managed to escape to France. I also know that, despite your friendship with Monsieur, King Louis refused to give you sanctuary. The next that was heard of you was when you were driving African slaves across the desert in the pay of Moulay Ismail, the Sultan of Morocco."

"That is no secret," Giles said disdainfully. In fact, it was the Moroccans who had given him the name of El Oued. It meant, in their language, 'the river', which was how they had likened the twisting scar which ran down Giles' cheek.

"But it is not so commonly known that, before you left the royal city of Meknes, you stole a quantity of gold and jewels from the Sultan's slave master, Suliman Bey. Monsieur de Louvois ascertained this from Suliman Bey himself when the Moroccan visited Versailles last year."

"What Suliman Bey probably did not see fit to tell Louvois was that the reason I helped myself to his treasure was that he had refused to pay me what I was owed," Giles said tartly.

"Probably not," d'Arsay agreed, "but Louvois suspects that these stolen goods were the very riches which you later contributed to help finance King William's expedition to England, and he wondered how pleased your new King would be to learn the origin of your generous donation to his cause."

"Is there much more of this?" Giles asked him in a bored tone that concealed the discomfiture he was starting to feel. There were many instances from his past that it was not convenient to recall now that he was in a position of importance, as Louvois would have known. William was no Charles Stuart. Charles had once rewarded a pirate with the governorship of Jamaica and pardoned, for his boldness, a thief caught stealing the crown jewels, but William was not a frivolous man. He required respectability and honesty from those he chose to place in positions of trust.

"Only one more thing, my Lord, but that, perhaps, the most significant of all. "When you left Morocco so hastily you took with you two slaves. One was a Negro," d'Arsay glanced at Ahmed, who still hovered menacingly over him. "The other was a Frenchwoman who had been captured by the Moroccan pirates when they made one of their raids on Marseilles." D'Arsay turned his attention now to Marianne. "That former slave is now your countess. She is not, however, your wife."

Marianne gasped. No-one, not even Philip and Theresa, knew that.

"Why do you say so?" Giles asked him in a tense voice.

"I say so because I know she is still married to a Frenchman, living in the village of Cassis. Her husband has never agreed to divorce her so if she has, indeed, married you, my Lord, then she is guilty of bigamy and must face the penalty of the law for that crime. If she has not married you then the child she is expecting must be considered a bastard and not eligible to inherit your estate or bear your name."

"We are not married," Giles said resignedly. He had hoped the truth would never come out but, now that it had, most of all he wished to remove any suspicion of guilt from Marianne. "All is as Louvois suspects."

"Now I come to the true purpose of my visit, Lord Wimborne. Since the Marquis de Louvois is sure there are certain facts which you would rather not have made public knowledge, he offers you the opportunity to ensure his silence by performing a small service for him."

"What service?" Giles demanded irritably. He knew that he could not win on this occasion, and he was a poor loser.

"You will be informed of that in due course but, whatever it is, my Lord, I do not believe you are in any position to refuse him."

Giles looked at Marianne, her belly swollen with the child that she was carrying, and then looked around at the rich finery he had accumulated as a reward for being highly thought of by King William

"No," he said bitterly, "nor do I."

The news that James had commenced his campaign in Ireland was received with satisfaction by King Louis but Louvois was not optimistic.

"This Ireland is a wild, unruly place I understand. He will never gain control of it in my opinion, not if he is fighting against the likes of Schomberg and Philip Devalle, who it is reckoned will be over there before long."

Schomberg was now William's General in Ireland but he had once fought in the French army. A Protestant, he had resigned his commission at the time of the persecution of the Huguenots, even though he had been offered special concessions to remain in France. Louis might have lost Schomberg but Philip was quite another matter.

"Philip would never turn his hand against me," he said. "He is half-French, after all."

"He must obey King William now." Louvois was too tactful to remind Louis that Philip's family upon his mother's side were Protestants and had nearly all perished during the purge of the Huguenots from Languedoc.

"He has never served a monarch so well as he has served me and he will serve me again, mark my words."

Louvois rarely disagreed with his royal master, indeed if he had he might not have raised himself from a humble bourgeois background to the important post of War Minister, but he looked dubious now. "Surely, your Majesty, he no longer has any cause to serve you since he is esteemed so highly by King William."

"Philip will always be my man." Louis said confidently. "We understand each other, he and I. However, it may be advisable to ensure his loyalty all the same."

"And how does your Majesty propose to do that?" Louvois said. "You can hardly invite him to France."

"No, I can't." Louis said thoughtfully, "but there are others who can."

He left Louvois abruptly and made his way to the Diana drawing room, where his brother, Monsieur, was playing billiards with Armand, the Comte de Rennes, although the thoughts of both of them were more upon the news from Ireland than their game.

Armand was in his forties with greying hair and a fine, aristocratic face. He still looked every inch the soldier he once had been, and would be still if a bullet had not injured his knee. Now the former Colonel was employed in supervising the rooting out of the last Huguenot rebels in the various regions. It was not a job that he enjoyed in the least and he would have much preferred to have accompanied James.

The same thoughts were passing through Monsieur's mind.

At first sight Monsieur was anything but a military man. His almost girlish prettiness was enhanced by the touch of rouge that he wore and the bows which decorated his dark ringlets. Exquisitely dressed, with his jewelled buttons and his high-heeled shoes, Monsieur looked decidedly effeminate and yet he, too, had been a soldier in his youth. His had been a brief career. He was acclaimed a hero after he distinguished himself during the French campaign in Flanders and he became too popular with the people for Louis' liking. Their uncle had made many attempts to take the throne from their father and Louis intended to make sure he did not have to spend his own reign fighting rebels who supported his brother. Although he loved him dearly, he had forbidden Monsieur to ever hold a position of any importance again.

Over the years Monsieur had adjusted perfectly to his life of aimless frippery. His role at Court was to be decorative, to organise balls, ballets and receptions, and this he did to perfection. As time went on he fell in and out of love with handsome young men and became so obsessed with his own appearance that he was a figure of fun to the less respectful, but Armand was not amongst these. He had fought alongside Monsieur at the Siege of Mons and he knew that, despite what most thought of him, Monsieur had qualities of leadership and courage that might have made this First Gentleman of France a great man.

Armand glanced across at him now. "I think you are probably envying your cousin James nearly as much as I am, Monsieur."

Monsieur agreed with a sigh. It was not often he allowed himself to ponder on what might have been.

Louis noticed his wistful expression as soon as he entered the room. "What's wrong?" he asked, concerned, for he was genuinely fond of his younger brother and did all he could to please him.

Armand shot Monsieur a warning look, for Louis would have been upset to learn the reason for his sadness.

"Nothing exciting ever happens here lately," Monsieur said instead, for it was part of the truth.

Louis had, for some time, been under the influence of the religious Madame de Maintenon. Since that had happened he had become a far more serious person and his Court was no longer the place of fun it once had been. For such as Monsieur, whose life consisted mainly of social gatherings, this was a great loss.

Louis looked at his brother sympathetically. "I fear Versailles is too quiet a place for you, lately, Monsieur. Perhaps you could get together with some old friends," he suggested. "That might cheer you up."

"Perhaps," Monsieur said, brightening a little at the thought. He still entertained quite lavishly at the Palais Royale, his own home, in Paris. "Who would I invite?"

Louis appeared to think for a moment. Armand watched him closely, wondering exactly what he was planning.

"I know who you have not seen for a very long while," Louis said, as if struck by a sudden inspiration. "What about Philip? You always enjoyed his company."

Armand had the highest regard for Louis' shrewdness and he saw immediately what he was up to. Philip was an experienced soldier who commanded an enormous following in England and he could pose a real threat to James' expedition. He was also one of Monsieur's favourites, even though he had never returned the Frenchman's devotion!

Monsieur looked elated for a moment and then his face fell. "But he won't come."

Louis looked surprised. "Won't come to see you, one of his dearest friends? Why do you say so?"

"How would it look for him to be visiting the brother of King William's greatest enemy? It would be the ruin of him."

"I'd not considered that." Louis looked directly at Armand.

Armand coughed discreetly. He had been associated with the Court for long enough to know when he should speak and when he should not, and he had followed Louis' drift closely enough to know what was expected of him on this occasion.

"Perhaps your Majesty will allow me to make a suggestion? It may be that, since Philip is a friend of mine also, I could invite him to La Fresnaye." La Fresnaye was Armand's estate in Brittany. "Then, if Monsieur would be gracious enough to honour my wife and I with a visit, he could meet Philip there."

Louis smiled. "What an excellent suggestion."

Monsieur clapped his hands delightedly. "When will you write to him?"

"As soon as you wish, Monsieur although, regrettably, I am not due to return to La Fresnaye for two months," Armand said pointedly.

Whilst it was not an onerous service that he was being put upon to perform for the King, Armand saw no reason why there should not be some advantage in it for him too and the greatest benefit Louis could bestow upon him was the opportunity to spend extra time with his wife at La Fresnaye.

"I believe it might be possible for you to return sooner than that," Louis told him, understanding perfectly. "In fact, if you wish, you might travel to Brittany tomorrow."

Armand bowed. "That is most gracious of your Majesty. I will send a letter to Philip without delay."

TWO

Philip was pleased, and somewhat surprised, when his servant, Thomas, handed him Armand's letter. In his eventful life he had learned to take very little, and very few, at face value, but his old army comrade was one of the handful of men he truly considered to be his friend.

When he had broken the seal of the package he saw that it contained two letters, the reason for which soon became clear. One was a simple invitation to a friend, which might be shown to King William to demonstrate the innocence of Philip's desire to travel to a country that might soon be England's enemy. The other outlined Louis' part in the proposal.

Philip smiled when he had read them both. "So, Armand, you have my interests at heart, as ever."

The letters had given him a great deal to think about. It would certainly be good to have a change of scene for a while, he thought, looking around the small apartment in which he and Theresa resided when they were at Whitehall. Philip had spent a great deal of his life in the palace, for he had come to Court at an early age. In King Charles' day it had seemed to be the centre of the whole world but now it had lost a great deal of its importance. William, hating London as he did, was favouring Hampton Court. Whitehall had an aimlessness about it now, like some discarded relic from a more colourful age, and Philip was beginning to feel the same!

Theresa charged in a moment later. Philip raised an eyebrow but said nothing as she slammed the door behind her.

"That woman is insufferable!" She picked up an orange from the bowl upon the table and threw it at the wall with such force that the skin broke and sticky juice trickled down. "How dare she speak to me like that?"

Another piece of fruit hurtled across the room, closely followed by a cushion.

Philip sat down on the couch and watched her impassively. Theresa had a hot temper but was generally over her passion very quickly and he had always reckoned it best to let her get it out of her system by hurling inanimate objects. So long as they were not being hurled at him, of course!

"She is not to be endured with her superior ways." Theresa flung herself down upon the couch beside him, her little fists clenched tight. "Who does she think she is when her husband is no more than a turncoat?"

"Sarah Churchill?" Philip guessed, recognising the description, for the haughty Sarah was married to John Churchill, who had been King James' favourite until, seeing where his best advantage lay, he had declared himself for William.

"Yes, Sarah Churchill, your pardon, 'Countess' Sarah Churchill, as she is constantly reminding me." Churchill had recently been created Earl of Marlborough. "Well I'm a duchess now and she shall not crow over me, even though I was born 'nothing better than a squire's daughter', as she says."

"Is that her game? Poor Tess." Philip put an arm around her. "She always was a bitch. Take no notice of her."

"That's alright for you to say." Theresa laid her head upon his shoulder. "I must put up with her all the time, and hear her boasting that her friendship with Princess Anne will one day make her mightier than the lot of us."

"Unfortunately, I fear that she may be right there," Philip said ruefully. In the twelve years since they had been wed William and Mary had been unable to produce an heir and Anne, Mary's younger sister, was next in line to the throne. "Let's hope the English air will be beneficial to the Queen's fertility but, if not, then it may well be Anne who succeeds her and then that termagant, Sarah, will truly come into her own, and so will her blasted husband."

Philip had known John Churchill for years and never liked him. They had been rivals always, both favourites of Charles' mistress, the Countess of Castelmaine, both soldiers in France and both dependent upon their looks and shrewdness to make their fortunes. As James' protégé, Churchill had risen in the last reign. It was Philip's turn now, but for how long?

He passed Theresa the letters Armand had sent him, hoping to lighten her mood, but it had quite the opposite effect.

"You won't go, will you?" she said anxiously, when she had read them.

"Why ever not?"

"Why ever not?" she repeated. "Have you not had your fill of scheming and deceit? For the first time in your life you are secure, valued by a king you helped to place upon the throne. You have a dukedom and a rich estate. You need want for nothing. Surely you will not risk all that upon some mischievous whim to see Monsieur again."

"There's more to it than that, as well you know. Since Louis put the idea into Monsieur's head then it is he who wants to see me and I am curious as to why."

"But you no longer serve the King of France, nor can you ever do so again," Theresa said. "You belong to William now, you need no other master."

"At present. The difference between us, sweetheart, is that you see only the pretty sunlit plains that stretch before you whilst I see the distant hills beyond! William is a sick man. That is obvious enough. What happens to us when he dies and leaves no heir? The Churchills and their kind rise to glory, that's what. We'll not flourish under Anne's reign, for she has never liked me much, and her precious friend, Sarah, will have already poisoned her mind against you."

Theresa sighed disconsolately. "For years, it seems, we have had to fight for our survival. Does it never end?"

"Not for the likes of you and me, my darling, but we must look to the future, not fear it."

"How can you say that when it was once foretold that you would end your days in prison?"Theresa said quietly.

Since that prediction had been made by a fortune teller Philip had been imprisoned both in the Bastille and in the Tower of London, where he had been held for plotting against King Charles.That time it had seemed certain he would lose his head and make the prophesy come true but once again he had triumphed, despite the best efforts of his enemies to destroy him.

He was convinced he always would.

"What harm would it do to hear what Louis has to say,Tess?"

"It will do a great deal of harm if by doing so you endanger everything you have worked so hard for here in England," Theresa said. "If King William, should become suspicious of your motives he would never trust you again, then the Churchills would indeed have cause to crow, and all the others who long to see you fall from grace.Whatever lies ahead for us we both must face in due course. For the moment we are safe and you would be a fool to hazard everything for King Louis, especially after he treated you so badly."

"It was Louis' friendship that protected us and our property under King James' reign," Philip reminded her. "Never forget that."

"Nor will I forget that he dealt with you no better than he did the French Protestants. You served him well, fought in his army risking your life to increase his territories and glory, yet he forced you to sell your Paris house and barred you from appearing at his Court."

"He had little choice in that," Philip said. "He could hardly make me exempt from his new laws against the Huguenots. Besides, I never really lost my house, since Monsieur bought it from me and allows me to rent it back from him. And there's another thing," he added craftily, "I owe a debt of gratitude to Monsieur for that. It would be churlish to refuse this invitation."

"It would be madness to accept it." Theresa flashed back. "If you won't think of yourself then think about your daughter. Have you stopped to consider her position should you lose the favour of King William?"

"That's unfair." Philip doted upon their six-year-old daughter, Madeleine. "It is for her future that I plan."

"But her future lies here, not in France. High Heatherton is her future." High Heatherton was Philip, family home. "That is all we need to fight for."

"Maudie's birthright is more than a Sussex estate," Philip said emphatically. "She must have a place at Court and a husband in a position of power and standing and, by God, she shall have all that, no matter what I must do to gain it for her."

On the matter of their daughter's prospects they could never agree. Theresa, with her modest upbringing, desired no more than to see her happy and loved by a good-hearted man, but Philip had very definite views as to how her life should be shaped. He had sired several bastards in his time and never given a thought to any of them, however Madeleine, the only child, so far, of his marriage was precious to him, almost as precious as his maddeningly practical little wife.

"You claim to be doing this for Maudie's sake?" Theresa leapt to her feet. "Nonsense! You actually want to go, that's clear enough, and it's not to see Armand or poor, besotted Monsieur. You have lived a life of intrigue for so long that you cannot enjoy a calm existence. You are bored and that's the truth of it, I don't doubt."

It was a good deal of the truth, though Philip did not want to admit it. "I would like to see Louis again," he confessed, "but I promise that I will do nothing rash."

"Of course you will, and don't say 'trust me' or I shall scream,"

Theresa warned. "You have fobbed me off with that too many times. You're not going and that's an end to it."

Philip knew that Theresa was capable of being very stubborn when she felt passionately about something, almost as stubborn as himself, and he recognised, only too well, the determined expression on her face now.

There was more than one way to approach the problem, however!

"Very well, Tess, I won't go."

Theresa eyed him suspiciously. "You mean you think I'm right?"

"Of course you're right, my darling, absolutely right. I must not let my desire for excitement override my good sense. My place is at King William's side, although I think perhaps that you might feel better for a short absence from Court."

"There is only one place I would like to be," Theresa said, "and that is Heatherton."

"That is what I have in mind."

"You mean I can go home for a while?" Theresa's face lit at the thought. "I can spend some time with Maudie?"

In one respect of their daughter's upbringing Theresa had managed to have her way. Philip had wanted the child at Court with them but Theresa, herself a country girl, had insisted that her precious early years should be enjoyed at High Heatherton, with space and freedom and healthy country air, away from the stench of the city streets and the restrictions of court life. It was a hollow victory for Theresa, nonetheless, for it meant she rarely saw her.

"I see no reason why you couldn't spend a month there if you wished," Philip told her. "It would do you good. Queen Mary appears to be planning nothing more thrilling than searching for a new house, so I am sure she will be able to manage without you for a while. I shall speak with her, for she can't resist my winning ways!"

Theresa laughed. "That's true enough. She blushes and grows quite nervous whenever you are near. You overwhelm the poor woman."

"I overwhelm most women," Philip teased her. "Why is it that I don't overwhelm you?"

"Oh, you do," she assured him, putting her hands upon his shoulders, "but I know you so much better than the rest. I know all your strengths and your weaknesses and I know, too, that despite the image you allow the world to see you are, at heart, an honourable man."

"I am nothing of the kind," he said, kissing her. "You see in me exactly what you wish to see."

"I see the man I love, for all his faults," she said simply, "and the father of my child."

"A child who had better not be turned into a savage by her mother's insistence that she be brought up like a peasant," he said severely.

Theresa giggled. "You spent your childhood years at Heatherton and you were not turned into a savage."

"But I was in the care of my mother's maid," Philip reminded her. His French mother had died when he was a baby.

"Well Maudie is in the care of my maid."

"That is not the same thing at all. Nanon had proper ideas of how the children of gentle-folk should behave. Mistress Bet probably has her running barefoot and climbing trees by now!"

"You're going to France after all?" Philip's servant, Thomas, stared at him.

"Yes, Thomas, that is why I asked you to pack my trunk," Philip said patiently.

"But you told the mistress that you would not be going."

"That's right, I did."

"You promised her in fact."

"I may have promised," Philip allowed.

"You certainly did. How could you do this to her?" Thomas was far more than a servant to Philip and he was permitted more than a servant's usual license. When Thomas was twelve years old, and an orphan of the streets, Philip had taken him into his household, after protecting him from a sergeant who was trying to arrest him for cutting a purse. Now in his twenties, Thomas had proved himself to be a brave and loyal servant to the master he adored and Philip thought the world of him. That was not to say he intended to justify his actions to Thomas or anyone else.

"She is far happier imagining that I am still in London," he said.

"But you can't let her go on thinking that, my Lord."

"Why not?"

"Well, because it isn't true."

"Truth is an adaptable thing, do you not think so, Thomas?"

Thomas shook his head. "Not really, no."

"Then let me put it to you another way. Which do you think would distress her most, to know that I am going to France against her will or to discover it later, when all has come out well?"

"You could always turn matters around to suit yourself," Thomas grumbled, beginning to pack Philip's trunk all the same. "I'll wager you had this in mind all along, before she even left for Heatherton. I don't know how you could ever lie to her. I couldn't, she has eyes which catch you out."

"Don't look into them, then," Philip said simply, "that's the best. Now stop nagging me, there's a good fellow or I'll leave you behind."

"I'd like to see you try! What clothes will you be needing?"

"Something decorative. I must impress Monsieur." Philip watched the servant folding one of his cravats. It was made of the finest Genoa lace, exquisite and expensive, and Philip knew that

Thomas had begun to hanker for such things. As the personal servant of a duke he had become a person of some importance in his own right and it was natural that he wanted to dress the part. "You can have that one," Philip told him.

"Truly?" Thomas rushed to the mirror and held the cravat up to his throat. He was a pleasant looking young man, despite the roughness on his cheeks left by the smallpox he had suffered the previous year. "Oh, thank you, my Lord. Wait until the Duchess of Dorset's pretty maid sees me in this!"

Philip watched him fondly. It was worth the loss of one of his favourite cravats to see the pleasure on Thomas' face. "Don't wear yourself out wenching," he warned him. "We'll be travelling in a day or two if all goes well. Now I have to go and deal with Giles, and I fancy," he added under his breath, "that a lace cravat will not buy my peace with him."

Philip was right. His brother-in-law regarded him in horror when he heard of his plans.

"I thought Theresa had talked you out of this madness."

"She thought she had as well. I am not here for a lecture upon my treatment of your sister, Giles. I have already endured that from Thomas. What I want from you is your assistance. King William turns to you for advice on everything and I desire you to advise him to let me go upon this visit."

"Why should I? I am in complete agreement with Theresa."

"The difference is that you can make it impossible for me to go. One cautionary word from you and William will refuse. I am at your mercy, Giles."

He smiled at him winningly, but it was apparent that Giles was in no mood for playing games and Philip suspected that he might have spent another sleepless night at the King's side. It did not occur to him that Giles might have problems of his own which, coupled with William's incessant demands, were placing an almost unbearable strain upon his nerves.

"I don't know what you're planning," Giles said irritably,

"nor do I desire to know, but surely you must see that any disgrace you bring upon yourself will reflect upon me and jeopardise the position I have worked so hard to attain at William's side."

Philip gave him a wry look. In his opinion, no rewards could be worth the sacrificing of personal liberty that Giles was forced to endure in order to be King William's aide. "I assure you that I have no intention of jeopardising the position of either of us, Giles. Credit me with a little more intelligence than that."

"I credit you with an ingenious brain that must be constantly employed in perpetrating some preposterous scheme. How often have you nearly come to grief through your plotting and conniving?"

"It was my plotting and conniving, as you call it, which helped to put the king you care so much about upon the throne," Philip reminded him.

"And what of the many times you have come close to losing your life and endangering those who love you, including myself. When will you ever learn to be content?"

"Perhaps never," Philip said frankly.

"My God, but you're a bloody fool, Philip Devalle. You will sacrifice all you have worked for and for what? To get back into favour with the King of France? How can he benefit you now?"

"I'm not quite certain," Philip admitted, "but I would indeed be a bloody fool not to find out. Don't be peevish with me, Giles," he begged. "Who knows, it may be to your advantage too."

"Don't drag me into this," Giles muttered crossly. "You may hurtle towards your own destruction if you please but I refuse, this time, to be involved in your misfortunes."

"Or my glories?" Philip said meaningfully. But for him Giles would never be holding the position he now enjoyed at William's side, as they both knew, for it was Philip who had persuaded Giles to support the Dutchman in the first place.

"King William offers you glories. You know he talks of sending you to Ireland."

"An honour indeed," Philip said dryly. "Fighting King James and his French army to uphold the rights of a handful of greedy Protestants."

"You may soon get the opportunity to fight the French army on their own soil," Giles reminded him. "I am expecting William to announce any day now that we are at war with France."

"That is one war I sincerely hope will never come," Philip said with feeling.

"But you would go, wouldn't you," Giles said anxiously. "William may insist upon it."

"All the more reason why I should take this opportunity to speak with Louis."

"Why, for heaven's sake? He is England's enemy."

"But he is my friend," Philip stressed, "and, as you well know, I have never held any man in such high regard. Certainly not our ailing 'Dutch William'."

"Go then and be damned!" Giles turned his back on him. "You always were too pigheaded to take advice. Why should I, or anyone else, care what happens to you when it's very plain you do not care a jot for any save yourself. You are an obstinate man, Philip. If you do this I am finished with you."

Philip was a little taken aback. He had expected Giles to argue but not to attack him quite so harshly.

"Giles, please don't let us part like this." He put his hand on his brother-in-law's shoulder but Giles shook him off. "I picked a bad time to approach you," Philip guessed. "I fear that if William drives you much harder he will wear you out."

"Why should that concern you?" Giles snapped back.

"I have always been concerned for you," Philip told him truthfully.

"Don't pretend to care about me, you contrary bastard! If you thought anything of me you would not even be considering this visit to France. With any luck you'll not return and I shall consider myself well rid of you."

Giles had gone too far this time.

Philip controlled his own temper with difficulty as he turned to leave. "Perhaps," he said quietly, "I have cared about you too much."

THREE

❦

"I never thought you would actually come," Armand said. "I feared it might not be safe for you to be visiting France now."

Philip shrugged. "It probably isn't."

"Then whatever induced you to take the risk?"

"An irresistible urge to meet Monsieur again?" Philip suggested wickedly.

"I doubt that, but it is good to see you anyway."

Armand's wife, Marguerite, agreed with him and Philip looked upon them both with real affection. They made a contrasting couple as they walked together in the gardens of their Brêton home. Armand, though he still had a good figure and was straight and tall, walked with a pronounced limp, whilst his young wife, pretty as a picture, danced along beside him, her dark curls bobbing around her animated face. Philip was pleased to see how happy his friend looked.

"It seems you have truly found contentment here, Armand."

"Here yes, but alas the King will not let me spend too much time at La Fresnaye," Armand said regretfully.

"Your duties still occupy so much of your time?" Philip said in surprise. "I thought most of the Huguenots had converted by now."

"There are not too many of them left, but I must still see to it that the converts are fairly treated."

Complaints had reached King Louis' ears of the brutal way Louvois' soldiers were dealing with the Huguenots. Armand had been appointed to oversee the situation and he had been chosen for the task because Marguerite herself had been a Huguenot. Her parents had been forced to flee to England and Philip had risked his own freedom by helping her to join them there but, when Armand had been prevented from following her, Marguerite had returned and converted to the Catholic faith, so that they could be together.

Even so, it seemed their life was still not their own.

"I tell you, Philip I am growing tired of it," Armand said. "I thought to have earned a little peace after the many years I spent at war in the service of my country but Louis is still not prepared to let me go."

"It appears that both you and my brother-in-law are held in bondage by demanding monarchs," Philip said.

"And what of you? Can you honestly say you have your liberty?"

Few men had ever managed to tame Philip's restless spirit. In his younger days, he had bound himself to the scheming Earl of Shaftesbury, and it had been that association which had nearly lost him his head, but since Shaftesbury's death no-one had truly owned him, or ever would.

"I am apparently in servitude to the King of France's brother," he said, producing a lace handkerchief and wafting it about his face in perfect emulation of Monsieur.

Marguerite giggled. "Whatever would your poor wife make of such a thing?"

"Believe me, sweetheart, the danger of my becoming enslaved to Monsieur is the very least of Theresa's worries on my behalf! I look forward to seeing the dear man, all the same."

Philip did not have long to wait for that pleasure. Directly Armand's messenger reached the Palais Royale with the news of Philip's arrival, Monsieur, delaying only long enough to have three trunks of clothes packed, set off hot foot for Brittany!

"I do hope everything is to his satisfaction," Marguerite said nervously as Monsieur stepped out of his coach at La

Fresnaye, resplendent in a coat of pink velvet covered all over in embroidered silver rosebuds. The fastidious Monsieur was the second most important gentleman in all France and they had never before received him as a guest.

He caught sight of Philip and gave a little cry of joy.

"Don't worry," Armand said. "It is!"

"I've missed you so much," Monsieur told Philip, throwing his arms around him and kissing him upon both cheeks.

"Have you really?" Philip himself felt quite affected by their reunion, for he was actually very fond of him. It was Monsieur's friendship which had originally paved the way for his acceptance at Versailles and it was Monsieur who had always stuck by him, no matter what trouble he had got himself into, pleading his case when none other would. Such devotion, Philip felt, should be rewarded with loyalty.

"How do I look?" Monsieur asked him anxiously.

"Handsomer than ever," Philip said, for Monsieur was a good-looking man who had no need to daub his face with powder and rouge, although he always did.

Monsieur beamed at the compliment and took the arm that Philip offered him. "We will have a splendid time. First, I thought we'd spend a few days here with dear Armand, catching up on all the gossip, and then you are to accompany me to Paris. You will want to see your house again, no doubt, but you are not to stay there. You are to be my guest at the Palais Royale and Louis says that I can bring you to Versailles, even though Protestants are not usually received there anymore."

Louis' gracious invitation came as no surprise to Philip, since he knew whose idea it had been for him to come to France in the first place!

As Monsieur teetered off upon his high heels to greet his host and hostess Philip noticed, for the first time, that Monsieur's coach had another occupant.

"Who's your travelling companion?" he asked him.

"Oh, that's Luc. I get so bored upon long journeys with no-one to talk to and he is such good company," Monsieur explained.

"Luc?" Philip queried, for he knew no-one in Monsieur's circle of that name.

"Luc Santerre. He's new at Court. His introduction came from Louvois, in actual fact, so I was quite prepared to dislike him but, instead, I find him a most pleasing young man."

"Surely you haven't started to chase young men again," Philip said severely.

Monsieur laughed. "No, I haven't, so don't sound so disapproving, but he is extremely handsome, as you will see, and most anxious to make your acquaintance. I think you must be a hero to him, for he has often talked about you and when he learned that I was coming here to see you he positively insisted upon accompanying me."

Certainly the greeting Luc gave Philip was that of a man at last in the presence of one he has longed to meet. He gazed at him for a moment as though mesmerised by the sight of him and then, recalling his manners, swept off his hat and bowed low.

"Your Grace, this is a pleasure I have dreamt of for many years, although I little thought to ever have the good fortune to actually meet you."

"Why, thank you," Philip said, a little surprised by the intensity of the young man's gaze. He was used to receiving admiration yet there was something more in Luc's look, something which made him feel uncomfortable in a way he could not quite define.

"Who is he? What is his background?" Philip asked Monsieur whilst Luc spoke with Armand.

"I've really no idea. Louvois said he was a fellow of good family, but I know no more about him than that, save that he tries very hard to please me. He is obviously much taken with you."

Philip frowned. He was not so sure of that. "I think you should find out a little more about the members of your retinue," he said seriously, "especially if they are introduced to you by Louvois."

"You don't think, surely, that he could be dangerous?" Monsieur said, laughing at his concern. "Why, he's as docile as a lamb."

"Perhaps," Philip said, "and perhaps not. Appearances can be most deceptive."

Armand knew very little about him either. "Louvois introduced Santerre to society saying only that he was well bred but of an impoverished family. I must say, he has made a great effort to ingratiate himself with everyone at Court and he goes nearly everywhere with Monsieur."

"And do you like him?" Philip respected his friend's judgement in such matters.

"Not entirely," Armand confessed," but then I rarely like Monsieur's choice of companions, other than yourself, of course! And there's another curious thing, Luc showed interest in me directly he learned I was a friend of yours. He has asked me countless questions about you."

"Has he now? I see I shall have to keep a careful watch upon this most engaging young gentleman," Philip said.

Luc made every effort to please during the few days they stayed at La Fresnaye. He was polite to his host, charming in the extreme to his young hostess and attentive to Monsieur. To Philip he was deferential enough yet many times Philip would catch Luc watching him with such a strange expression on his face that he began to wonder who was observing who!

Thomas also became the object of Luc's attention, but Philip had no worries on that score. He knew that his loyal servant could be relied upon to divulge nothing of his business, but he was intrigued when Thomas told him that Luc had been attempting to question him about Jules Gaspard.

Jules was a crippled poet who Philip had befriended in his younger days, when he had discovered him making a meagre living writing verses for the gentlemen of Paris to give their ladyloves. Under Philip's patronage, Jules had written several plays, some of which had been performed on the Paris stage. Two had even been performed before the King at St. Germain.

Philip's early introduction to Court society had made him cynical beyond his years, but Jules Gaspard had taught him much about patience, trust and genuine friendship. Unfortunately, Jules' health was fragile and, despite the best care Philip could buy for him, he had died. The loss had affected Philip deeply at the time and he was still extremely sensitive concerning any reference to him.

Philip ignored Luc as much as possible after that, although he knew he would not be able to do so on the long journey back to Paris in the confines of Monsieur's coach.

"Shall you be visiting your house, your Grace?" Luc asked him as they were preparing to leave.

"I hope so." Philip was greatly attached to his Paris home. It was the first property he had owned and, filled as it was with associations of Jules, it recalled a particularly poignant period of his life.

"I wondered if I might accompany you there," Luc said.

Philip looked at him in astonishment. "Why ever would you want to do that?

"Monsieur has told me a great deal about it and I am curious to see inside."

"Well your curiosity will have to wait for a while," Philip told him, a little irritably. "It has been many years since I have been there and on the first occasion, at least, I will wish to be alone."

"With your memories of Jules Gaspard?"

Philip looked at him sharply. "What of it?"

"I meant nothing by the remark," Luc said, "But it is common knowledge that he once resided in your house."

It was, indeed, common knowledge that Philip had once given over part of his house to Jules, so that he could live and work in comfort, and yet a bitter note had entered Luc's voice when he alluded to Jules. Philip could not fathom it at all, any more than he could fathom Luc's desire to see inside the house.

"What is your interest in me, Luc Santerre?"

"Why, only the interest any man of my age would show in such a great person as yourself," Luc said. "You are a famous soldier, a famous lover, a…"

"Yes, yes, I know very well what I am," Philip interrupted him, "but I have not yet discovered what you are, or even who you are."

"My family, I regret to say, is nowhere near as illustrious as yours, your Grace, and I am merely trying to advance myself in the world by studying those I consider worthy of esteem."

"You say so, yet it is very clear you disapprove of me," Philip said. "No, don't protest, I've see the way you look at me, particularly when I'm with Monsieur. I thought at first that it was jealousy because you feared I was usurping your place at his side, but you don't particularly like Monsieur either, do you? Oh, you are prepared to be pleasant to him in order to, as you say, advance yourself in the world, and I don't blame you too much for that. I did much the same at your age but the difference was that I was at least his friend. You are using him and I don't like to see that, for he has not the guile to realise it."

Luc's eyes narrowed. He had blue eyes, as blue as Philip's own. "You insult me, your Grace."

"Only if I have assessed you wrongly and I don't believe I have. How old are you, Santerre?"

"Eighteen, your Grace."

"At a little more than your age I was serving in King Louis' army. I suggest that, instead of wasting your time upon cultivating the friendship of people you clearly despise, you use your influence with Louvois to obtain yourself a commission and fight for your country. The army is the best way I know for a person with no fortune to advance himself and I am sure the Comte de Rennes will be pleased to give you any help or advice you need."

"Thank you, your Grace," Luc replied stiffly. "I would, indeed, like to be a soldier one day, for it is in my blood, but I have made a promise to myself to avenge someone very dear to me and until I have fulfilled that promise I am not free to choose the direction that my life will take."

"Oh well, suit yourself." Santerre was too intense a person for Philip's liking. He left him and sought out Armand.

"I will return here just as soon as I discover what Louis wants with me," he promised him

"I beg you to take every care, my friend. I feel responsible for your well-being," Armand said worriedly. "I was instrumental in bringing you to France and I would be distraught if anything happened to you."

Philip laughed. "Whatever could happen to me here? All my enemies are in England!"

FOUR

❧

The Palais Royale was a popular gathering place for the fashionable members of French society. It was a place where they could have some fun, uninhibited by the sombre presence of Madame de Maintenon and uninterrupted by the interminably long religious services which they were now expected to attend at Versailles.

The week that followed Philip's arrival in Paris was hectic. As well as the nightly gambling parties, Monsieur organised a ballet and even a full-scale ball in his honour. It seemed that no amount of trouble or expense was spared but by the time the week ended even Philip, who could drink with the best and had a passion for cards, was beginning to flag.

He had managed to fit in two visits to his house, but Luc did not again ask to accompany him. Although the young Frenchman was present at every social occasion, he had evidently decided not to approach Philip again. Even so it was obvious that his interest in him had not diminished and Philip often found himself to be the object of that almost obsessive gaze but he had other, more important, matters on his mind.

Whilst he was quite enjoying the novelty of sitting up until the early hours playing lansquenet with Monsieur, this was not the prime reason for his visit to France. He was delighted when he finally received Louis' invitation to attend upon him at Versailles.

It had been a long while since Philip had looked upon the three impressive blue and gold palace gates surmounted by an image of the sun, Louis' own emblem. As he was travelling with

Monsieur they could pass through the central gate, reserved for the King and Queen and Princes of the Blood. They could also go through the next gate, which led directly onto the Marble Courtyard in front of the palace, whilst lesser visitors must stop their carriages at the Court of Ministers and hire a sedan chair to take them further.

Monsieur had not stopped chattering all the way from Paris. He had not stopped eating either, for he was always hungry, so that Philip was very glad when the journey was over. As they alighted he glanced up at the first floor and at the windows overlooking the courtyard, the windows to Louis' own apartments He wondered what would be the outcome of the interview for which he was risking so much.

He left Monsieur in the Hall of Mirrors and went through the door concealed behind the fifth mirror in the long gallery. This door led to Louis' cabinet.

Philip scratched upon the door with his little fingernail, as was the custom, for none were allowed to knock on doors at Versailles. He received the command to enter and paused for a second to compose himself. It was no small thing to be about to confront the mighty King Louis, who had made France one of the most powerful countries in the world. A man hated and feared by many, but not by Philip.

Louis was still good looking, even if the loss of his upper teeth four years before had caused his mouth to sink a little. The blue-grey eyes which surveyed Philip over the prominent Bourbon nose were as clear and penetrating as ever.

"Philip! Always pleasing to the eye." Louis regarded him approvingly. Philip had dressed flamboyantly for the occasion in a coat of scarlet brocade, for he knew that Louis liked those around him to wear gay colours, although he himself was nearly always dressed, as he was now, in his favourite brown coat.

Philip bowed low and kissed the hand Louis offered him. "I do endeavour to be pleasing to your Majesty."

"Sometimes you do! The years have been kind to you, Philip, perhaps kinder than you deserve. I used to fear you would be ruined by your drinking and debaucheries."

Philip laughed at that. "On the contrary, your Majesty, I am as fit as ever I was. I scarcely drink at all now and I am changed into a respectable person of regular habits."

"Never!" Louis said, "I know you better, though I would like to think that Theresa has succeeded in reforming you a little."

"She does pretty well," Philip allowed.

"That lady is too good for you. I have always said it! Perhaps, though, it is your new monarch who has managed to control your unruly temperament?"

"Certainly King William's Court is not a place where unruly temperaments flourish, your Majesty," Philip said carefully. It would not be politic, he knew, to extol William's virtues but neither did he intend to be too disloyal to the Dutchman whose accession had benefited him so much.

"And what do you think of your sickly king?"

Philip smiled. There was almost a trace of possessiveness in Louis' tone, but this king was the sort of man that Philip understood and knew how to deal with, much better than he did the cold and withdrawn William.

"Even in the best of health King William of England could not compare in the slightest way to King Louis of France, your Majesty," he said, knowing how much Louis loved to be flattered.

"Yet you have advanced under his rule, have you not?"

"So I should, for I helped put him where he is, for which action I trust your Majesty will not indict me. My life was quite intolerable under James' rule. We were virtually prisoners on our estate."

"I cannot blame you entirely for what you did. Your brother-in-law, though, is a different matter. I shall not receive him should he show his scarred face here again," Louis warned him.

"Giles and King William have become so inseparable that the King can scarcely bear him out of his sight."

"And it is my opinion that they richly deserve each other," Louis said tartly. "How have your countrymen taken to their new ruler? I heard there were some Protestants who wanted James back even at the time William was appointed."

"There were a few, but they only wanted him with the assurance of his good behaviour, and he would never have given them that. There were also suggestions of allowing him to keep his sovereignty and making the Princess Mary the Regent, but the majority were for making her Queen and wanted William, as her husband, to be joint ruler."

"An elected king," Louis said disdainfully, "required to accept parliamentary conditions for his succession."

Philip hid a smile as he imagined the magnificent Sun King being bound by such restrictions. Louis was the absolute ruler of his country and the French parliament was there to pass the laws he had created, not to dictate policy.

"It was essential that the will of the people prevailed, your Majesty." He was tempted to add that the country had not had any intention of accepting a monarch who would rule with as little regard for them as had King James but since James was, after all, Louis' cousin he thought he had better not!

"But the army mutinied, did it not?"

"James' own Scottish forces rebelled," Philip admitted, "but the Dutch cavalry soon subdued them. Morale was low amongst all the troops at first, as you might expect when they were forced to serve a foreigner who had defeated their sovereign, but they are loyal enough to him now."

"So there are none who work for James' cause?"

"A handful, that is all, your Majesty. Certainly, insufficient to pose a threat. Ireland, now, is a different proposition. King James will make a nuisance of himself there without a doubt and the worst of it is that I believe King William intends to dispatch me there to fight him. I hear it is a land of bogs and mist and savages."

"Then it can't be worse than the fighting you did for me in Holland," Louis said pointedly.

Philip had wondered how long it would be before that was raised. He had taken part in the sack of Holland, under the Maréchal-Duc de Luxembourg's command, fighting against William!

"Luxembourg still speaks highly of you," Louis continued. "You became a true Hero of France on that campaign."

"Thank you, your Majesty."

"What were you in those days, a major? You acted like a general when you defended your garrison at Woerden with a mere handful of troops against the might of the Dutch army, and to think that the attack upon you was led by William himself, and that it was Luxembourg who arrived to relieve you."

The irony that he might soon be called upon to fight on William's side against the French had not escaped Philip. "Does your Majesty imagine I could ever forget those glorious days," he said quietly, "or the Maréchal de Luxembourg? He was an inspiration to me, as were Condé and Turenne, under whom, thanks to your Majesty, I also had the honour to serve. The example of such men has shaped my whole life, but the person who has had by far the most influence on me is yourself."

"Yet now you talk about the likelihood of your striking a blow against French troops. Against me," Louis stressed.

"You wound me, your Majesty, if you think I could enjoy the prospect," Philip protested. "The war which threatens to divide our two nations is, in my opinion, senseless and unnecessary."

"Yet there are some who reckon that William only wanted England in order to add it to my enemies."

"I don't believe that. The English hate you chiefly because you harboured King James," Philip said.

Louis gave a slight smile. "That comes well from the person who helped both James and his wife escape from England! Why did you do it?"

It was a question many people would have asked if they had known the truth!

"I came across the Queen's party quite by chance the night she was escaping with her baby son," Philip said. "I have never born her any malice and I considered it no more than my honourable duty as a gentleman to see her safely on her way."

Louis nodded approvingly. He always treated women kindly and politely, even the lowest serving wenches in the palace. "That I can understand, but King James has been your sworn enemy for years. Why would you help him?"

"Because I hoped it would redeem me, in some small way, in the eyes of your Majesty," Philip said frankly.

"So I thought! You have not yet, then, become my enemy?"

"I would never wish to be that, your Majesty," Philip said in all sincerity, "but I am placed in a most unenviable position. On the one hand I owe allegiance to William and on the other I cannot forget the deep regard I have for you or the love I have for France. I feel I am both Frenchman and Englishman."

"You are a soldier and if you are sent to Ireland then you must do your duty, but I tell you this, Philip," Louis said, "I have forgiven you a great deal in the past, but I am not certain I could forgive you if you ever led troops against me on French soil. You still belong to me, and you always will."

Philip had already guessed that this was the reason for Louis' invitation. What he did not yet know was what Louis would be prepared to offer him in exchange for his loyalty.

"I will refuse to fight in France," Philip promised, "although a great many will think me a fool and a traitor for it. I suspect the honour of the French campaign will then go to Marlborough, whilst I am condemned to years of fruitless war-mongering in Ireland. No matter," he added, after a short pause to indicate that he had made his offer and that it was now time for Louis to make his, for Philip knew all about this particular game. "What does concern me, however, is the effect my decision will have upon my personal affairs."

"Such as the future of your daughter?" Louis said.

"Madeleine's future is a matter always uppermost in my mind," Philip said. Whilst he would have bargained, at one time, for power or purely money, other issues interested him now, for he had achieved the rest.

"It is in my mind too." Louis said.

Philip hadn't expected that.

"Why should that surprise you?" Louis asked. "It has long been my desire that she should one day wed a Frenchman. Would that please you?"

Philip eyed him coolly. "That would very much depend upon the Frenchman, your Majesty."

"A prominent one, of course. I already have one in mind for her, and it is a better union than you could ever hope to arrange for her in England, even though you are now a duke. What I am offering you, Philip, is the chance to ally yourself to me by ties of blood. I wish to take your daughter into my own family, as the wife of the Comte de Touraine."

Philip swallowed. Even he had never aimed as high as that. Louis had a great many illegitimate children, all of whom he had acknowledged and treated with every honour and advantage. Touraine was the ten year old son of Louis by Philip's old friend, Madame de Montespan. To wed Maudie to him would be a coup to outshine them all. Whilst Philip himself came from a noble line, Theresa did not and he had always feared that fact would mar his daughter's chances of a good match. "I am overcome by your Majesty's generosity," he told Louis truthfully.

"It would be my dearest wish for you and Theresa to reside here too, but in the meantime I shall be happy to make the compact, which can be kept a secret between us for now and, for my part, shall be binding for as long as you refuse to turn your hand directly against France."

"Why would you do so much for me?" Philip said, still astounded at the magnificence of Louis' offer.

"Many reasons. For one thing you have a large following in England, indeed I would say you have become a legend there, and I would sooner not have a legend for my enemy."

Philip rather liked that. He had never before heard himself described as a legend! "I wonder, then, that your Majesty does not simply have me killed if you fear I could be so much trouble."

"I said there were many reasons," Louis reminded him. "The chief amongst them is that I am fond of you, troublesome individual though you are!" He offered his hand, indicating that the audience was at an end, for Louis was a busy man and kept to a timetable. "Return early tomorrow, when you have had the chance to properly consider my proposal. In the meantime I will have the necessary documents drawn up and we can sign them there and then."

Philip disclosed nothing of his conversation with Louis to Monsieur on their return journey to Paris, for Monsieur could not keep even the meanest secret. He did discuss it with Thomas that night, however, for Philip trusted him implicitly.

"It is a generous offer," Thomas said, "but I don't know what the mistress will make of it."

"She won't have the chance to make anything of it," Philip said. "This is a decision I must make alone, and now."

"You don't propose to even tell her? That's not right!"

"I know it, but I have little choice. Louis will not wait whilst I return to England to discuss the matter with Theresa. It is, as you say, a generous offer, more generous than I deserve or expected, and to ask for more than one day to consider it would be to insult the man."

"I say it is unreasonable of him, no matter who he is, to allow you so little time to make a decision that will influence your daughter's whole life, my Lord."

Philip smiled at his earnestness. "It's not really so difficult to make, in fact I would say that matters have worked out very much my way, wouldn't you? By simply refusing to fight in France I shall ensure all our futures after William's death and make a better match for Maudie than I could ever have dreamed of making, for all my ambition."

Thomas sighed. "As usual you have not considered any of the problems."

"Problems? What problems?"

"There are several I can think of," Thomas said, sounding exasperated. "To begin with, won't Maudie need to become a Catholic in order to marry into the family of the Most Christian King of France?"

"Quite possibly, but that is not uncommon. Monsieur's wife changed her faith in order to marry him and so have many others when they wanted to make an advantageous match."

"I suppose so, but the mistress is opposed to the very idea of an arranged match for her."

"How absurd! Practically all good marriages are arranged," Philip said. "Was not our own? Not by our families, it is true, but it was arranged all the same, and I don't believe she is discontented with it."

Their marriage had been arranged by the Earl of Shaftesbury, for whom they both had worked at the time, helping him in his plot against the Papists. Scheming for him had landed Theresa in trouble and Shaftesbury had insisted that Philip marry her so that his title would enable her to remain at Court.

"She loves you now, my Lord, but she has often said how unhappy you both were about it at the time. She wishes to spare her child such unhappiness."

Philip made a dismissive gesture. He cared a great deal about his daughter's happiness, of course, but he honestly could not see how she could be other than enraptured by the prospect of gaining such a husband. "Maudie will obey my wishes when the time comes, just as Theresa will obey them now."

"I don't think she will," Thomas warned. "I think she will be furious."

"Let her be. Ultimately she will see it is for the best. Any other problems you envisage, little worrier?"

"Only one, and that my biggest worry of all. What will people say if you refuse to fight in France?"

Philip shrugged. He knew exactly what Giles would say but, after the way they had parted, he cared little for his brother-in-law's opinions.

"I have been giving that thought and I believe the best thing would be for me to volunteer for duty in Ireland right away. It is not a duty I relish but if I am already on active service then it will be easier for me to find some excuse not to go to France."

"You may already be too late to volunteer for Ireland," Thomas said. "If you stay here much longer the war with France may be declared before you even get home. Then you would be placed in a devilishly tricky position."

That fact had already occurred to Philip. He regretted now his promise to return to La Fresnaye before he left France but, because he had real regard for Armand, he was determined to keep that promise, even though the trip to Brittany would delay him for several days. "You're right, Thomas. We must leave Paris as soon as we can. There is, after all, no longer any reason for me to stay."

"What about Monsieur?"

"I'll think of something to tell him. Whilst I'm at Versailles tomorrow you can be packing my things."

"I think I should accompany you," Thomas said.

"Whatever for? You didn't accompany me this morning."

"That was different, for you were travelling with Monsieur. No-one with any sense would try to get at you whilst you were with him, but to travel totally alone, is that wise?"

Philip patted his cheek affectionately. "You fret over me too much. I am merely driving to Versailles and back again. Surely not much can happen to me doing that. Besides, I don't believe I have too many enemies in France at the moment. It is in England where I shall shortly have to watch my back!"

FIVE

༄

It was barely light when Philip left the Palais Royale. Since he had needed to borrow one of Monsieur's coaches, Philip had been forced to tell him that he was returning to Versailles, but he had said no more than that. He had also broken the news to him that he would be leaving Paris the following day and Monsieur had been too upset to ask him any questions.

There was hardly a soul out on the streets as they drove past the Louvre and only three men on the Pont Neuf, instead of the noisy throng that would come later in the day to see the street singers and pedlars who plied their trades on the bridge. At any other time Philip would have paid more attention to those three men, who were leaning against the railings which surrounded the equestrian statue of King Henry IV, but his mind was on nothing save his business at Versailles. He was weary too. He had managed to snatch only a few hours' sleep by the time Monsieur had finally allowed him to retire.

In the unaccustomed stillness, the pump that supplied the Louvre with water from the river sounded loud as they passed over the bridge's second arch, where it was housed. Philip was distracted by it from the thoughts of his forthcoming meeting with King Louis and, as they drew level with the statue, he noticed that the three men had disappeared.

He had a soldier's instinct for danger. Despite the efforts of La Reynie, the Chief of the Paris police, the city was not a safe place to be abroad during the quiet hours. Philip feared he might be about to be set upon by thieves and his hand went to his sword.

He was too late. Before he could draw the weapon, the coach door was thrown open. His reactions had been nowhere near as swift as usual and Philip cursed to find that he was looking down the barrel of a pistol.

The man holding it wore a mask that covered most of his face. Philip saw that another masked man stood beside him, also brandishing a pistol, whilst a third had grabbed the horses' reins and was pointing his weapon at the driver.

"Out of the coach, Lord Southwick."

"So you know who I am?"

"All Paris knows you, your Grace."

"And why should you believe me to be travelling with any valuables?"

"Your valuables do not concern us. We are executioners, not robbers."

"Executioners?" Philip repeated, looking about him. There was not another soul in sight and he saw no way of receiving aid or escaping.

He stepped out of the coach, since he had no other choice. He had been caught with an ease which made him feel ashamed. "Oh, Thomas," he muttered, "what will you say when you learn of this?"

His courage had never deserted him in times of crisis and it did not do so now. "Upon whose orders are you acting?" he demanded as one of the masked men motioned him to the side of the bridge.

"Let us just say, Lord Southwick, that there are people who think the world would be a better place without you."

"But King Louis is not one of them," Philip said. "He will punish my murderers."

The man, who he took to be the leader, laughed harshly. "You should never have come back to France, your Grace."

"I am beginning to agree with you." Philip had been in hazardous situations before but he had never felt quite so helpless.

With two cocked pistols pointing squarely at his chest he could not draw his sword or risk the slightest sudden movement. He edged closer to the parapet of the bridge. "Won't you at least tell me why I am to die?"

"For the inconvenience your life causes your fellowmen."

"Anyone in particular?" The only people in France that Philip thought he could possibly have offended by his presence were the supporters of James Stuart, but he didn't think James was so popular with the French that fanatics would be acting on his behalf.

"Let me hear the great Hero of France beg for his life," his assailant said mockingly, "then I will tell you who intends to take it from you and the reason."

Philip had been weighing every chance whilst he talked and he had backed away until he could go no further. He was pressed against the very edge of the bridge and he looked down at the fast-flowing waters of the Seine. He had only one way of escape and that was a desperate one. Five feet below the stone parapet of the bridge ran a ledge about a yard wide and he knew that if he simply jumped he would not be able to clear it.

"I see little point in begging for a life you have already decided to take," he said calmly, bracing himself against the top of the parapet, every muscle tense and ready as he prepared himself for one of the most dangerous feats he had attempted in his reckless life.

"Then know now, Englishman, who takes your life."

Philip would dearly have loved to learn the identity of his enemy but, since he guessed that he would die the instant he discovered it, he decided he would have to remain in ignorance.

He took a deep breath then threw himself backwards over the side of the bridge, to land on the ledge below.

It was obviously the last thing the two men had expected him to do. Both their pistols fired as he hurled himself from the ledge but their bullets only sliced the air.

Philip hit the water with an impact that almost stunned him and he sank like a stone. Frantically he struggled with his shoes and managed to wrench one off. He had no breath left to attempt to remove the other and he tried to fight his way to the surface, throwing off his heavy sword. It seemed hopeless. The pockets of his velvet coat had filled with water and it was pulling him down. His strength was waning.

He had almost ceased his struggles and accepted his fate when an image of Theresa came into his head. His lungs were almost bursting and his muscles were numb from cold but the vision gave him one last spurt of strength.

Philip felt the air upon his face and took a gulping breath but immediately a shot sounded and he forced himself once more below the surface. This time he succeeded in kicking off his other shoe.

That was better. Another swift gasp of air and he was able to slip out of his coat. Freed from that encumbrance, he tried to swim under the bridge but a bullet hit the water dangerously close to him and he knew he was not yet out of peril.

He felt sure that he would be safe if he could only hide beneath the arches of the bridge, for it could not be too long before the sound of the shots attracted attention from the houses in the nearby Place Dauphine and the three masked men would be forced to flee.

Philip was a powerful swimmer and he fought against the strong current as he strained to reach the cover of the bridge, but he had reckoned without the other objects the Seine held in its watery grasp. A piece of driftwood, part of a dead tree, was coming straight for him.

Weakened already by coldness and exertion, Philip could not avoid it. As he collided with the branch it all but knocked the breath from his body. A jagged piece caught the sleeve of his shirt and Philip could not free himself. The branch pulled him back out from under the bridge and in full view of his assailants once again.

This time he was truly at their mercy. Another pistol shot sounded and he cried out in pain.

There was a burning sensation in his right shoulder and then the world went black.

∽

Thomas was folding Philip's clothes into a trunk, ready for the journey home, when he heard a carriage driving in great haste into the courtyard below. He went to the window and recognised it as the same vehicle in which his master had left less than an hour earlier. Thomas peered down, expecting to see him alight in a foul mood because he had forgotten something, or perhaps even to call out to him that he could come to Versailles after all. Then he realised there was no sign of Philip in the coach.

The coat he was holding dropped from his hands and he rushed down the stairs. He was beside the coach before it had even stopped. "Where the hell is he?"

The driver looked considerably shaken. "The Duke is dead. Shot by assassins on the Pont Neuf."

The words seemed to rob Thomas' limbs of their strength. He grabbed hold of the harness of the nearest horse for support as the courtyard reeled around him.

"It's not true," he said huskily. His throat had gone so dry he could hardly form the words.

"I swear it is. We saw him shot and then he fell from the bridge into the Seine."

That was, indeed, what they had seen.

"But do you know he is dead?"

"Oh yes, no doubt about it," the driver said. They shot him again when he was in the water. We never saw him after that."

Thomas stared at him, still unable to properly take in the

news, and then something seemed to snap inside his head. Numbness was replaced by anger; anger at Philip for being so stubborn, anger at himself for letting him go alone and anger at Monsieur's men who had stood by whilst his beloved master was murdered.

"You let them do it?" he cried out in a rage, grabbing the driver's leg and pulling him to the ground. "You watched them kill him and you never tried to stop them? You cowardly bastards!"

The driver landed heavily. "There was a pistol held on us," he yelled as Thomas dragged him to his feet and threw him with all his force against the carriage door.

The footman jumped down and joined the fray and Thomas, white with anger, set about them both.

Windows had begun to open upon all sides of the courtyard and Monsieur himself heard the commotion and sent for his valet.

"What is happening down there?" he wanted to know.

"It appears that the Duke of Southwick's manservant is fighting with two of your men, Monsieur."

"Bring him to me," Monsieur ordered. "I always told Philip that his servant was an unruly fellow but it is not to be borne when the ruffian disturbs me at this unearthly hour."

Thomas came up to him a few minutes later, neither struggling nor protesting, for his anger was spent. He regarded the irate Monsieur unconcernedly. The fury of the First Gentleman of France at being woken at dawn was the least of his troubles.

Monsieur stopped in mid-sentence as he became aware that the object of his anger looked dazed and seemed unaware of what was being said to him.

"Monsieur," Thomas said quietly, "I advise you to sit down and listen to me."

"Sit down?" Monsieur repeated in an outraged tone. "Why ever should I do that?"

Thomas shrugged. "Then don't." He had no idea how

Monsieur would react to what he was about to tell him, but he was prepared for hysteria at the very least. "It appears that my master has been murdered."

Monsieur gave a strangled cry and slumped, unconscious, onto the floor at Thomas' feet.

Thomas shook his head. "Wonderful!" After years of pretending to swoon for effect, Monsieur had finally managed the real thing, and with only Thomas there to witness it.

"You," Thomas told the inert figure, "are all I need at this moment."

∽

"Hey, daughter, bring the boathook. Swift now!"

A young girl struggled across the deck of the barge with the long hook. "What have you spied, father?"

"A body, I think, though it may be a trick of this river mist. Quicker, girl, the current is bearing it away."

He grabbed the boat hook from her and jabbed it at the object floating past. He cursed as the hook failed to grasp its target but then cried out triumphantly as, on the second attempt, it snagged on the belt of the floating figure. "It is a body," he cried out triumphantly, "and I have it fast!"

The girl gasped as she looked down at her father's catch. "He's not drowned, he's been shot – see the wound upon his shoulder."

"A pox on that, have you seen the rings on his fingers? A gentleman, I'd reckon, and well worth hooking for those jewels."

"You'd steal the rings from a dead man?" The girl looked at her father in disgust.

"And why not? What use has he for them now? He'll be at the bottom of the river soon and those prizes with him, unless we can wrench them from his fingers."

The girl shuddered. "It can't be right to do that. I'll not touch him."

"You'll do as I tell you," her father snarled. "Over the side with you and help me haul him up or I shall beat you so hard you'll wish yourself as insensible as he."

It was no idle threat, as the girl, who had been beaten many times before, knew only too well. Resignedly she kicked off her shoes and took off her skirt and blouse then, clad only in her petticoat, lowered herself from the barge into the cold, grey water. "He's stuck fast on a log," she panted, struggling to free Philip's sleeve.

"That must be what's kept him afloat. You mind he doesn't sink when you release him or it will be the worse for you."

"Can't I just take the rings off his fingers?" the girl begged, her teeth chattering with cold.

"And let him go when he might be carrying other valuables about his person? We'll have him up on deck and search him properly."

It took all of the girl's strength but eventually she managed to prise Philip's shirt from the log and hold his arm high enough for her father to grasp it and haul him aboard. "He's still bleeding," she noticed. "It can't have happened long ago."

"All the more reason to be rid of him quickly."

His daughter climbed back aboard and looked at Philip. "He was a pretty one and no mistake," she sighed.

"Don't waste your time admiring him," the bargee said. "His kind wouldn't have given you a glance when he was alive, much less good will he do you now. Help me turn out his pockets."

Still the girl could not take her eyes from the pallid face. Even streaked with river mud, Philip was the handsomest man she had ever seen. As she looked at him it seemed as though his eyelids fluttered, but the movement was so slight as to be almost imperceptible. Certainly the bargee, who was already engaged in searching through the pockets of Philip's waistcoat, never noticed it but the girl drew closer to him. He was ice cold to the touch yet, as she put her hand upon his heart, she could feel a heartbeat, faint yet unmistakeable.

"He's alive!"

Her father looked up from his search for barely a moment. "He'll not stay alive for long after we throw him back."

"You can't be meaning to return him to the river?"

"Why not? The man is nothing to us and he had no more valuables on him, or if he had the Seine has them already." He examined the three heavily jewelled gold rings he had pulled from Philip's fingers. "No matter. These should be worth a fine few pistoles."

His daughter thought quickly. There was only one way she could think of to persuade her mercenary father to an act of humanity. "If he truly is a rich man then would he not reward us for saving his life?" she said craftily.

The bargee grunted. "Aye. You're making sense now. Let's get him inside and see what you can do for him."

Together they dragged Philip into the living quarters of their boat and stripped off his wet clothes.

"Look at his back!" The bargee turned him over onto his stomach and pointed to a crisscross pattern of scars that covered most of Philip's back.

The girl drew away in horror. "He's been lashed. Poor man!"

"I wonder for what? Perhaps he is no gentleman after all. He has another ugly scar upon his side, see?"

Philip's body, which was nowhere near as pretty as his face, told of a life that had not been without its misfortunes.

"I'm sure he is a gentleman," the girl said hastily, afraid that her father would, even now, throw her prize back into the water. "See how delicate his looks are and how fine his hands."

"And yet he's a strong man, by the look of him, whoever he is." The bargee touched the firm muscles of Philip's arms. "I doubt we'll ever discover the truth. He's lost a lot of blood, I'd say, and God knows how long he's been in the water. If he lives out the day I'll be surprised."

SIX

✍

Ahmed tapped upon Giles' and Marianne's bedroom door. "King William has sent a message that he wants to see you right away, Master."

Giles cursed. He was warm and comfortable in bed, with Marianne in his arms.

"Don't go," she said. "Ahmed could tell him you're unwell."

Giles shook his head. "One does not advance to an influential position by refusing to attend upon one's sovereign, my darling. I'll go right away so that I can return to you all the sooner."

"He probably wants to talk all night about his problems again," Marianne said with a sigh.

But William did not look in the mood for conversation. His face was solemn as Giles entered.

"I have something to tell you, Giles," he said quietly, "and I wish it was anyone but me who had to do it. I have just received news that has distressed me and will devastate you."

Giles stared at him, uncomprehending, and then an awful suspicion crossed his mind. "Not Philip?" he asked, in a strained voice.

"I fear so. He was drowned in the Seine, Giles. Murdered, by all accounts, for there were witnesses who saw him shot."

"Shot?" Giles repeated. William's words seemed to be making no sense. "Who would shoot him?"

"His assassins have not been caught, nor has his body been found."

"Then can we be sure that he is dead?"

"I have been sent a full account and it appears a pistol was fired at him at close range," William said flatly. "He fell from the Pont Neuf and the current carried him off. Oh, Giles, there are no words of comfort I can give to one who loved him as you did. I feel my own loss acutely enough. But for Philip I would likely not be here in England now. He was a great man. Please convey my condolences to your sister when you write to her with the news."

Giles left William's chamber in a daze, remembering only too vividly how he and Philip had parted.

"Oh, Philip, Philip," he murmured, "why did you cause me to say such bitter things to you in our last moments together? Why, damn it, did you have to go?"

∽

England officially declared war on France in the first week of May.

For Giles, still numbed by the news of Philip's death, the declaration had but a fraction of the import it would have had before his loss.

"I have decided I will send Marlborough to Flanders at the head of the English army, in place of Philip," William told him.

"Marlborough?" Giles face perfectly portrayed his opinion of John Churchill, the Earl of Marlborough.

"He is the logical choice. Oh, I don't like the man any more than you do," William said, "nor shall I ever really trust him after the way he deserted King James, but he is a fine military commander, you must acknowledge that."

"He is a good soldier," Giles allowed, somewhat grudgingly. Marlborough had been his enemy at Sedgemoor, for it had been Marlborough who had led King James' troops against Monmouth, during the Duke's doomed rebellion. "He was never comparable with Philip of course. However, since we go to fight against King

Louis, I think perhaps that Marlborough is not only the logical choice now but would always have been the better choice."

"You think Philip would have refused to go?"

"I think he would not have enjoyed to go," Giles said carefully. "Whilst upon the subject of my brother-in-law, my sister has written to me from Sussex that King Louis has invited her to attend a magnificent service he is holding in Philip's honour at Versailles. Theresa will naturally wish to be present and I think, under the circumstances, I should accompany her, if your Majesty will give me permission."

William looked dismayed. "You want to go to France now, when I have so much to do and need you by my side?"

Giles felt a stab of annoyance that he had difficulty in concealing. William, he felt, was being totally unreasonable. It was a week since he had heard about Philip and he had not even had the chance yet to visit Theresa to console her in her loss. "Yes, your Majesty. I do."

"You spent some time in France yourself and made important friends before you joined with me," William reminded him sharply. "Do you suffer from Philip's conflicting loyalties too?"

Giles stiffened. "I am wounded to the quick that your Majesty should ask me such a question."

William looked contrite. "Forgive me, Giles. I should never have made that remark to one who has served me so devotedly. You, of all the English, I should not doubt, nor do I, but I am under such strain that I fear mightily to lose those I value."

"Your Majesty will never lose me," Giles assured him, "but I do have a duty to my family."

"Your sister will be in less danger than you in France," William said. "I understand she is most highly thought of by King Louis whilst you, despite your friendship with Monsieur, will have no guarantee of safe conduct now in a country with whom we are at war. I beg you to reconsider."

"I wish to go," Giles said firmly, "and not only for my sister's sake. Philip and I occasionally had our differences, it is true, but without him I would have had no hope of making my way in the world, let alone holding the post I am now honoured to hold with your Majesty. I owe him this."

"Yes, I can see why you would feel that way," William admitted. "Very well, you may go, although it is much against my better judgement. How long would you expect to be away?"

"Not long. A month at most," Giles said.

"I want your word on that, for I am not certain I can manage without you for longer."

"I am flattered that your Majesty considers me so indispensable!"

"They are not empty words, Giles," William said. "You are the only English person I really trust. Without you to protect me I shall be at the mercy of those self-seekers who only want to cultivate me only for their own benefit. Unless you positively swear to be back within a month I shall refuse to let you go."

"Only death or imprisonment could keep me away from your Majesty's side for longer," Giles said.

He knew that William had come to depend upon him very much, which was why Giles was prepared to make himself available whenever William needed him. This time, however, he knew what he had to do and, for once, William must take second place.

Marianne was even more unhappy than William about Giles' proposed trip to France.

"Don't go," she begged him. "William is right; Theresa will be safe enough at Versailles."

"That is not the only reason I am going," he reminded her, "or have you forgotten the little matter of your husband in Cassis? What better opportunity shall I ever have to perform this task that Louvois expects of me? I propose to take Ahmed to help me, if you can spare him."

"It is you I cannot spare," she sobbed, clinging tightly to him. "I want you beside me when our child is born."

"My dear girl, that is not until September," Giles said. "William says I am to be gone no longer than a month. All the same I don't much like the idea of leaving you at Court alone for that long so I thought you could accompany me to High Heatherton and stay there with Bet whilst I am gone." Bet, who had been Theresa's maid for many years, was now the housekeeper at High Heatherton. "There are none in whose care I would rather entrust you in your condition, for there is very little that woman does not know concerning medical matters. She has her own cures for most ills and what she does not know I reckon she invents, with every bit as good a result! It is decided then."

Marianne rarely argued with Giles. In any case he was not a person who was used to considering the opinions of others very much, not even of those close to him.

"Very well, Giles," she said meekly.

High Heatherton was sad and silent. The entire estate mourned Philip deeply, for he had brought prosperity to those who earned their livings upon his land and he was loved by all. The property had first passed to Philip's elder brother, Henry, who suffered from the madness that had touched his family line for generations. Henry had manifested signs of the illness early. The lash marks on Philip's back were the result of his brother's vicious attacks upon him when they were younger, but he had managed to have Henry committed to Bedlam and had gained the estate for himself through the courts.

By the time Heatherton had finally become his it was a sorry place but Philip had restored it all, working in the woods beside his own tenants to cut the valuable timber to sell to the boatyards at Shoreham. That income had been the means of undoing the years of neglect the once thriving estate had suffered under Henry's control.

59

Now, bereft of their leader and their inspiration, the heart had gone out of everyone.

John Bone, Philip's farm manager, met Giles, Marianne and Ahmed at the gate. The normally jovial giant was subdued as he greeted them. John had been Philip's childhood friend. Isolated from the outside world because his father had not wanted people to know of Henry's sickness, Philip had learned to wrestle and swim with John and had become adept at many other pursuits not normally engaged in by the sons of gentlefolk. It was an upbringing he had often had cause to bless, for he had learned rough skills that had stood him in good stead during his adventurous career.

Giles had always considered Bone to be rather uncouth, but he warmed to him now as he saw how affected he was by the loss of his master.

"It is said Lord Philip drowned," Bone said to him, "yet he was the strongest swimmer I ever saw. I can't believe he met his end that way."

"Not even if he fell from a high bridge into the River Seine, hampered by his clothes and sword, and with a bullet in him?" Giles asked sadly. "By all accounts he was not capable of swimming by the time he hit the water."

"Still, my Lord, his instincts would have made him try. If he was not killed instantly by the bullet I reckon he would have had the strength to save himself. After all, his body was not found."

"It may have been by now," Giles pointed out. "I wish I, too, could hope for a miracle, but I cannot."

They found Theresa calm, almost too calm it seemed to Marianne, but Giles was not surprised. Frail though she might look, he knew his sister had considerable strength.

Even so, her first words astonished him.

"He's not dead, Giles. I know it."

"Bone thinks that as well, but you have to face the facts, Theresa."

"Morgan feels as I do," she said defensively. "He wants to go to France to find him."

That was different.

Morgan, Philip's Welsh steward, had been very close to Philip. They had met in the French army when he had joined Philip's troops. He had later saved Philip's life, dragging him from under the hooves of a Dutch cavalry charge and, since that time, a bond had been forged between them which neither time nor distance, nor even death, it seemed, could sever. Morgan had a dark past, but Philip cared nothing about that and had kept the Welshman by him as his personal servant. He had later made him steward of the estate, although it was difficult at times to judge which was the servant and which the master. Philip would often defer to Morgan's judgement and allow his own strong will to be ruled by the Welshman's good sense.

Giles and Morgan had never truly liked one another.

Morgan was small and thickset, with a swarthy skin and wild black hair, and he was missing half of his left ear. Most found him a fearsome individual. Giles was not afraid of him, but he had always been able to sense the resentment the Welshman bore him.

"We have not always agreed, you and I." he said, a little awkwardly, when Morgan came in to see him. "I know you think me selfish and believe I only wanted Philip for the advantages he brought me, but there are things which must be discussed between us now and we must try to set aside our differences."

Morgan nodded. He was ever a man of few words and it seemed that as he grew older he became even more taciturn.

"My sister tells me that you are convinced Philip still lives."

"I am."

"She also tells me that you desire to go to France and search for him."

"That is my intention, if I can be released from my duties here."

"However would you go about such a task?" Giles wondered.

"I would speak first with the Comte de Rennes and learn all I could about the incident and then join forces with Thomas. I am certain that, together, we could discover the truth."

"Do you not think the Comte de Rennes will have already done all he can?" Giles said. "He was a good friend of Philip's."

"That's as maybe but the Comte is not a free man to do as he pleases. He is a servant of King Louis and would not, perhaps, be able to investigate the matter as thoroughly as it should be investigated."

"You surely don't believe the King of France was involved?" Giles said, shocked.

"It is my contention that King Louis feared to have him as his enemy and that he lured him to Versailles and then arranged his death to ensure that he never fought against France."

Giles regarded Morgan silently for a few moments. He could not, in his heart, believe Louis capable of such deceit, at least not where Philip was concerned, but it was a possibility that ought to be considered. "Yet you reckon he might still be alive," he said at length. "Why do you say so?"

"I can give you no reason other than I feel it to be so," Morgan admitted, "but he may be injured and in need of help. Whatever his condition, if he is alive then he will be in danger, since it is certain that another attempt will be made. Especially," he added grimly, "if the order for his murder came from King Louis himself. He should never have gone to France."

"I tried to talk him out of it, believe me." Giles paced the floor, turning the matter over in his mind. Unwilling though he was to allow vain wisps of hope to cloud his thinking, Giles had to admit that the Welshman did seem to have a sixth sense where his master was concerned. If there was the slightest possibility that Philip still lived then he knew that he, too, must join in the search, regardless of his promise to William. "Can you be spared from Heatherton for a while?" he asked Morgan.

"I believe so. John Bone is more than capable of running things in my absence and Bet can help him, for she has a head for figures which is better than mine."

Bet was Morgan's wife.

"Then perhaps you should come," Giles said. "You could accompany my sister and I and then, as soon as I have attended to a little business of my own, I will join you and Thomas in your quest. William has allowed me to be away for a month, but if it takes longer then so be it."

"Will you not be endangering your own position if you delay your return?"

"That is a risk I will have to take. I am leaving Marianne here, where she will be safe, so I will be at liberty to hazard my life and my reputation as I please. I hope this will not prove to be my ruin but the matter must be resolved. We will find him or we will find his killers. What do you say? Shall we join forces?"

"I would be glad of your assistance," Morgan told him. "You have your faults but I have never been able to claim that you were lacking in either courage or resourcefulness."

Giles raised an eyebrow. From the surly Welshman that came close to being a compliment!

SEVEN

∽

When the bargee had predicted that Philip would not live out the day he had sadly underestimated his constitution.

The bargee's daughter, whose name was Françoise, nursed him as well as she was able with the facilities on hand in the boat. Luckily the bullet had not lodged in his shoulder and she cleaned the wound with oil and bound it firmly, but Philip had become ill from exposure and the amount of dirty water he had swallowed.

The bargee moored in the city and unloaded his cargo of wood, but after a couple of days he was anxious to leave Paris.

Françoise, who had hardly left Philip's side, looked at her father worriedly when he told her they were leaving. "Can we take him with us?"

Her father scowled. "It's one thing to waste your time on him when we are moored but I shall need you to work along the way."

"I'll work," she promised, "and look after him as well."

"Suit yourself. Surely you don't think he's going to fall in love with you for tending him so fine," he mocked her.

"I know he won't," Françoise said quietly. "How could he, or anyone, love me?"

They travelled all the next day. Philip's temperature had risen alarmingly and Françoise picked some of the wild strawberries growing along the river bank and boiled the roots and leaves in barley water to cool his fever.

That night they moored near a tavern, where the talk was

all of the war with England. The bargee spoke as loudly as any against the foreign troops who were positioning themselves to march upon Flanders, but as he staggered back aboard Françoise begged him to be quiet.

"His fever has turned at last, praise God. He's sleeping peacefully."

The bargee followed her down the steps and looked at Philip. It was true. There were no longer beads of sweat upon his brow. He was cool to the touch and his breathing was regular.

"How long has he been like that?"

"About an hour. Before that he was calling out, but I could not understand the words. I think they may have been in a foreign language."

"A foreigner eh?" The bargee looked interested. "Let's hear him speak again." He gave Philip a nudge, despite his daughter's protests, and continued to shake him until he awoke.

Philip opened his eyes and attempted to focus on the flickering lamplight.

He closed them again, unable to properly see or to fathom his surroundings.

"He needs to rest," Françoise protested.

"He has rested long enough." The bargee shook him again and, this time, Philip did wake.

With a little cry the girl sank back into the shadows and Philip found himself looking into the bargee's coarse features.

He recalled jumping from the bridge and the gunshot that had sounded whilst he struggled in the water, but nothing after that.

"Who are you?" said the bargee.

Philip blinked, momentarily surprised to hear him speaking in French but, as his thoughts became more coherent, he adjusted himself to talking in that tongue, which came as easily to him as his own.

"A traveller, sir, who met with misfortune. My name is Guy."

Guy was Philip's second name and the one which came most promptly into his head. He was not so addled as to have forgotten there had been an attempt on his life and he knew he might still be in danger.

His throat was so dry that he could barely mouth the words at all and, as a cup of water was held to his lips, he became aware of someone else in the darkened room, keeping well out of sight. He drank gratefully. "Where am I?"

"Aboard my barge. I fished you out of the water, and a sorry state you were in, too, with a bullet wound in your shoulder."

"Then it seems I owe you my life, sir," Philip said when he had slaked his thirst, "and my thanks."

"My daughter tended you, not I."

Philip looked around but the other person, who Philip now took to be his daughter, was once more hidden from view. "I thank you anyway. I wish there was some way I could repay you."

"That is exactly what I have in mind," the bargee said. "Thanks to my daughter's time and trouble you have survived a plain attempt at murder. What do I get in exchange?"

Philip heard the girl gasp in horror at this, but her father spun round on her. "Be silent, you. You've played your part. I can still throw him back into the river."

It was the truth. Phillip felt as weak as a kitten and knew he could do very little to defend himself against the hefty bargee. Indeed, it was as much as he could do to even keep awake and he drifted once more into unconsciousness.

Philip spent the next day in a half-dozing, half-awake state where time had no real meaning and he was aware only of the throbbing of his shoulder when he moved and the sick feeling that never left his stomach. Water was offered him at frequent intervals, although by whom he could not say, and when the bargee appeared again beside him he was so confused in his mind that it might have been an hour or a week since their last conversation. The bargee continued it as though it had been but a minute.

"We were talking of how you might reward me for saving you from the river," he reminded him.

Philip recalled it now. As his head cleared he recalled also that he must give the mercenary bargee no clue as to who he really was. He needed to regain his strength and figure out a proper plan of action.

"Alas, there is nothing I can give you," he said. "You would have been welcome to my rings," he added, looking at his naked fingers, "but it would seem that I have lost them already."

"Rings? I know nothing about any rings," the bargee said quickly. "They must have come off in the water, but you have more things of value at home, don't you? You are a gentleman."

"Am I?" Philip asked guardedly. "Why ever should you think that?"

"From the look of you."

"I am flattered. I have certainly earned my living, on occasions, by posing as a gentleman."

Philip suspected that his rings were not lost in the river's depths at all but were now in the bargee's possession, and he knew he must invent some feasible tale as to how he came to have such treasures on him.

"A trickster!" the bargee snarled. "So that is why they shot you. I told my daughter you were not worth saving." He made a gesture of disgust to the girl, who was pressed against the cabin wall, out of the lamplight. "Wait, though, you could be lying. She said she heard you talking in a foreign tongue."

"I only thought the words were foreign," Françoise put in. "I wish now I had not mentioned it."

"Be quiet," her father ordered, studying Philip more closely. "Are you an Englishman? We are at war with England now and you could be a spy."

Philip closed his eyes. He needed to rest in order that he might think more clearly, for that piece of news had added to his problems.

"Let him sleep now," Françoise begged. "You can ask him more questions tomorrow. He cannot escape you."

"Very well, but if he is a spy then there might still be money to be made from him."

"You wouldn't turn him over to the authorities?" Françoise cried.

"Yes, if I could collect a fat reward. If not then let your pretty trickster ply his trade and make some money for us."

"But you already have his rings. Aren't they enough?"

The bargee raised his hand and fetched it across her face so hard that she fell to the floor. "Hold your tongue, Françoise, or I shall bring you out into the light and make him look at you."

Philip's hands were itching to deal with the greedy, lying bargee who treated his defenceless daughter so harshly. As he drifted off to sleep he vowed that he would speak with her tomorrow and thank her for her kindness to him.

When he awoke he guessed it was morning, although the cabin was still dim, for it was served for light only by a tiny porthole. Even so he could make out a shape under a heap of blankets in the corner and he suspected it must be the bargee's daughter. He raised himself up a little to look at her, for he was curious as to why she would not show herself to him, but he was weaker than he thought and groaned as he fell back on his sore shoulder.

The sound woke Françoise and she jumped to her feet. "What is the matter?" she asked him, her voice full of concern.

"Nothing but my own impatience," Philip said. "I am not yet as strong as I thought. But why were you asleep upon the floor? Have I taken your bed?"

"Yes, but I don't mind," she assured him. "Do you think you could manage a little food today, Guy?"

The prospect was not too inviting, but Philip knew he must eat if he was to restore his strength. Somehow he had to return to Paris and contact Thomas, who he knew would be out of his mind with worry and might even think him dead.

"A little bit, perhaps, if you would be good enough to get some for me."

"Of course." Françoise sped out the door so quickly that Philip still had no opportunity to see her and, when she returned and handed him a bowl of caudle made with ale, she turned her head away so that he should not see her face.

Philip noted the rest of her all the same. She was a young girl with thick, black hair and a dark skin, too dark for his own taste, but her figure looked good, so far as he could tell.

"Your name is Françoise, is it not?" he said, as he forced himself to eat the thin gruel. "Tell me about yourself."

She shrank back once more into the dark part of the cabin. "I am but a clumsy, ignorant girl, not fit to wait upon you," she said, in a small voice.

"Is that why you will not let me see you?" Philip said, putting down his bowl. He had managed to eat a little, but it had been a great effort.

"You wouldn't wish to see me, Guy. My father says I shouldn't be seen by anyone."

"For heaven's sake! Why?"

"I had the smallpox. It has left me very ugly."

"I see." Philip held out his hand to her. He was angered at the bargee's insensitivity toward the gentle girl who had cared for him. "Not too ugly, surely, to be looked upon by one whom, but for you, would never have seen anything in this world again. Come here to me."

He spoke the words not as a request but as an order and, as he had hoped, Françoise dare not do other than obey. She took his hand and slowly and unwillingly, stepped out into the light. She had evidently suffered the disease badly and, Philip guessed, had been left untreated, for her complexion was rough and pockmarked.

"I told you that you should not look at me," she tried to pull away from him, but Philip held her firmly. "Let me go, Guy," she begged, tears in her eyes.

"Not until I have thanked you for all you have done for me."

"It was a pleasure, please believe that. You looked so handsome as you lay there in my bed and there were so many times I wished myself a beauty so that you might open your eyes and see me and fall straightaway in love with me," she confessed. "Was that not foolish?"

"Very," he said severely. "How old are you, Françoise?"

"Twenty."

"Tsk! I have a bastard daughter older! You should find yourself a sweetheart of your own age."

"Whoever could love me?"

"A good many people if they knew of your kindness and compassion."

Françoise blushed. "Don't make fun of me, I beg you, Guy."

Philip shook his head. "I promise you I would never do that. Sit down here on the bed beside me, for I wish to talk to you."

She did as she was bid, although she turned her face a little away from him.

"I am going to tell you about two people who are very important to me, Françoise." He relaxed his hold upon her, but this time she did not try to get away from him and he patted the hand he held. "That's better! The first person I shall speak about is my brother-in-law. He used to be a very handsome man."

"As handsome as you?" Françoise ventured.

"Well very nearly, until the day he helped to rescue his sister, who had been kidnapped. He saved her life but, whilst defending her, a sword blade sliced his cheek from here to here." Philip drew an imaginary line down his own face and Françoise shuddered. "After that he was regarded not with admiration but with pity by everyone he met and he thought of himself as the ugliest creature in the world, yet now he has a wife who loves him and he holds such an important position that many people would gladly sacrifice their own looks to change places with him."

He glanced up at her and, this time, Françoise did not look away.

"Now to the second person," Philip continued. "Thomas is about your age and a year ago he, like you, was smitten by the smallpox." Philip put his hand to her cheek and touched it gently. "He, too, will carry the scars of the illness all his life."

Françoise trembled at his touch. "Does he hide himself away from the world too?"

"Indeed he does not! He travels with me everywhere I go and is the most impertinent and self-assured young man that you could wish to meet! When I see Thomas or my brother-in-law I don't see their disfigurement but their selves, who are dear to me."

Philip felt her cheek damp where he still touched it and saw that tears had started from her eyes. "I did not wish to make you cry," he told her softly, "but to make you happier, if I can."

"You have, Guy, oh, you have," she said, "and you have just repaid me for what little I did for you."

"What little you did for me was to save my life," Philip reminded her. "For that I shall remember you with gratitude for all my days, but you must not fall in love with me for I have a wife and a little daughter, and I must return to them as soon as I have the strength to do so."

Françoise nodded. "I will help you all I can," she promised. "I will even try to get your rings back for you when my father is asleep."

"I think you had better not," Philip said. "I would sooner lose them than have you beaten for my sake."

"Did you steal them?" Françoise asked uncertainly.

"No. They were mine. I did not tell your father quite the truth, I'm afraid, and I cannot tell you either, but be assured that I am neither a criminal escaping justice nor a foreign spy endangering your country."

"I believe you. No-one who looked like you could possibly be other than an honest, upright man," she said staunchly.

Philip laughed at that. "You should not judge too much by appearances, Françoise. I did not claim to be an angel! Now, if you can help me from this bed and up on deck into the fresh air I should be a lot obliged."

"You won't be leaving right away will you?" Françoise said anxiously.

Philip held on to her tightly, for the cabin was reeling around him as he tried to stand and all he really wanted to do was lie down again. "No, sweetheart, I shall not be leaving you just yet awhile, of that you may be certain!"

EIGHT

⁂

"Allow me to offer you my sincere condolences, Lady Southwick."

Theresa was at the Palais Royale visiting with Monsieur's wife, known as Madame. She turned to find herself looking into the face of an exceptionally good-looking young gentleman. She had no idea who he was.

He made her a low, elaborate bow. "Allow me to introduce myself, my Lady. My name is Luc Santerre and I was great admirer of your husband."

"Did you know him well?" Theresa said.

"Unfortunately, I met with him only a few times during this last visit of his to France, yet I do feel I knew him well, for I had made it my business to find out a great deal about him."

At any other time Theresa, with her inquisitive mind, would have wanted to know why, but it hardly seemed to matter now. She smiled politely at him and would have passed by but he stood in her way.

"Was your daughter much upset by the news?"

"My daughter?" Theresa looked at him in surprise, for only close friends would have thought to ask that. "Well, she is only small. She doesn't properly understand yet, for she was not with her father all the time."

"He did not have her living at Court?"

"Why no. We have a house in the country."

"Ah yes. High Heatherton."

Theresa excused herself and hurried on. The questions

had been put conversationally enough and yet she had found them strangely intrusive. She decided to tell Madame about the encounter.

Madame was frank and jolly, though not at all pretty, and she had always been a real friend to Theresa. Some found her coarse and outspoken but Theresa liked her. Although they had not met for several years their occasional correspondence had kept their friendship fresh and Madame had welcomed her to Paris with a warmth that had touched Theresa's heart.

She pulled a face when Theresa mentioned Luc Santerre. "He is one of Monsieur's hangers-on. You know how my husband likes to surround himself with handsome young men."

"He is handsome," Theresa allowed, "and, to be fair, he said nothing out of place, yet I sensed something strange about him. Why should he care how either Maudie or I feel since, by his own admission, he only met Philip a few times?"

"Perhaps he fancied himself in love with him!" Such things had become commonplace to Madame since her marriage to Monsieur.

"Perhaps. He did describe himself as an admirer."

"Then there is your answer."

"I suppose so." It made sense, although Theresa found the thought distasteful. She could not take these matters quite as lightly as Madame did.

"I never approved of your husband, of course," Madame told her candidly. "He was far too gaudy and he wore more jewellery than a man should."

Theresa only smiled. There was no need to fly to Philip's defence. Madame was saying no more now than she had always said to his face and it used to amuse him. She criticised Monsieur constantly for similar things. Not that it made the least difference.

"Philip always thought I was a stupid woman, I know that," Madame said.

"No, he didn't, truly," Theresa said. "He respected you. In

fact, fond though he was of Monsieur, he never knew how you endured him."

"Nor do I." Madame's taste was for more red-blooded men than her effeminate husband. Monsieur had once accused her of having an affair with one of the Chevaliers of the Royal bodyguard, and Theresa had always thought it very likely true! "Monsieur leads his own life, as he ever did, and I lead mine. He spends vast sums upon his favourites and gives me nothing, and invites his ridiculous friends to parties here at the Palais Royale. They don't think anything of him really. It is just that life at Versailles is now so dull they crave diversions."

"Is it honestly that bad?" Theresa said. Madame had always complained that Versailles was a tame place compared with the German Court which she had known in her youth, but to Theresa it had always seemed very exciting.

"You will shortly find out, since Louis will no doubt insist upon your staying there, whether you want to or not," Madame said. "He takes no account of the wishes or comforts of anyone, even his closest family. We ladies are expected to be lively and pleasant at all times, whether we are sick or tired or pregnant. Can you believe that only six weeks after I gave birth to my son I had to endure a journey with Louis to Fontainebleau, during which he insisted that I ate sweetmeats the whole way, even though I felt like death? He wouldn't even stop the coach when I needed to relieve myself. I tell you, the moment I alighted from the damn thing I rushed into the gardens and did it there and then, in the bushes!"

Theresa giggled. Despite her melancholy situation, the irrepressible Madame had managed to cheer her up, as she always did. "You are outrageous," she reproached her, "but we were talking of Versailles. What has caused it to change so much?"

"My dear, there is nothing but religion there now, and for that I blame 'La Pantocrate'." That was name Madame had given to Madame de Maintenon. "Even holidays are celebrated with extra-long sermons." Madame pulled a face. "I have never been a good Catholic, you know that. To me the monks and priests are worse than the devil, although it is heresy to say it now. They make such a to-do of their religion yet, for all their lengthy sermons and their singing, it is nothing but sham to them. They do not feel it in their hearts."

"You really should not say such things," Theresa chided her. "If Louis was not so fond of you it would be your undoing."

"He is not so fond of me as he was," Madame said, "and for that I blame the Dauphin. I confided to him one day that, in my opinion, a person of such low birth as La Pantocrate should not be allowed to remain seated in the presence of the King and Monsieur, and he only went and told her! There are few I can depend on now, for all wish to be in her good books so as to keep their favour with Louis, and even he has changed."

"Not too much, I hope," Theresa said. Louis had always made a fuss of her and she had grown extremely fond of him during the time she and Philip had resided at Versailles.

"You will find him very different, I'm afraid. He is not to be trusted any more. There are even some who think...," Madame checked herself mid-sentence, a thing she rarely did, for she believed in speaking her mind.

"Who think what?" Theresa prompted her, and then gasped in horror. "Not that he arranged Philip's death? You can't mean that, surely. Louis had the highest regard for him."

"Did I say anything to imply that he did not?" Madame said brusquely. "You put your own meaning into my words, but people do talk, you know. Your husband could be counted as an enemy to France now. At the time it happened it was no secret that war was about to be declared between our two countries. Make of that what you will."

"I will make nothing of it," Theresa said firmly. "I can't believe King Louis could be so wicked."

All the same, Madame's words did cause an awful inkling of

suspicion to awaken in her. The next day, when she went to visit Louis at Versailles, she almost dreaded meeting with him as she waited in the antechamber, where he had asked her to attend upon him.

The Swiss Guard opened the door for her and Louis turned around to greet her. As she came face to face with him every unkind thought she had entertained about him fled from her mind.

Louis' face betrayed his feelings only too well. There was so much concern evident in his features that Theresa's eyes began to prick with tears she had never intended to shed in his presence. The strength that had sustained her since the dreadful news was broken to her seemed to drain from her now that she needed it most, and she stood rooted to the spot, unable to move or even speak, like a clumsy country maid.

Louis did not wait for her to make the deep curtsey normally expected of a lady visitor, but took her silently in his arms and held her to him. It was the gesture of a friend, almost a member of the family, and Theresa was touched by it.

"Poor Theresa," he said gently, when he released her. "Philip was never good enough for you, as I often told him, but I know that you will grieve most deeply for him."

"I still can't quite believe he is dead, your Majesty."

"Nor can I, and it is especially ironic that he met his death in a river, for it was in another river, twenty years ago, that he first demonstrated his courage to me." Louis led her to a chair and indicated that she was sit down, which was a very great concession. "It was in the Dutch Wars, when he was serving as a captain under Condé, fighting for France against William of Orange," he could not resist pointing out. "Our troops were crossing the Rhine and several lines of cavalry were already in the water when some guns were fired from a fort at Tolhuys. As our men fired back at the fort from the river bank, the horses panicked and many soldiers were thrown and swept to their deaths by the strong current. Condé's son, Monsieur le Duc, was amongst those unhorsed and I saw Philip leap from his own mount into the water to save him. Although they were both weighed down with boots and weapons he managed to tow him to the bank through the floating bodies of men and horses. As well as an act of extreme bravery, it was also a most prodigious feat of strength."

Theresa had known that Philip had saved the life of Condé's son but she had never heard the story told in so much detail, for Philip had always been dismissive of the incident, and she said as much to Louis.

"I'm not surprised. For all Philip's ridiculous conceits, he rarely bragged about his truly great achievements. In fact your husband was a contradiction altogether, Theresa, for he was one of the most likeable and yet most infuriating men I have ever known."

"What steps have been taken to discover his murderers?" Theresa asked, wondering how she could have ever doubted him, but his next words shook her.

"I am responsible, Theresa, and I take full blame."

She stared at him, unwilling to believe what she had heard. "You, your Majesty?"

"Yes, I killed him as surely as if I had fired the bullet into him myself," he said bitterly. "Only the previous day I had offered him a proposition to consider. He was on his way back to me with an answer when he was killed. If I had left him in England then Philip would be alive today, even though it might be him instead of Marlborough now advancing upon my northern frontiers. I underestimated the hatred that his enemies bore him."

"But who in France hated Philip enough to want him dead?"

Louis went over to the window and stood for a moment watching the people in the marble courtyard below. "Many people hated him," he said at length, turning back to her.

Theresa's heart sank. His tone left her in no doubt of his meaning. "You are not going to try to find them, are you, your Majesty?" she asked, fearing she already knew his answer.

"No, Theresa, I am not, for it is useless. In any case, how could I carry out investigations into the death of one Englishman, however well he served France in the past, when there are eight thousand more preparing to attack my troops in Flanders? It would anger every loyal Frenchman in the land."

"But Philip was your ally."

"Yes, I truly believe he was. That is why I am prepared to hold a service for him fitting for a Hero of France, as he will always be considered by me. More than that I cannot and will not do. I hope you understand."

Theresa understood well enough. The ceremony was Louis' last gesture to a man who had once played his part in increasing France's might. It salved his conscience and demonstrated his generosity of spirit to the world. To risk the discovery that Philip's murderer was a member of his own Court would bring nothing but embarrassment to him.

She sighed. Theresa had come to know the world too well to expect much different, but she was bitterly disappointed nonetheless. "Philip would have been delighted to think that such a grand occasion was to be held in his honour," was all she could find to say.

"Of course he would. It is the final tribute his vanity would have most desired, and it is more than his own king is doing for him," he added pointedly.

"I don't believe King William has the time or inclination to involve himself in ceremonials at the moment," Theresa said.

It was true. William, beset by the problems of Europe on the one hand and Ireland on the other, had far too many other things upon his mind.

Louis' expression was one of plain disgust. "Not even for one to whom he owes so much? Some of us do not forget out debts so easily, Theresa. And now to you," he continued in a softer tone. "You will, of course, stay here at Versailles whilst you are in France. That is decided."

Theresa smiled, recalling Madame's prediction. "Yes, your Majesty."

"I have allotted an apartment to you near to that of the Comte and Comtesse de Rennes, who are here for the ceremony. I am sure you will find comfort in their company."

"Thank you, your Majesty. Armand and Marguerite are good friends and very dear to me," Theresa said, pleased.

"I am your friend also," Louis said, "and to prove it I have a matter which I would discuss with you, but I shall not trouble you with it now. Rest and restore your spirits."

"I can do that in the peace of your Majesty's gardens," Theresa told him, for she loved the gardens that Louis' gardener, Le Nôtre, had created at Versailles. "There are lots of little hidden ponds and bosquets, and I know them all. Sometimes you can find a quiet grove and not be disturbed for ages."

Louis put out his hand and touched one of her auburn curls. It was a simple gesture, yet filled with warmth and tenderness, "Since you desire peace, Theresa, you may visit me when I go to Trianon."

It was great honour to be invited to Trianon, the small palace Louis had built in the grounds of Versailles. It was to this more intimate residence that Louis went to escape the pressures of the Court and very few were invited to accompany him, normally only his family and courtiers of the highest rank.

Theresa was quite astonished by the offer since she herself was not of noble birth and, without Philip's name, would never even have been entitled to appear at Court.

"I am overwhelmed by your Majesty's kindness to me," she said as he helped her to her feet and escorted her to the door.

"You will find I can be a good deal kinder than this, Theresa, if you allow me to be," Louis' eyes met hers for a moment, "but that is a matter to be discussed on a future occasion."

∽

Monsieur was less than delighted when the Minister of War presented himself at the Palais Royale.

"Louvois, have you no heart? Don't you know that, save for a few of my closest friends, I have shut myself away from the world during this time of grief?"

Monsieur sniffed loudly and dabbed his eyes with his handkerchief, taking care not to smudge the black paint which he always daubed heavily upon his eyelashes. Whilst there was no doubt that he was genuinely grieving over Philip, the theatrical side of Monsieur's nature was being given full reign and, for the benefit of onlookers, Monsieur would register despair with more art than any player from the Comédie Française!

Louvois, it appeared, had known the First Gentlemen of France too long to be impressed with anything he did. "It is on account of one of your closest friends that I am here, Monsieur," he said crisply. "I refer to Giles Fairfield, who is a native of the country with whom we are now at war and is, in addition, of high political importance in his own land."

"Giles is permitted to stay in France for Philip's ceremony, provided he does not go to Versailles for any other reason, or cause disruption of any kind. My brother said so," Monsieur told him smugly.

"King Louis may well have agreed to that but, as Minister of War, it is my responsibility to ensure that he has every intention of keeping to those conditions."

"He has hardly been out of my sight for one instant since he arrived," Monsieur declared, "and I assure you that, since I am not normally permitted to associate with him, I shall keep him close by me until he leaves France."

"A fortunate man indeed," Louvois said dryly, "nevertheless I insist on speaking to him, Monsieur, for he has shown himself in the past to be a person not to be trusted."

Louvois' plump features were resolute and Monsieur sighed tetchily. "Oh, very well. We were to have gone for a carriage ride around the Tuileries gardens to try and lift my spirits," he gave another dab at his eyelids, "but I suppose that will have to wait. I'll send him to you now."

Giles had been expecting Louvois to contact him so he was not at all surprised at the summons although, for the sake of appearances to Monsieur, he pretended to be incensed about it.

He greeted Louvois curtly, for he saw no reason why he should exchange pleasantries with the man who had placed him in such a wretched position.

Louvois did not seem too surprised by that. "May I begin by expressing my sorrow at your loss, Lord Wimborne, a loss which myself and all France shares with you," he began smoothly.

Giles shook his head, marvelling at Louvois' hypocrisy. "You hated Philip, didn't you?"

"Hated a Hero of France? You would hardly expect me to admit to that, but we are not here to talk about the sad fate of your brother-in-law. His part in the affairs of France has ended – whilst yours is just beginning."

"It has turned out most conveniently for you that I am able to be in France at this time, almost too conveniently some might say," Giles said with a sidelong glance at Louvois.

Louvois' face was bland. "It is irony indeed that Lord Southwick's untimely death has afforded you the opportunity to comply with my wishes."

"Your wishes?" Giles said sharply. "More like your threats, Louvois."

"As you please, my Lord. Now to the business between us. Your royal master, King William, employed a network of spies long before he gained the English throne. He has them in every Court in Europe, in fact I have reason to believe that your brother-in-law was his agent in your country during King James' reign, even though he was supposed to be working for the interests of King Louis."

He paused but Giles was not about to be led upon that subject. Philip had been devious, it was true, and it was that very deviousness which had earned him Louis' protection during James' reign and William's gratitude after his accession!

"What is your point?" he prompted Louvois.

"My point is that King William will have an agent at Versailles and I am certain that you, being William's confidante, know who he is. I am not asking you to reveal his identity," he said, before Giles could protest. "That would be pointless, since he would be replaced directly he was compromised. What I want is for you to make contact with him and relate whatever information I shall give you which he, in turn, can transmit through his usual channels, in order to misinform the Duke of Marlborough."

Louvois paused, as though expecting some fiery reaction on Giles' part, but Giles regarded him coolly.

"I understand."

"The prospect of this evidently does not trouble you too much then," Louvois said.

"Not as much as it would trouble me to have you broadcast to the world that my Countess has another husband."

Louvois smiled. "You are everything I expected you to be, Lord Wimborne. Once this task is accomplished, and the results of it are evident, I shall be prepared to forget that I have ever heard of a certain baker from Cassis, or you either, for that matter."

Giles had to take a lot on trust, he realised that. He would have no guarantee that Louvois would keep to his side of the bargain, but he was really in no position to argue with the French Minister of War, and he knew it.

"Very well. What information am I to give him?"

"Firstly, I need to know how well are you acquainted with the Allies' plans," Louvois said.

"I know they are to divide into four separate forces," Giles told him. "In the north the Spaniards with some of the Dutch, under the command of the Prince of Vaudemont, are to capture

Courtrai. Beyond the Ardennes, the Elector of Brandenburg will lead the Germans and Prussians towards Bonn, and to the south the Count of Lorraine will attempt to take Mainz."

"And the English?"

Giles saw no point in holding back or lying. Louvois would soon discover if the information he had been given was false and then Giles would have gained nothing.

"The English are to join with the Swedes and the rest of the Dutch, under the command of the Prince of Waldeck. They plan to take Walcourt and claim the territory between the River Sambre and the River Meuse." Walcourt was an old town, strategically placed on a hill.

"Walcourt's defences are crumbling but it will not be easy to take," Louvois said, "especially if I can find a way to ensure that Marlborough and his English forces are split from those of the Prince of Waldeck. And to think," he added, "but for misadventure it might have been your brother-in-law at the head of those English troops. I fear it would have been far more difficult to obtain your cooperation under those circumstances, Lord Wimborne, whilst I imagine you are none too fond of Marlborough."

"No, I'm not, although he is an able enough soldier."

"One who was once your bitter enemy." Louvois recalled. "Was it not his troops who slaughtered the Duke of Monmouth's supporters at Sedgemoor?"

"I wish to ensure my future, not discuss my past," Giles said heavily. "Give me whatever information you wish me to pass on to William's agent and then please do me the favour of never communicating with me again."

"As you wish." Louvois handed him a sealed note. "This concludes our business, my Lord Wimborne."

Giles snatched the paper from him and looked the Minister of War levelly in the eye. "It had better, Louvois, it had better."

NINE

⌇

Theresa peered out at the gardens of the North Parterre. A gardener was sweeping the steps that led down to the fountain of the Pyramid and she suddenly envied him the simplicity of his life. The spring sun shone brightly, so that she longed to be outside herself that morning, but she dutifully ascended the winding staircase which led to the Royal Chapel. Mass had not quite ended and, from the first floor window, she could not resist glancing out once more. From here the view was even wider. She could see one of the great marble ponds, whose water sparkled in the sunlight, making patterns. She half-closed her eyes so that the flashes of light seemed to dance before her vision like brilliantly clad water fairies.

Theresa was still standing there when Louis came out of the chapel and she turned quickly.

Walking beside him was a soberly dressed woman, who drew back immediately she saw Theresa and assumed a more subservient place behind him. It was Madame de Maintenon.

As Theresa curtsied to Louis, Maintenon, in turn, curtsied to her, for no matter what inferences were put upon her relationship with the King, she was deferential to all of higher rank. Almost too deferential, thought Theresa, who was not fooled by either the pious expression on the face of 'La Pantocrate' or her outward humility.

She had tried to be fair, for such was her nature, and not be too much influenced by the fact that Madame did not like the woman but, so far, she had found nothing endearing about her whatsoever. There was little of warmth evident in Madame de Maintenon. When they had first been introduced she had asked to be permitted to express her regrets at Theresa's loss, but the words had plainly been mere words of duty and Theresa would rather not have received them at all, although she was polite to her for Louis' sake. If anything Maintenon seemed to resent her and Theresa suspected that she might have actually disliked Philip.

She was pleased when the solid figure of Louis' consort had departed, along with the rest of the retinue, and she was left alone with him.

He did not speak for a moment but he was evidently glad to see her, for he was smiling.

"Your Majesty desired me to attend upon you directly after the service," she reminded him.

"I had not forgotten but, tell me, what were you thinking of just now?" he demanded. "You had such a wistful expression on your face."

Theresa knew that the Sun King liked to be aware of even the innermost thoughts of those around him. "I was wishing I was one of your Majesty's gardeners," she told him frankly, indicating the man who was working below them. "Then I would be fortunate enough to be able to spend the whole day in the gardens."

That was at least part of the truth, the part that Louis would like to hear. He loved his gardens and always warmed to those who shared his pleasure in their beauty. Unfortunately for him, Madame de Maintenon was not one of them.

"Did I ever give you a copy of the guide that I prepared of the gardens?" he asked her.

"Indeed you did, your Majesty, and I followed it faithfully," Theresa said, for she had.

He looked pleased with that and led the way into his Cabinet of Curios. There many wonderful things to be found in this room, which was filled with Louis' personal treasures, some of which had been left to him by the late Cardinal Mazarin. Theresa looked around for her favourite piece. It was called a nef and was made of lapis lazuli, decorated with enamel flowers and with a face upon the front. I remember this well," she told him. "May I hold it?"

"Of course." He lifted the precious piece down for her and she fingered it reverently. A small bronze Neptune graced the top of it, sitting on a shell with his trident, and a gilded animal's head, fangs bared, looked out upon the opposite side.

"What do you think of this?" he asked her, taking it back and handing her a fluted dish made of agate. "It is my latest acquisition."

The dish set on a gilded base, was streaked with a dozen shades of green and a face was cleverly carved upon the side. "It is beautiful," she said, "like all your treasures."

"It is not only for their looks that I desire to own such things," Louis said. "Remember, we were poor when I was a child, so poor I had to wear patched clothes. Why, I even had to borrow money from Cardinal Mazarin in order to buy a farewell gift for his niece."

Theresa had heard that the Cardinal's niece, Marie, had been Louis' first love, but he had been forced to relinquish her upon his marriage.

"Mazarin had money," Louis said, somewhat bitterly, "and fine things too, though I inherited some of his treasures when he died. I have resolved now to surround myself always with articles of value, particularly those whose beauty is pleasing to me. I have a discerning eye, you know, Theresa."

He was watching her steadily whilst he talked, so that she could not take the remark other than as a compliment to herself and she blushed, which seemed to amuse him.

"I cannot believe that any woman who has been married for ten years to Philip can have remained so modest," he teased. "I never understood how you two suited each other so well, for you were not a bit alike. For one thing you appreciate beautiful objects whilst he never did, except, of course, portraits of himself!"

Theresa smiled, for she knew that the reference to Philip's vanity was meant fondly. "There are no busts or portraits of you in this room, your Majesty," she noticed, for Louis himself had been a trifle vain as a young man. Philip had told her that when Bernini, the great Italian sculptor, had been a little too faithful in his representation and had shown the slight irregularity of the King's nose he had been forced to alter his work to depict perfection!

"I have had enough of all that," Louis said dismissively. "I am constantly being troubled by commissions for statues of me to adorn provincial towns. I tell you, France is rapidly becoming disfigured by likenesses of me."

"You have changed," Theresa laughed.

"Not toward you, my dear." The blue-grey eyes caught hers and Theresa felt her cheeks grow hot again.

Louis nodded, as though satisfied with the effect his words were having on her. "Tell me, do you still wear the brooch I gave you?"

"Yes, of course I do." The ruby brooch had been a gift from him a few years before and she was very proud of it. It was not everyone, after all, who could boast of receiving a personal present from the King of France. "It is my greatest treasure," she assured him, "but it is not seemly for a new widow to be wearing jewellery."

"Not even Philip's widow? I don't think he, of all people, would mind too much but, if it troubles you, then I believe there are none who would find this inappropriate."

So saying he picked up a velvet box from the table and handed it to her.

She looked at it and then at him, taken completely unawares.

"Well open it, then," he smiled. "What an unusual woman you are, Theresa, to stand looking at a gift without attempting to discover what it is!"

In fact Theresa was usually as excitable as a child when it came to gifts, but this one was quite unexpected. She flipped open the lid and gasped as she saw, nestling on purple silk, a necklace made of shiny jet beads.

"Why, it is lovely, your Majesty," she said, quite overcome, for she guessed the necklace must be very valuable.

"When I married the Queen I could not afford to give her jewellery that did honour to France," Louis told her, as though reading her thoughts. "Now my fortunes have improved and I am in a position to give whatever I like to whoever I like. You will accept this, please, as a token of my great affection for you, and you will be able to wear it because even a widow may adorn herself with jet."

"I will wear it," she promised. "Thank you, your Majesty."

"Let me fasten it for you."

He stood behind her and she felt his fingers touch her neck as he closed the gold clasp. His nearness and his touch made her feel a little strange.

"You are very good to me," she said as she turned to show him the black beads, which gleamed against the whiteness of her skin.

"Why should I not be good to you, Theresa? I want you to turn to me for help when you need it, for you are alone in the world now. Are you happy at the English Court?"

The question caught her off guard. "Truly, I am no longer a courtier by nature," she said. "I am happiest of all when I am home with my daughter."

"I am pleased to hear that, for you see what I am about to say concerns your daughter."

Theresa was surprised. Louis loved children, yet she had not expected him to talk about Maudie.

"How do you agree with Queen Mary?" he wanted to know.

"Oh, fairly well, I suppose. I feel a little sorry for her," Theresa confessed. "She's not happy to be back in England."

"Not happy, when she has taken her father's kingdoms away from him?"

"Your Majesty should not judge her too harshly on account of that, for she was torn between her duty as a daughter and her duty as a wife," Theresa said loyally. "She put a brave face on it when she first arrived, so brave that some folk put about malicious tales of how she was gloating in triumph, but she loved Holland and she hankers for a much more private life than she can possibly expect to have as Queen of England. She spends all her time upon domestic matters or at her knotting."

Louis looked at her suspiciously. "Knotting? You jest with me!"

"Not at all! It has now become the most fashionable thing for a lady to be seen intent at work upon her knotting, whether she is in her carriage or in the Privy Gardens. The Queen sits working on hers so furiously you would think her livelihood depended on it!"

"And do you disapprove of such behaviour in a royal personage?" Louis still looked as though he did not believe her.

"Why no, but the fact is I can't do it!"

Louis laughed. "Theresa, you are a delight! There is little wonder that I am so fond of you. That is why I want to keep you here with me."

"But I cannot stay in France, your Majesty," Theresa protested, flattered all the same.

"And why not? Have you so many loved ones in England that you could not bear to leave?"

Theresa thought for a moment and then shook her head. She still had brothers and sisters in Dorset but her mother was dead and she had little to do with her father, who disapproved of Philip and the life they led. "It is only my brother Giles who I would truly miss, and he is always busy with his own affairs. The rest I could leave, and cheerfully, but England is my home. I have a duty there."

"You also have a duty to your daughter to consider," Louis said. "Listen now and I will put a proposition to you exactly as I put it to your husband the day before he died."

Theresa did listen, in amazement, as Louis outlined his plans for Maudie.

"I am overwhelmed, your Majesty," she said quietly, when he had done.

"Of course you are, but the decision must be yours now that you alone are responsible for your daughter's future. We can only surmise what Philip's decision would have been, but you knew him well enough to understand the ingenious way in which his mind worked."

"His 'distant hills'," Theresa said. She smiled at Louis' puzzled look. "It is just something he said to me before he left England, meaning that one should always look beyond the present, even when all looks well and you are happy." Her smile faded. "I really was happy then. He was still by my side and my world was quite complete. I keep imagining he is here with me."

"Oh he is here," Louis said dryly, "and never far away from us, for Philip is embodied in the very decorations of my palace."

It was Theresa's turn to look puzzled now.

"Decorations?" she repeated.

"Why, yes. The next time you go to the Marble Drawing Room glance up at the ceiling and you will see him."

"There are pictures of courtiers looking down on us from the frieze in that room," Theresa recalled.

"Indeed there are, and study with particular care a young man who stands alone over the first window by the door. He is handsome with long blonde curls, and he is dressed distinctively with a scarlet knot upon his shoulder and a scarlet bow at his throat. We are both aware of Philip's penchant for such adornments, as was Coypel, the artist, whose paintings decorate that particular room."

"You believe Philip persuaded Coypel to include him in the

frieze?" Theresa forgot herself sufficiently to giggle at the notion, but Louis did not seem put out.

"What greater triumph could there ever be for his conceit? Coypel never admitted to it, naturally, but Philip was in my service at the time and in a position to influence him. No matter, he was a pretty enough adornment for any room, but in achieving immortality in this way he also revealed a good deal of his nature. You will notice that he wears his hat, as though about to go upon his way. That signifies to me that even when he was a courtier it was but a part of his life, for Philip was like an actor, shifting constantly from one scene to another, and look closely at his expression. He appears to be smiling thoughtfully upon those below, as though considering how best he might manipulate them for his own ends."

Theresa looked at Louis in astonishment. It was evident that he had given considerable thought to the likeness and to Philip's nature too.

"I knew him very well," Louis said. "Better than Charles Stuart or James ever knew him, better even than Lord Shaftesbury, in whose service he nearly destroyed himself, and better, most certainly, than King William."

"And he respected you far more than he did any of them, even Shaftesbury," she confided. "He always said you were the man he revered most of any in the world."

"That is gratifying to know, but what of you Theresa?" he asked, looking directly at her.

"I have the most profound admiration and the deepest affection for your Majesty," Theresa told him, nervously fingering the necklace he had given her. She had not forgotten how his touch had affected her, in spite of herself.

Then you should not find the proposition that I offered Philip too hard to accept."

"I am a little surprised that you offer it to me," she admitted.

"There are several reasons why, even with Philip dead, I

am still offering my son as your daughter's husband. One is a statesman's reason, and you may not like it much," Louis warned her. "By this gesture I am showing the world that Philip and I were still friends and that those who have once served me do not all turn against me, as Schomberg has."

This reason Theresa could comprehend. Even though his country was now at war with France, Philip was to be remembered always as a French ally. It would be a snub to William and demonstrate that Philip's actions to put the Dutchman on the English throne were not directed personally against the King of France. Louis was right. Theresa didn't like it, although she suspected Philip would not have minded.

"The second reason is because I am a man of honour," Louis continued. "I offered Philip the opportunity of wedding your daughter into my family because I thought highly of him, and I did not make the offer lightly, you may be assured of that. To my mind he has fulfilled his part of the bargain, for he will never turn his hand against me now, therefore I should fulfil my part, and I am prepared to do so. The third reason I believe you know, if your modesty will allow you to admit it."

She looked at him uncertainly and he took her hand in his. "Theresa, would the admiration and affection you profess to have for me permit you to become my occasional companion?"

Theresa's heart pounded as he took her hand and raised it to his lips. The attraction between them had always been apparent to them both, yet he had never before made any advances towards her.

"You must have known how I felt about you," he said softly. "It was only on Philip's account that I have not pursued you before. You loved him much too well and, anyway, I feared he would not make a contented cuckold."

Theresa knew he was right about that. Whilst other men might have deemed it an honour to have their wives selected for favour by the King of France, Philip most definitely would not! All the same she was still astonished by his words for, by all accounts, he led an exemplary life now that he was dominated by Madame de Maintenon.

"What exactly is your Majesty proposing?" she said, when she could organise her thoughts sufficiently to speak.

"I am not suggesting that you openly become my mistress," he reassured her. "Such frivolities are behind me now, but I would enjoy to have occasional relief from the burdens of kingship. Our liaison would need to be discreet," he stressed, "for both our sakes, and for the sake of Philip's memory, but for me that would enhance the pleasure, and I promise to be kind to you always."

Theresa's head was spinning. She could not quite take in all he had said. Also she felt a little guilty. She should have protested at the prospect of having an affair, even with Louis, so soon after Philip's death, but she had not.

"It is too soon yet, I realise that," he said, when she did not speak. "We must both mourn our dead hero for the proper amount of time, but we have years ahead of us, Theresa. Stay at Versailles with me and you may command your King when you are ready for him."

He relinquished her hand and turned away, business-like once more, for Louis arranged his whole life as he did his work. He had put his proposition. If she agreed to it then, Theresa knew, a space would be found for her in his busy schedule. It was as simple as that.

She bit her lip, still unsure of quite what to say.

"Perhaps I am being a little unfair to you," he said gently. "I gave your husband time to consider my proposal; maybe I should give you the same."

Theresa collected herself quickly. Philip's proposal had not included the offer to become Louis' lover! To take time to consider that, even an hour, might be construed as an insult to the great man who had offered her so much. She knew that he was sincere and she had no doubt that a relationship would be pleasurable to them both but, all the same, there was someone she very much needed to consult with before she made up her mind.

"I need no time to discover the feelings I have for you, your Majesty," she said, "indeed I don't believe I have ever been able to properly hide them, even from Philip, but I must admit that I would like a day or two in order that I might arrive at a decision regarding my daughter."

"Of course." Louis looked pleased at her words, although Theresa doubted whether he had seriously expected to be refused. "You will not offend me by making me wait a little while for your answer, in fact, if you accept, I shall be all the more delighted knowing that you have given the matter the deepest thought. Let me have your decision after Philip's ceremony. That might be more fitting."

Theresa thought so as well and went to find Armand's wife, Marguerite, who had become her comfort and her confidante. The pair had bonded from their very first meeting, for Marguerite was not of noble birth and, like Theresa, had only acquired a title by marriage.

She looked horrified when she heard Louis' proposition. Marguerite did not share Theresa's affection for him, for she remembered only too vividly his persecution of her fellow Huguenots. That was a lot for the young Comtesse to forgive, too much, in fact.

"Whatever shall you do?" she asked. "If you refuse then neither you nor your daughter will ever find favour at Versailles again."

"I know it, yet there is one person I must see before I finally decide."

"Your brother?" Marguerite said.

"Giles? Lord, no! I would never ask him what to do, for any advice he gave me would be loaded with self-interest. The person I must ask is the mother of the boy Maudie has been invited to marry, for without her approval the proposal can go no further. I'll not have my child thrust into a world of hatred where she must fight for her survival against bitches who scheme to put her down. I've seen too much of that, at this Court and at Whitehall. I have to talk to Athénais de Montespan."

Marguerite made no reply to that but only pulled a face.

"You do see that I am right?" Theresa pressed her, for the opinion of her little friend was important to her.

"Yes, I agree that you must do it, but I have my own reasons for hating Madame de Montespan. Armand once had an affair with her."

This was news to Theresa, but she was not unduly surprised. Armand had cut a dashing figure in his military days. "I understand," she told her, "and in your place I would probably feel the same, although, now that I think about it, she most likely had an affair with my husband too, for I know they used to be great friends."

"How can you bear to meet her then?" Marguerite said.

Theresa laughed at her earnestness. "You have to remember that Philip, in his time, has had amours with half the women at two Courts! I couldn't possibly avoid them all. I'll leave right now, while I am determined on it. The ride will do me good. I will choose a horse from Louis' stables, for he assured me that everything in his entire household was at my disposal during my stay here."

"I'm not sure Armand would approve of your going off to Clagny all alone," Marguerite said worriedly. Clagny was the house which Louis had given Athénais when she had been his mistress. "He said I was to watch over you, but I'm sure you understand why I can't accompany you there."

"I understand perfectly, but don't fret, I will take Morgan with me," Theresa promised her.

She could not find Morgan, however, and recalled that she had given him leave only that morning to ride into Paris to find Thomas. Armand had told them that Thomas was making his own enquiries into Philip's murder, since no official one had been started. Theresa was not too concerned for Thomas' safety, for he was well able to take care of himself and there was never a person more at home in city streets, be they those of London or Paris.

She made up her mind to go to Clagny with or without Morgan., for the house was only a few miles from Versailles.

Before she left the palace Theresa made her way to the Marble Drawing Room and looked at the frieze above the first window by the door. She smiled to herself. Now that she looked closely at it she could see that Philip was, indeed, the handsome courtier in the painting, although it had not occurred to her before and he had never once mentioned it.

She noticed, too, all that Louis had said about the figure poised above her, and she noticed something else besides — the courtier's face seemed to be lit by the radiance of the sun, and she felt this to be, somehow, an omen. If she accepted Louis' offer then she would likely bask in the Sun King's affection all her life.

It was a point very much to be considered.

TEN

❧

Philip's strength had come back to him slowly, too slowly for one impatient to return to Paris. He had begun to take a turn, each day, walking the powerful black and white barge horse along the towpath, at first for only a mile or two but soon he was spending the greater part of the day leading the animal in its patient plodding.

The clean country air was revitalising him and the gentle pace of river life seemed to restore his powers of thought as he quietly plotted his revenge against his unknown enemy. His first action, he knew, must be to somehow contact Armand. With his help he could let those who loved him know that he was safe and, hopefully, set about discovering the identity of whoever it was that desired him dead.

The barge had travelled as far as Montereau, where the River Seine joined with the Yonne, and it had picked up a cargo of the wood which had been floated down the Yonne from Morvan. They were on their way back to Paris and would soon be passing near the forest of Fontainebleau.

Philip intended to quietly slip away as soon as they reached the next lock. He was sure that the bargee was still convinced he was a spy and would likely inform the Paris authorities of the fact if he thought he could profit by it with a reward, so Philip suspected he might have trouble if he openly announced his intention to depart.

Françoise was walking along beside him that day; indeed, she was rarely out of his company, and he saw with satisfaction that his encouraging words to her seemed to have had good effect. She no longer shrank from the sight of those she encountered along the riverside. Instead, with Philip's reassuring hand upon her arm, she faced them cheerfully, gaining confidence by the day.

All the same, she grew quieter the nearer they got to the lock.

"What is it?" Philip said. He had come to observe her very closely.

"There is a young lock-keeper here. We used to be good friends."

A sad look came into her face and Philip noticed it. "Were you in love with him?"

Françoise blushed. "I think I was. Each time I passed this way we would spend a happy evening in each other's company whilst my father and his cronies sat drinking together." She smiled at the memory, but her smile faded as she came back to reality. "But he is the one person I cannot face."

"Well, I'm afraid you must, that is if you intend that he shall ask you to marry him," Philip said. "Of course if you would sooner spend your life trudging up and down the river bank and caring for that ill-natured father of yours then you could always hide from him as you have before."

Françoise hung her head. "That's not fair."

"It is extremely fair upon your father, who no doubt hopes that he has persuaded you to withdraw from the world so that he will have a skivvy to slave for him for the rest of his life."

She did not speak for a moment and Philip feared that he might have gone too far, but the pathetic little creature had struck a rare chord of sympathy in his cynical heart, and he was determined that she would overcome her self-doubts. Also, a meeting between her and her lover would serve his own purposes quite nicely, for he was not relishing taking his leave of one who had become so dependent on him.

"Look at me, Françoise," he said, sternly. "Do you think this young man loved you too?"

"I'm sure he did."

"Then you will face him, just as you face me now."

Françoise bit her lip and Philip knew how daunting it would be for her to show her pock-marked face to the man she loved, but he was determined to persuade her to do it.

"Use those dark eyes to best advantage and employ every feminine wile you know. In a short time you could be a wife and your father will have to employ someone to lead his horse for him and cook and clean. God knows he can well afford it with the money he will get from the sale of my rings. What do you say?"

"When I talk to you it seems as though anything is possible," she murmured, looking into his eyes.

"And so it is. Then you'll do it?"

"Yes," she said emphatically. "Yes, I will. If he no longer likes me then he never did care for me enough to make me his wife."

"Good girl! Go tidy yourself up now. Put on your prettiest dress and comb those lovely curls."

She turned to do as he said, then hesitated. "You're leaving, aren't you?"

"Yes," he said truthfully, for he could not lie to her. "Yes, I am, but shall never forget you, or that I owe you my life." He kissed her on both cheeks. "Now go and make me proud of you."

She smiled at him, although her eyes were moist. "I will, Guy. I promise that I will."

Françoise had not reappeared by the time the barge entered the lock so that Philip feared her courage had failed her after all. He took a special interest in the young man who was turning the handles of the lock's mechanism. He was not especially handsome but Philip noted approvingly that he had a kind and amiable face.

The young man appeared to be observing him too. "What are you doing on board?" he called out.

Philip smiled. Jealousy might be the very thing to fire the

smouldering embers of this particular love affair. "I am just a traveller who Françoise and her father have befriended."

"And how long do you propose to stay with them?"

"That depends." Philip looked meaningfully toward the boat.

The young man's jaw tightened. "How is Françoise? She would not see me the last few times they passed by this way. Her father says the smallpox marked her badly."

Philip made a gesture of indifference. "I've seen worse. Such things do not trouble me."

"Nor me."

"Then why not go on board and tell her so?"

The sound of the water rushing out of the lock drowned out their conversation then but Philip noted with satisfaction that, as the barge began to descend, the young lock-keeper did leap down upon the deck of the barge.

Françoise's father, holding the boat steady with a rope, scowled but there was not much he could do.

They moored on the other side of the lock and Philip led the horse into a nearby field. Françoise's father was in a huddle with two men upon the quayside and Philip feared that he might well be the subject of their conversation.

It was time to go.

He felt he had more than paid his debt to both of those who had saved his life. The bargee had his rings whilst Françoise, if she was shrewd, had a husband. All Philip had at that moment was the dirty shirt and breeches he was wearing; a barefoot duke without a sou in his pockets, wandering the highways of a country at war with his own.

It was a prospect many would have found daunting but Phillip still had one valuable possession – an ingenious mind that had extricated him from tricky situations many times before and would, he was certain, do so again!

Athénais de Montespan was still a very beautiful woman. She had been superseded as Louis' favourite by Madame de Maintenon but Theresa could not see how he could possibly prefer that austere matron to this lovely, animated creature, with her fascinating voice.

Although he had discarded her as his mistress, it was said that Louis still cared for her and saw to it that she wanted for nothing, but Theresa guessed this would be scant comfort to a passionate woman who had loved him enough to dye her dark hair blonde for him and endure rigorous treatments to reduce her weight.

She had met Athénais before but she still felt overawed to be alone with this voluptuous woman who had been such a close friend to Philip in the past. However, she was quickly made welcome and put at her ease.

"Philip's death was a great blow to me. I was always very fond of him," Athénais said frankly, "although I was never his lover, and that is the truth. I was Armand's lover once, though, and I fear your friend, the Comtesse de Rennes, still hates me for it."

"She does," Theresa said, "but I have no reason to hate you, quite the reverse, for I know you helped to have Philip released when he was in the Bastille. What I came here to discover is whether you hate me, or rather my daughter."

"I suspected that was why you came," Athénais said. "Louis has already discussed with me the proposition he was going to put to Philip. So now he has offered it to you. That is like him."

Theresa thought it hardly tactful to tell Athénais what else Louis had offered her!

"I need to know your feelings on the matter," Theresa said, "for I love my child too much to ever want her to advance against the will of her husband's mother."

Athénais laughed. She had a lovely laugh; in fact her whole manner was so very pleasant that Theresa could well understand the affection that Philip had felt for her.

"Why ever should you think that?" she said. "What reason would I have to hate the woman who made Philip so happy, much less his little daughter? I should be pleased to have her for my daughter-in-law, you silly girl!"

"Forgive my foolishness." Theresa hung her head, feeling ashamed of her fears. "My thoughts are in turmoil. I must make decisions when I am least capable of making them, and I want to do what Philip would have wished."

"He would have wished for you to marry your daughter to my son," Athénais said emphatically. "I beg you to treat me as your friend, Theresa, for that is what I will be, if you let me."

Theresa nodded wearily. "I would be glad of your friendship."

Her voice wavered and Athénais came over to her, looking concerned. "You poor thing. How I feel for you, but I had heard that you refused to believe Philip was dead."

"I am no longer so certain that he is alive," Theresa admitted, "not at Versailles with all the preparations being made for his memorial service. I think the awful truth finally came home to me today, during my talk with the King. This is the first important choice I have had to make without him and it occurred to me suddenly that I shall be making decisions alone for the rest of my life. Oh, Athénais, I am going to miss him so very much."

"I know you are," Athénais said quietly, putting a comforting arm around her, for Theresa could not control her tears. "He is the very worst kind of man to lose, for he was so very much alive, but perhaps you should not give up on him quite yet. I once persuaded him to see a fortune teller and she was quite explicit as to the method of his death. It was certainly not predicted to be in water."

Theresa dabbed her eyes and looked at her. "Yes, he told me about that. She predicted he would die in prison, did she not? I think he treated it as a jest."

"He should not have done so, for she said a great deal more than that although, no doubt, he has chosen to forget it." Athénais shuddered. "You probably think I am a very foolish woman, but to tell you the truth I have always been a little scared of such things."

"What exactly did she say about Philip?" Theresa wondered, but Athénais shook her head.

"Some other time, perhaps. Now tell me, how are you getting on with Maintenon?"

"She doesn't seem to like me very much," Theresa admitted.

Athénais laughed. "Well she wouldn't, would she? You are Philip's wife, and he stood for everything she dislikes, but there is quite another reason why she hated him."

"Really?" Theresa said, intrigued.

"Oh yes. It was years ago, when Philip was introducing his crippled poet friend to literary society," Athénais explained. "She was a widow then, known simply as Madame Scarron, and she was visiting Philip's salon with me, but she had no more tact than to make disparaging remarks about Jules Gaspard's talent and even nasty inferences about their relationship. Philip was furious and promptly ordered her out of his house, in front of everyone, and told her never to return."

Theresa smiled, despite her sadness. "How wonderful of him."

"Yes, it was rather wonderful," Athénais agreed, "but a trifle foolish, as matters turned out. Who could have predicted that she would someday be Louis' favoured one? Not me, for sure," she said bitterly. "And to think it was through me that she advanced so far. When I engaged her as a governess to our children Louis could not abide her, but I persuaded him of her worth. I even obtained the money from him so that she could buy the estate of Maintenon. I little thought the bitch would go behind my back, telling such lies to Louis about me that he took her part." Athénais sighed. "Enough of my problems, you have your own. Shall you stay and dine with me? I would enjoy to have your company."

"I would enjoy it too," Theresa said truthfully, for she liked

Athénais more than she had ever thought she would, "but I should be leaving now if I am to return to Versailles before dark."

"You are most welcome to stay the night, if you prefer it," Athénais offered.

"Thank you, but I must get back. Armand worries dreadfully about me and will be convinced that something awful has happened if I don't return."

Athénais smiled. "He is a sweet man. Would you like one of my servants to accompany you? I don't think you should go alone, for it is already dusk."

Theresa declined the offer, for she enjoyed to ride by herself, but she soon began to wish she had accepted Athénais' invitation to stay the night, for she had not even reached the outskirts of Versailles before the skies darkened rapidly and a loud clap of thunder startled her horse.

It had been a warm day and she was wearing only a light riding outfit and had no protection from the impending weather. She debated whether to turn back but decided there was little point, having come so far, and pressed on, resolving to make for Trianon, for she knew she would be quicker travelling that more open route than attempting to negotiate the streets of the town.

The thunder sounded again and rain began to fall. As Theresa urged her frightened mount faster she became aware of a figure riding some way behind her. She had vaguely seen someone near the crossroads when she had turned toward Trianon and it seemed as though he had made the same decision. He kept a steady distance behind her until they drew closer to the palace, then she noticed a marked increase in his pace.

`Theresa was not unduly alarmed, for she could already see the white stone palace of Trianon though the trees and pick out its marble columns. Not being of a nervous disposition, she was more absorbed in the problems of the weather than her own safety, but she did look round at the sound of the fast approaching horse's hooves. She frowned, pushing her wet hair from her eyes. She recognised the rider now but could see no reason why he should wish to catch up with her, and she decided that he, like her, was merely fleeing from the downpour.

As the rider drew near a flash of lightening illuminated the sky, startling Theresa's horse. It reared and her damp gloves could not grip the reins.

Theresa hit the ground heavily. Bruised and shaken, she struggled to her feet, expecting her follower to dismount and help her, but he did not.

"Won't you at least try to catch my horse?" Theresa panted, angry that, on top of his lack of consideration for her plight, he had not even tried to stop the animal from bolting.

Luc Santerre was watching her with a strange, triumphant smile upon his handsome face. "You won't be needing him, Lady Southwick, for you are coming with me."

"Indeed I am not," Theresa said furiously, attempting to brush the mud from her sodden skirt.

The next lightning bolt seemed to be directly overhead and, by its brief brightness, she could see that Santerre had a pistol levelled at her.

"You must be a madman," she shouted over the roar of thunder that followed closely.

"I possibly am, but you have been very stupid to ride out alone, and on such a night."

"I see that now." Theresa realised that their meeting could not possibly be a coincidence. Luc must have followed her to Clagny and back, hoping for just such an opportunity, and she had played right into his hands. She looked about her frantically but there was nowhere to run for cover, besides she would not have got far, for she was hampered by her skirt, which now clung to her legs like a soggy sheet. "Why are you doing this?" she demanded in as steady a voice as she could manage.

"I have my reasons, as you will discover in due course. Now mount up here behind me. My horse can carry us both."

This time he did offer her his hand, but Theresa stood fast.

"I will do no such thing."

He shrugged. "Then walk. Whatever way you choose I intend that you shall, accompany me."

"And if I refuse? Shall you kill me," she paused as a dreadful thought struck her, "...as you did my husband?"

He laughed, but it was a dry, harsh sound that was unpleasant to her ears. "You think *I* murdered him? He has more important enemies than me, of that you may be assured. In any case I did not want him dead. It would have suited my purposes better for it to be him, not you, here with me now."

"You would not have crept up on him so easily, I am certain," Theresa muttered, accepting, with very bad grace, the hand he still held out to her, for she did not fancy trudging along besides him in the pouring rain.

"He was taken easily enough upon the Pont Neuf," he reminded her sneeringly. "The great Hero of France, it seems, was not a match for three hired assassins."

He said no more as they rode back the way they had just come. This time, when they reached the crossroads, they turned towards the town of Versailles.

Theresa could not imagine why Luc would have wanted to ambush Philip if not to do him harm but she had other problems to contend with at that moment.

He slowed as they reached the edge of the town and halted before a dingy, single storey cottage which was little bigger than a hut.

He dismounted and helped her down. Theresa decided to have one last attempt at reasoning with him, for she had no idea what fate might be awaiting her inside. Whatever it was she felt far from able to deal with it. The day had been eventful enough, even before her encounter with Santerre!

"Luc," she began, shivering as she spoke for, although the rain had stopped, she was soaked right through to her skin and it was most uncomfortable. "It would be wise for you to let me go. I have some very powerful friends who will soon be looking for me and then you will find yourself in a great deal of trouble."

"I know all about your powerful friends, my Lady. Even King Louis himself is a friend to Lord Southwick's wife, but I do not intend to hurt you."

"Then why have you brought me here?"

"I want you to see inside the hovel where I lived as a child."

"Whatever for?" Theresa asked him, mystified.

"Let us just say, Lady Southwick, for a lesson in the unfairness of life."

ELEVEN

ᴄ᷍ᴐ

Philip spent the night in the forest of Fontainebleau. He had hunted there in the past, and stayed at the chateau at Louis' invitation but he was in no position now to boldly announce himself at the main doors. For one thing he was no longer sure who was his friend and who was his enemy and, for another, he was hardly dressed for visiting a royal palace!

Very early the next morning he approached the chateau cautiously. What he had in mind to do, which was to take a horse from the royal stables, was extremely risky. Philip was accustomed to the taking of risks but, even for him, the plan was hazardous. If he was caught, looking the way he did, the guards would be likely to shoot him before he could explain who he was or, if he did manage to explain, it would then be known that he was still alive. That would seriously damage any chance he had of finding his would-be killers, or even avoiding them should they try again.

As he went past the coach house he glanced in to see if he recognised any of the equipages there. The coat of arms upon one of them was unmistakeable.

He laughed softly to himself. It belonged to Mary of Modena, the wife of James Stuart and the previous Queen of England.

Philip could scarcely believe his luck. If there was any person who owed him a favour it was she. The only question was whether or not she was a lady who paid her debts.

His problem now was how to contact her.

Philip looked about for a means to make himself look less

conspicuous. There was an apron hanging on a peg in the stables, left there by a groom he guessed. He put that on to cover his grubby clothing and then found a pair of riding boots in the tack room. They were too large but they sufficed to make him look a little more respectable. He would have liked to find a hat, partly to cover his tangled hair and partly to hide his face, but there was not one conveniently left there. In any case he doubted he would be recognised in the garb he was wearing, so he walked boldly toward the servants' courtyard.

One of the palace guards was walking from the nearby parade ground and Philip cursed beneath his breath as the guard intercepted him.

"Where do you think you're going, fellow?"

"I have a message to give Her Majesty, Queen Mary," Philip told him, with as much dignity as he could muster under the circumstances. "Would you be so good as to ask if she will see me?"

"Who is the message from?" the soldier demanded.

"Tell her, if you please, that it comes from a gentleman who comes to claim a favour that she owes him."

The guard looked him up and down suspiciously

"What gentleman?"

"That I am not at liberty to say. My words are only for the ears of the Queen," Philip said firmly.

The guard still looked dubious but obviously thought that, as the English Queen was a guest at the chateau, he had better serve her interests as best he could. "I will fetch one of her servants who will take you to her. If she agrees to see you, that is," he added.

Philip hoped fervently that she would, otherwise he might find himself in a devilishly tricky position.

He had hoped that the wording of the message might intrigue her and it seemed that it had, for a servant appeared before long and beckoned Philip to follow him up the stairs to one of the chambers on the first floor.

"I wish to see the Queen in private," Philip stressed, as the servant made to precede him into the room.

"I will need to ascertain Her Majesty's wishes in the matter," the servant informed him pompously.

"I'll see him in private, if he wishes," Philip heard the Queen say. "I can't believe a man would walk boldly into this palace to do me harm, since he must know that his own life would certainly be forfeit before he left the building."

She looked up interestedly as Philip entered and her face paled. "Philip Devalle?" she said incredulously. "Can it be?"

Philip breathed a sigh of relief.

"Well it is not his spirit come to plague you," he assured her, taking up her hand and raising to his lips. "I am sorry if I have given you a shock, your Majesty."

"You have indeed," she said. "I was told that you were dead, drowned in the Seine after your carriage was attacked on the Pont Neuf."

"Have the men who attacked me been found?" he asked hopefully, but she shook her head. He thought he saw a sudden look of embarrassment cross her face, although he could not fathom why.

"In that case it would be better if I was still thought to be dead," he told her. "The fact is I have no idea who tried to kill me or who employed them. Until I have discovered that, my life remains at risk and there are few people I feel I can truly trust."

"And you trust me, the wife of the king you helped to depose?" she asked archly.

Philip was not put out. "The king I aided in his flight to France," he stressed.

"You helped me too, I have not forgotten that," she assured him in a gentler tone. "You could have prevented my leaving London; you could even have taken my son from me." She shuddered at the memory of the dark, rainy night when Philip had come upon her and her party making good their escape from the capital. "I have many times thanked God that it was you we encountered and not a person of less honour and compassion."

Despite his own allegiance to Queen Mary's enemy, William of Orange, Philip had not detained her on that fateful night but had helped her to the boat which waited for her and her baby son. Few people knew of the incident for not too many, he reckoned, would have understood his decision, but Philip had never regretted it.

"I trust the day will never come when I wreak revenge on women and children," he said sincerely, "but now it is I who am in need of *your* assistance."

"I will do anything that does not betray the trust of King Louis, who has been so kind to me," she promised.

"I have no reason to suppose that Louis is involved in this, but I cannot be sure," he told her honestly. "All I ask of you is that a message be sent to the Comte de Rennes, for I know I can rely upon him, and also that I might be given sanctuary here until he receives my letter and travels down from Brittany. I throw myself on your Majesty's mercy."

"I will aid you in that and gladly," she agreed. "It is little enough after what you did for me, but you will not need to hide at Fontainebleau. In fact, you were fortunate to find me here at all for I am returning to Saint-Germain today and you could accompany me, that is if we can find you some decent servant's clothing. As for Armand, well he is closer than you think for he is at Versailles in readiness for the ceremony."

"Ceremony?" Philip asked, perplexed.

"Yes. The grand memorial ceremony that is to be held in your honour."

That came as a complete surprise.

"You know nothing of this?" she asked, seeing his expression.

"Indeed not, but I rather like the notion," Philip admitted.

The Queen smiled. "Yes, I thought you would! Wherever have you been not to have heard tell of it?"

"I was wounded," he reminded her. "I have had barely any contact with the world."

"Then you won't know either that your wife is also here for it."

"Theresa is in France?" Philip's heart lifted at the thought.

"Yes, poor, sad little thing. I ought to hate her for the trouble she has caused my husband yet, when I saw her, I felt only pity. She mourns you deeply, Philip, and so does Monsieur. I declare I have never seen the man in such a state; pale as a ghost and unable to say more than a few words about you before he dissolves into tears."

Philip was flattered by that but he knew he could not entrust Monsieur with the knowledge that he was alive. Not yet. Monsieur was quite unable to keep secrets and the news would be broadcast in no time, which did not suit his plans.

Servant's clothes were found for him and the journey to Saint-Germain together passed pleasantly enough. The Queen became quite animated as they reminisced over old times at Whitehall, for they had known each other for many years and Philip had always treated her courteously.

. "How is King James?" he asked her.

"Obstinate as ever," she said frankly, "but in other ways he has changed. He has even begun to stammer lately, as his father did, and I fear for his health."

"His health?" Philip said, surprised, for James had always been very strong and seemed to suffer from nothing worse than the occasional nosebleed.

"Not his physical health," she stressed. "He can still hunt with the best and outlast many a younger man in the saddle. He's even found himself two scarecrows to dally with in Ireland, I am told! Not only must he always make me a figure of ridicule with his mistresses but, as his brother, Charles, used to say, he has not even the good sense to like them beautiful!"

Queen Mary was very beautiful, with jet black hair, pale skin and a dainty oval face. She was James' second wife, although it was widely known that she had once intended to be a nun, for she was deeply religious. She was also spirited. Philip smiled as he remembered the many times she had set upon her husband in public on account of his infidelities, indeed the domestic scenes between them when they were still the Duke and Duchess of York had enlivened many a social function at Court!

Philip had seen for himself the beginnings of a change in James mental state the previous year, when he had helped the King to leave England. He had never rated James' intelligence particularly highly, yet it seemed that an almost childlike unreasonableness had developed in him. Still, he figured, as traumatic an event as losing three kingdoms would have affected a person far less irrational than James Stuart!

"Perhaps some active service in Ireland will restore him," he suggested.

"He is up against Schomberg," she reminded him.

"I know. William was going to send me there too."

The irony of the situation struck him. But for misadventure, Philip could be, even now, upon an Irish battlefield facing the husband of the woman who was helping him.

He had long ago ceased to ponder upon such twists and turns of fate.

The Palace of Saint-Germain was, to Philip's mind, a grey and somewhat unattractive place, but it held poignant memories for him as they arrived. He had once seen a play performed there that had been written by his friend Jules Gaspard and he wondered what Jules would think if he could see him now, dressed as a servant, arriving in attendance to the exiled English Queen!

The Queen wrote a note to Armand as soon as they arrived, saying nothing except that she wished to see him without delay. Philip thought this would be the safest course in case the letter fell into other hands.

༄

When Armand got to the palace he was shown into an ante-room to wait for Queen Mary, so he was told. As Philip opened the door he turned, ready to make a deep bow.

He froze as he realised who had actually entered.

Armand began to laugh softly, shaking his head as he held his hands out to take Philip's own. "It's true, you really are indestructible! Dear God, but you're a welcome sight."

"And so are you, believe me, my old friend," Philip said truthfully, for this was the one Frenchman he knew he could trust implicitly. "How's my Tess?"

"Brave in her grief and strong. You would have been proud of her."

"And Thomas? Is he with her?"

"No. Thomas is still in Paris. He took the news of your death very badly," Armand warned him. "He blamed himself for allowing you to travel alone."

"I knew he would. Poor Thomas." Philip had thought a lot about his servant lately.

"He has sworn to avenge you, even if he never returns to England. When I last heard he was scouring the lowest dens of evil in the city for some clue as to your murderers. I only hope he has better luck than I have had with my enquiries."

"An official investigation has discovered nothing?" Philip said.

Armand looked uneasy. "There is no official investigation, Philip, nor will Louis allow there to be one."

Philip's heart sank. He understood now the embarrassment the Queen had shown when he had brought up the subject. "That must means he suspects someone close to him, unless of course…," he paused as an even worse thought struck him.

"It wasn't Louis himself, you may be sure of that," Armand insisted. "He loves you far too well."

"I hope you're right," Philip said darkly. "If it was at his instigation then I may as well take my own life here and now, for what use will it be to me? If there is one man in this world I cannot fight it is King Louis."

"But if he was responsible why would he be planning to hold this most magnificent ceremony to honour you?" Armand said.

"Lots of reasons I can think of." Philip had been involved in intrigues long enough for him to be a cynic.

"But there is something else. Only yesterday he repeated to Theresa the same offer he had made to you."

"Did he indeed?" That was more hopeful, until a worrying thought struck Philip. "She never turned it down, did she?"

"Why no. She was considering the proposal; in fact she rode out to Clagny yesterday to ascertain Athénais de Montespan's feelings in the matter."

"Clever girl! Athénais would convince her it is for the best."

"I assume she did, for it appears Theresa stayed the night at Clagny, which we took to be a good sign, so you see you need have no misgivings on that score."

"But the fact remains that the only people in the whole of France who are searching for my attackers are you and Thomas," Philip said crossly.

"Not quite. Your steward came over from England with Theresa."

Philip was overjoyed at that news. "Excellent! He is just the person I need."

"He is not alone. Lord Wimborne came as well."

That was more of a surprise. "I thought Giles was never to be allowed into France again."

"Well he's here now and a guest of Monsieur, so make of that what you will. I can't pretend to like your brother-in-law very much," Armand admitted.

"Not everyone takes to Giles," Philip said with a fond smile. "I tell you frankly there have been occasions when I have wanted to kill him and other times when there is no-one in the world whose company I enjoyed more."

"And does he feel the same?"

"Oh, yes. We are fated for each other, Giles and I, but we parted badly the last time and I expect he has suffered on account of it. In fact I very much hope he has," Philip added, recalling Giles' parting words to him, "the sanctimonious little bastard!"

"Well he has promised to aid the search for your killers anyway," Armand said, "but I don't see how much use the man can be. In the first place your King William has given him a leave of absence for no more than a month and in the second he has been forbidden to leave Paris except for the ceremony. Louvois has been most insistent on it. He even visited him at the Palais Royale."

Philip frowned. "Why would Louvois do that?"

"He told Monsieur it was a formality because England is at war with us."

"But you think there is more to it than that?" Philip guessed.

"I'm afraid I do. Have you considered the possibility that your brother-in-law might be a traitor to your country?" Armand asked quietly.

"Giles a spy? Never!" Philip said emphatically. "He has too much eye for his advancement to risk his considerable interests in England, and for a French king he detests. Besides he is devoted to William."

Armand nodded thoughtfully. "That is what I thought. In that case I believe I may know the answer to the mystery."

"Well," Philip urged as Armand lapsed into silence. "Do you propose to keep in to yourself?"

"No, but it is a little difficult to say."

"Even to me?"

"Especially to you, my friend. It is a trifle delicate," Armand explained. "I will relate to you an incident which happened shortly after the subduing of the Huguenots. Louvois accompanied me upon a grand tour of the regions which had been most troublesome and one of the places we visited was Marseilles.

On the way we passed a small town called Cassis but, whilst we were there, a disturbance broke out. My soldiers arrested the local baker, who was a Catholic convert and had apparently spoken out against the King. It was suggested that an example be made of him in front of Louvois and I must confess I was angered enough to do it at first. The Minister of War was none too well disposed towards me at that time and would have delighted in reporting to King Louis that I was failing in my duties.

Nonetheless it is not in my nature to judge without being fully appraised of the facts and so I had the man brought before me in order that he might have the opportunity to regret his rashness and pledge his obedience to the law."

"I assume this charming little tale will soon prove to be relevant to my brother-in-law," Philip prompted as Armand paused, as though unwilling to continue.

"You will find it most relevant," Armand said. "Louvois insisted on being present when the man was brought in and when the fellow began to speak it transpired that his protest was not against the King at all but on account of the baker's treatment by one of his Majesty's courtiers who, he claimed, had stolen his wife."

Philip started to laugh but he stopped, for Armand's face was grave. "Surely you don't think Giles stole her?"

"Oh, I am certain of it."

"But what would Giles have been doing in Cassis?"

"He was never there, but the baker's wife had run away to Marseilles and had been unlucky enough to be taken by pirates in one of their raids upon the city. They apparently sold her into slavery in Morocco, where she was purchased by an Englishmen working for Sultan Moulay Ismail. He brought her back to France and she went home to her husband, but she left him again a few months later and the baker was convinced that, this time, she had gone to join her rescuer in Paris."

Philip nodded slowly. The story was beginning to make more sense now.

"I suspect there are not too many English courtiers who have also been employed as slave procurers to the Sultan of Morocco!" Armand continued. "I always knew it had to be Giles."

Philip was forced to agree. "Marianne was the slave girl and she is now married to Giles. Are you telling me she is also married to a baker in Cassis?"

"Perhaps and perhaps not. Your brother-in-law had no wedding in Paris so far as I am aware. Unless they were wed in Holland, it is possible that she has been merely posing as his wife all this while."

"And now she is expecting his child, as Louvois is doubtless aware," Philip said with a groan. "Oh, Giles, what have you been persuaded to do in order to buy his silence? What happened to the baker, by the by?" he wondered.

"Why, nothing at all. I told him that I would mete out no punishment against one who had already been treated so harshly. As far as I am aware the man still bakes bread in Cassis."

"He will probably not be baking it for too much longer," Philip said grimly, "not now that he has become such an inconvenience to Giles Fairfield!"

"But he has had no opportunity to do anything about it," Armand said. "I told you he is forbidden to leave Paris."

"He'll find a way," Philip predicted. "Tell me, is his servant, Ahmed, with him?"

Armand frowned. "I don't know."

"Well if he was you would have noticed him," Philip said. "Ahmed is another of his slaves, and this one would not take his freedom when Giles offered it. He is a Negro who wears a knife at his belt and he is usually no more than a few feet from Giles' side. It is my guess that Giles has already dispatched him to Cassis to dispose of this unfortunate man and break whatever hold Louvois has on him."

Armand looked shocked. "He would do that?"

Philip laughed. "Armand, we are talking about a man who, before he went to fight for Monmouth, organised his own escape plan in case things went awry for him! Giles is devious and ruthless, with strong instincts of self-preservation! You should never underestimate him. I don't."

TWELVE

Armand looked concerned as his coach drew nearer to the gates of the Chateau of Versailles.

"Don't worry, no-one will recognise me like this," Philip reassured him.

He was still dressed as a servant but now he was wearing a dark wig, as well as a hat pulled down low over his eyes. He was quite enjoying the deception, although it was obvious that his friend was not.

"I am still not convinced that this was a good idea," Armand said.

"But once inside the palace there is no telling what I can't discover," Philip pointed out.

"And there are a great number of people who might discover *you*," Armand said, "including the King himself."

"I will keep clear of him and anyone else who knows me well. No-one will look twice at me in this disguise."

"I hope not, but you have yet to try behaving as a servant," Armand reminded him, with a slight twinkle in his eye, "particularly mine. I am not like you, who allow your attendants such liberties of speech. I am known to be abrupt with those who work for me, even my faithful Eugene, who has been with me for so many years, and to treat you differently in public would arouse suspicion."

"Speak to me however you like, I'll not be offended," Philip said. "Besides, I doubt you will have cause to reprimand such an exemplary lackey, for I shall be most assiduous in the performance of my duties, Monsieur le Comte!"

"I hate being fussed over," Armand warned.

"Do you really? I adore it." Philip sighed wistfully. It seemed a long while since Thomas had brushed his hair for him or massaged his back when it ached from a hard day's riding, and he missed such attentions.

They were at the gates now and Philip had his first chance to appear inconspicuous. He did it well. The blue-uniformed Swiss guards did not even glance at the Comte de Rennes' servant.

Once inside the palace he kept a respectful distance behind Armand and, fortunately, they did not meet any who recognised him, although Philip caught sight of a Frenchman he knew only too well.

"What the devil is he doing back in France?" he asked Armand when they had passed him by.

Armand followed his gaze. "The Marquis d'Arsay? He returned from England directly war was declared."

"He was posing in London as an escaped Huguenot seeking sanctuary," Philip said. "The bastard must have been spying for Louvois all along. You see I have learned something already!"

Armand and Marguerite had a tiny room allotted to them at the palace, although they rarely used it. There was very little comfort to be found in the cramped, almost airless quarters and they both preferred to spend what little time they were able to spend together at La Fresnaye.

Marguerite greeted her husband with a kiss. "What did Queen Mary want with you, my darling?"

"She wished to tell me she has found me a new manservant." Armand indicated his companion. "I think you will be agreeably surprised when you see his face."

At that cue Philip swept off his hat. "Your servant, Madame la Comtesse."

Marguerite gave a little shriek. "Is it truly you?"

"Truly," he laughed, pulling off his wig and shaking down his blonde curls. "Do you recognise me better now?"

"Yes, oh yes." Marguerite hugged him hard. "How wonderful! I can't wait to see Theresa's face."

"Where is she?" Philip could not wait to see her either.

"Not returned from Clagny yet but I have dispatched Eugene to escort her back."

"I could go and fetch her myself," Philip suggested.

Armand look stern. "You promised me you would do nothing rash if I indulged you in this masquerade."

"Did I really?"

"Yes, you know you did. Now behave yourself!"

Philip waited impatiently for Eugene's return and was disappointed to see him enter alone.

The servant's mouth dropped open in surprise when he saw him, but he quickly collected himself. "I know not how you came to be restored to us, your Grace, but I am glad to find you still alive, though sorry that the first words I must speak to you shall be distressing to your ears. It would appear that Lady Southwick has disappeared."

Philip stared at him. "What are you saying, Eugene?"

"She left Clagny early last evening but it seems she never returned to Versailles."

Philip forced himself to stay calm. "But I understood she was accompanied by my steward, Morgan."

"No, your Grace. Apparently she had already given him leave to go to Paris. She rode to Clagny alone and declined Madame de Montespan's offer of a servant to escort her home."

"It's my fault," Marguerite cried despairingly. "I should never have allowed her to leave."

"If Tess had made up her mind to go it would have taken more than you to stop her, sweetheart," Philip comforted her, turning to Armand, whose face was grim. "I believe my little game is over now. The most important thing is to find my wife."

"Not at the risk of your own life," Armand said firmly. "That will benefit no-one. I shall go to the King and tell him exactly what has happened to Theresa. If he is as fond of her as I think then he will act quickly and far more effectively than you could."

"And what am I supposed to do?" Philip said. "Stay in hiding until she is found murdered? Damn it, Armand, what do you expect of me?"

"I expect you to be reasonable," Armand said. "An impetuous action on your part will solve nothing. You are still in danger yourself, must I remind you of that?" Even as he spoke Armand donned his coat and sword again. "I shall request an urgent audience with King Louis."

"Where the hell is Giles at this moment, or Morgan or Thomas either, for that matter?" Philip drove his fist into his hand in a gesture of frustration. "I am deserted by everyone save you three." He looked gratefully at his two friends and their servant.

"And are you going to be sensible and allow us to help you?" Armand said, "Or at least remain here and do nothing until I return from the King?"

"That much I will promise you." Philip had the greatest regard for Armand, who was already leaving at as fast as his injured leg would let him.

He paced the floor of the tiny apartment like a caged animal as he awaited Armand's return. He had been a man of action all his life and one who liked to be in control of every circumstance. To sit calmly by was not in his nature, especially when someone dear to him might be in peril.

Armand was back within the hour. The search has begun," he said. "I have rarely seen Louis so upset. I am to take charge of a company of Swiss guards and scour the entire town of Versailles and question any who might have seen her. Already the grounds of the palace are being searched for any clue to her disappearance and every courtier and palace servant alerted."

"Good. I will come with you," Philip decided, reaching for his wig, but Armand stayed his hand.

"No, Philip, that would be madness."

"Amongst all this activity do you think anyone would notice the Comte de Rennes' new servant?" Philip said.

"One person would, and that is the King. He proposes to join the search himself."

"But today is Thursday!"

Thursday had always been Louis' day for private audiences and Philip knew he was unshakeable in his routine.

"Be that as it may, he has decided that this matter should take precedence over all else. He is already upon his way to speak with Madame de Montespan and instruct her to begin a thorough search of the environs of Clagny."

Philip whistled softly through his teeth, "Even I am impressed with that! Very well Armand, you win. I shall stay away from him; in fact I shall make quite certain that he does not see me."

"Now what do you have in mind?" Armand asked him despairingly.

"A plan that even you cannot object to, worrier." Philip put a fond arm about Armand's shoulders, for he knew the Frenchman was trying to do his best for him. "I am going to Paris to see Giles and to find my elusive servants."

❦

"Santerre is behind this," Louvois said angrily to the Marquis D'Arsay. "I am certain of it."

"What makes you so sure?"

"I have my reasons. Besides, who but a madman would abduct the woman King Louis intends to make his mistress?"

This last was news to d'Arsay. "How did you know that?"

"I know a great deal d'Arsay," Louvois said. "I also know that only yesterday he offered her the self-same proposal he offered

Southwick, on the pretence that he was fulfilling his obligations to her dead husband. Frankly I don't believe him to be that honourable."

Nor did d'Arsay. He had been a Huguenot until the troubles and he had seen too many of the others of his faith crushed by the will of the King to believe in Louis' honour. D'Arsay was not that honourable either. He had resolved never to share their fate.

Not only had d'Arsay been prepared to change his faith in order to save his life, he had also been prepared to profit from it. No-one in England had suspected him to be anything but the Protestant fugitive he had purported to be. London was full of them; tradesmen, lawyers, teachers and many of his own class, for the harsh laws instigated by Madame de Maintenon, passed by King Louis and implemented ruthlessly by Louvois ensured that no Protestant in France was able to be employed by, or employ, a Catholic. Their schools and churches were destroyed, they could not be admitted to a hospital when they were sick or buried during daylight hours when they died and, perhaps the most inhumane of all, their children could be taken from them to be educated in the Catholic faith.

It took a particular kind of person to be able to abuse the very people who had offered him sanctuary from such oppression and d'Arsay was that kind of person. His title gave him access to the English Court and his previous religion gave him access to every other Huguenot in London. He had shamelessly reported back to Louvois every useful piece of information he had gleaned.

"That still does not signify that Louis was planning to take Lady Southwick as his mistress," he pointed out to Louvois.

"I know the signs," Louvois said. He had been in King Louis' service for a long time and he had made it his business to keep a very close eye on his royal master. For someone who had advanced himself from lowly beginnings, as Louvois had, this was essential. Not for him a noble name to bring to his defence should he ever make an error of judgement, or influential relatives to intervene on his behalf. Men such as Louvois needed to be constantly vigilant, able to justify their every decision, never for a moment allowing themselves to forget that, more than anything else, they needed to retain the royal favour.

This was exactly the reason Louis preferred to give important posts to men of Louvois' background.

"I fail to see why Luc Santerre would abduct her all the same," d'Arsay said.

Louvois did not reply. D'Arsay had been invaluable to him and yet the Minister of War could not entirely trust a man who would so lightly betray his own kind.

Most Huguenots had converted, of course; he had seen to that himself, treating the order as purely a military operation. As with any war, there had been some brutality, although the King had not been aware of it until the Comte de Rennes had brought the matter to his attention. Louvois would never forgive the Comte for that, for Louis had never quite forgiven Louvois. It always seemed unfair to him that he should be blamed for his methods when, after all, he was merely ensuring that the numbers of converts were in line with the quotas given him by King Louis and Madame de Maintenon.

"I want Lady Southwick rescued," he told d'Arsay.

"Yes, I can see why you would." D'Arsay played with the corners of his moustache regarding Louvois sympathetically. "After all if it is Santerre who has her then the King will hold you responsible, since he was your protégé."

Louvois was not taken in by d'Arsay's apparent solicitousness. No matter how much the Marquis had profited from their association, Louvois knew that d'Arsay resented him. He was accustomed to resentment, particularly from those who were better bred than he and yet were now subservient to him.

"Luc Santerre must die," he said grimly.

"What difference will it make to kill him?" d'Arsay said.

"Unless you are prepared to kill Lady Southwick also then the world will still know it was him."

"Don't jest about that," Louvois advised him. "It would not take too much, as it is, to put the idea into folk's heads that whoever has taken her us the same person who killed her husband." This was a sore point with Louvois, who had been given direct orders by King Louis to suppress any reaction to the murder. "It is not enough that I must have Southwick's servants watched to prevent them from unearthing anything that might upset the King, now I am put in a position of embarrassment by some young hothead who I employed solely to inform me upon the movements of Monsieur. I think I know where Santerre might have taken her. He must be disposed of quickly, before anything else happens."

"But what if Lady Southwick tells the King who took her?"

Louvois smiled. "I think I can rely on Lady Southwick's silence."

D'Arsay could not for the life of him understand why, but he guessed he would get no more out of Louvois. "Who do you propose to send to take Santerre?" he wondered, hoping it was not going to be him. D'Arsay did not much enjoy doing Louvois' dirty work and he found it demeaning in the extreme to take orders from him.

"I have a person in mind for the job." Louvois scribbled a note on a piece of paper and handed it to d'Arsay. "This is the address of the house where I believe Santerre may be holding Lady Southwick. I want you to take it to her brother at the Palais Royale."

THIRTEEN

Monsieur pulled a marzipan fruit from his pocket and nibbled at it absent-mindedly. Giles regarded him with distaste. The sweetmeat had a piece of fluff attached to it, but his royal companion did not even seem to notice!

The plain fact was that Giles did not enjoy Monsieur's company half as much as he had a few years before. If he had been honest with himself he would have had to admit that he only enjoyed it then because there had been the prospect of advantage in it. In those days, when Giles had been a fugitive from King James' justice, it had seemed unlikely he would ever be able to return to England. He had been extremely grateful for Monsieur's friendship then, for the Frenchman had promised to help him buy lands and a title in France. It was Philip who had persuaded him to invest the money he had acquired from his loathsome trading for the Moroccans not upon a French chateau but upon William of Orange.

Giles had found William to be a man he could respect, and he respected few. His commitment to the Dutchman had been absolute. Giles had not only contributed to William's funds, he had helped train his troops and organise the expedition to England. This time 'Rebel Fairfield', as he was known after Monmouth's rebellion, had left no options open for himself, as he had when he fought at Monmouth's side. He had staked his all on William's success, and it was a gamble that had repaid him well. The one-time exile, who had escaped with his life but very little else, now had more wealth and power than he could ever have anticipated in his wildest dreams, and his success had been well deserved.

Giles sighed. He longed to be back in England now. He was finding that he actually missed William, demanding as the King was. Compared with him, Monsieur and his friends seemed ridiculously trivial and Giles could not imagine how he had once thought he would be content to live amongst such superficial creatures. William had given his life purpose and made him an altogether more discerning person.

Already a week had passed of the four allowed him for his absence and Giles had managed to achieve very little. It was true that he had concluded part of his business with Louvois but he had been placed under such restrictions during his visit that he was no further forward in discovering the identity of his brother-in-law's attackers. Philip's wish had been realised – Giles was suffering a very great deal on account of the way they had parted. To make matters even worse Monsieur, still sorrowing over Philip's death, would hardly let him out of his sight, and the frustration of that was making him less than appreciative of the Frenchman's gossiping.

Fortunately Monsieur was blissfully unaware of that and was prattling on as ever, seeming to not even notice that his English guest had hardly spoken a word for nearly an hour.

A servant interrupted them. "Lord Wimborne, you have a visitor."

"Do I?" Giles came out of his dark reverie. He was expecting Morgan to call and report the progress he and Thomas were making, for they were free to move about as they chose. "I will see him in my room."

"Return directly," Monsieur instructed him. "I thought we might go to the theatre. There is a new production of Molière's 'Le Bourgeois Gentilhomme' at the Comédie Française. I always liked that play, you know I did."

"Could you not take Luc instead, Monsieur? I'm feeling rather tired."

"I don't know where he is," Monsieur complained. "He's not been near me in days. You have to come."

"Not this time," Giles vowed under his breath as he hastened away. When he got to his room, however, he discovered that the visitor awaiting him was not Morgan but the Marquis d'Arsay.

"What the hell do you want?" Giles snapped. He had not set eyes on d'Arsay since he had seen him in England, and had no desire to ever do so again.

"I come from Louvois," d'Arsay said, not seeming too put out at his welcome.

"What? Is the man hounding me now?"

"Oh no, my Lord. This time he wishes to do you a favour. It concerns your sister."

Giles had not heard the news and he listened aghast as d'Arsay related what had happened to Theresa. It had never once occurred to him that she might be in any danger at Versailles.

"Are any searching for her?" he cried.

"Yes, half the Court, including the King himself, but Louvois believes he knows where she might be."

"So has he told the King?"

"No, my Lord. He thought it best if only you were to know."

"Me? What good does it do for me to know?" Giles said, irate. "Unless my sister is hidden in this palace I should be unable to discover her whereabouts, since I am barely ever permitted to leave it. Between your master and Monsieur I am practically a prisoner."

"I cannot, of course, speak for Monsieur but Louvois has bade me tell you that, so far as he is concerned, all restrictions upon you have been temporarily lifted, Lord Wimborne."

That was unexpected. Giles raised an eyebrow. "Damned good of him, I'm sure," he muttered tartly. "Well, where is she then?"

"He believes she is still in the vicinity of Versailles and is being held in a shack in the poor quarter of the town." D'Arsay passed him a piece of paper on which Louvois had written an address.

"But who took her?"

"Have you met a gentleman of Monsieur's acquaintance called Luc Santerre?" d'Arsay asked him.

"I have."

"Louvois believes it may be him."

Giles stared at d'Arsay. He was staggered at this information given him so coolly by the French spy. "Does Louvois know why?"

"I assume so, but he did not see fit to confide in me."

From d'Arsay's tone Giles deduced that he was not at all happy with that. "And after you have proved to be so valuable to him too," he said mockingly.

"Shall you go to find her or not?" d'Arsay demanded.

"Yes, of course I'll go." Giles was already buckling on his sword and taking up his pistol.

D'Arsay looked curiously at the weapon. "What manner of pistol is that?" he asked.

"It is an English invention," Giles told him. "It fires several shots without reloading. Don't tell me this was something you missed when you were studying us so assiduously," he added pointedly, fastening the weapon to his belt.

D'Arsay ignored the slight. "Louvois requires this matter to be kept as secret as possible," he stressed.

Giles knew what that meant. "So I am expected to dispose of Santerre?"

"Exactly so, my Lord. No-one but you and Lady Southwick are to ever know of his identity."

"And what is to prevent my sister speaking out?" Giles said. "Louvois has no hold upon her as he does on me."

"Nevertheless he thinks she will be prepared to keep silent."

Giles really could not imagine why she would. In fact there was something very strange about this whole affair. He could well understand why Louvois would not want it known that Theresa's kidnapper was Luc Santerre, since any scandal would reflect on him, but Giles could see no reason for Luc to have abducted Theresa. Unless...

"Is Santerre connected with the murder of my brother-in-law?" he demanded.

D'Arsay smiled, an annoying, smug smile that Giles suddenly longed to wipe from his face. "That we may never know, my Lord, but I do have a piece of advice for your two English friends, and that is to meddle no more in this business."

"Meddle?" Giles repeated incensed. "You are referring to Philip's servants when they only seek to discover what it seems few care to discover – the identity of those who brutally murdered him."

"Precisely, but if Louvois wanted them discovered he would have employed his own investigators, if you understand my meaning."

Giles did understand, perfectly. It meant that Thomas and Morgan were being watched very closely.

"Speaking of servants, my Lord, what a pity it is that you cannot take your blackamoor with you upon this mission," d'Arsay added as Giles showed him to the door.

Ahmed's safety was already a matter of great concern for Giles and the remark, designed to let him know that little escaped Louvois' attention, did nothing to help his peace of mind.

He was still pondering upon that when Morgan arrived a few minutes later.

"Was that the Marquis d'Arsay I saw leaving?" the Welshman asked. "What did he want?"

"I'll tell you presently. First of all, is Thomas planning to meet his contact in the Café Procope again?"

"Yes, this evening."

"Then you must stop him. From what d'Arsay said I fear he may be walking into a trap."

"Why would the Marquis warn you?" Morgan wondered.

"I think Louvois has slighted him and he wants to upset his plans a little. Come, I'll explain all as we ride, for if Monsieur discovers I am going I shall have the devil's own job to get out of this wretched building."

"Are you coming with me to find Thomas?" Morgan said when they were safely out of the palace stables and riding down the Rue St. Honoré.

"No. I have other matters to attend to, I fear." Giles told him briefly of Theresa's kidnap and the rest of his conversation with d'Arsay.

Morgan listened grimly. "I should never have left her side."

"If it comes to that she should never have gone to Versailles," Giles said. "Had she stayed here at the Palais Royale with Madame, as I suggested, I could have kept an eye on her myself, but matters may yet turn out well if the information Louvois sent me is correct."

"And there's another thing that bothers me. Why should Louvois do you the great service of informing you of her whereabouts?" Morgan said. "There was never any love lost between him and my master, so why should he care what happens to her?"

"I suppose, as d'Arsay says, because he fears he will be judged as guilty by association."

"But why should he trust you to tell no-one of it?" Morgan persisted. "What are you to him?"

Giles felt a stab of irritation. He had sufficient problems to contend with at the moment without suffering Morgan delving too deeply into his relationship with Louvois. "What should I be to him for heaven's sake?"

"I don't know, but I suspect he may have something to do with this devious business you had to deal with whilst we were in France."

Giles was incensed at the Welshman's impudence. "Why should you assume my affairs to be devious?"

"I have known you too long to believe any other. Why, for instance, has Ahmed not been seen since we first arrived in France?"

"Damn you, Morgan Davis, I do not have to answer to you. I am not Philip, who you could bend to your will, and I care not, frankly, if you approve of me or not, for I do not require the devotion you showed my brother-in-law."

"Just as well," Morgan retorted.

They were to part company shortly after, Giles to ride out of the city toward Versailles and Morgan to go to Philip's house, where he hoped Thomas would be waiting for him.

"Take every care," Morgan said, their differences forgotten for the moment. They were often at odds with one another, but Philip had been the common ground between them and when they reached the Pont Neuf they both looked toward the fateful spot where he had been attacked. Even with him gone they were bound together, like it or not.

"It will not be the first time I have been called upon to rescue my sister," Giles reminded him, running his finger down his scarred cheek. "Let us hope that, on this occasion, her freedom will not be bought at such a high price."

"But it may be that you, as well as Thomas, are walking into a trap," Morgan warned.

That thought had occurred to Giles as well, but he only smiled. "Now why in the world would they want me?"

Morgan watched him go upon his way until the white plume upon his hat was no longer visible amongst the traffic on the bridge. He could think of several reasons why Giles might be at risk, not least of which was his closeness to King William, but he knew that no threat of danger would have prevented Giles from attempting to rescue his sister.

It was late afternoon when Morgan arrived at Philip's house, near the Place Royale. Although it was a dull day, he could see no lamps lit and he feared Thomas must have already left for the

Café Procope. He noticed something else too. A horse was tied to the railings in front of the house. Morgan dismounted and felt the animal's hide. It was hot and damp, as though it had been ridden hard.

He tethered his own horse beside it and pulled out the knife he always carried. The message Giles had given him from d'Arsay had left him in no doubt that he and Thomas were themselves in peril so long as they were pursuing his master's killers.

He stood completely still, his senses alert, and after a moment he heard the sound of movement around the back of the house. Moving softly as a shadow, he crept down the side path and, as he turned the corner, he picked out the shape of a man. As he crept closer it was evident that the stranger was attempting to force an entry through a downstairs window.

Swiftly Morgan pounced. His left arm went around the intruder's throat, choking him as his head was forced back, whilst the knife in the Welshman's other hand pressed into his spine.

"What is your business here?" he demanded, pushing harder upon the blade so that the tip pierced his victim's skin through his clothes.

Philip ceased to struggle at the sound of that voice. Those few French words had not been spoken by any Parisian!

"Morgan, for God's sake loose your grip. You're going to kill me!"

Morgan did release him, and so suddenly that Philip all but lost his balance. Steadying himself, he turned around to find the Welshman standing as though rooted to the spot.

"I am returned to you, Morgan," he said softly.

Morgan's face showed barely a flicker of emotion but Philip saw that the hand holding the knife was trembling. "I never truly thought you were dead, my Lord," was all he said.

Philip understood perfectly. "Of course you didn't. When I die you will feel my death throes, as I will feel yours." The bond between them was so strong that they had become almost a part of each other over the years and no more words were needed.

"Why were you breaking in anyway" Morgan asked as he let him into the house.

"Believe it or not my key was lost in the Seine, together with a perfectly good sword and one of my favourite coats!"

"You should have been more alert on that occasion as well," Morgan said.

"Well thank you, Morgan." Philip gave him a sidelong glance. "I shall try to benefit from your good advice!"

"If you ever listened to advice you would not be in this mess now," Morgan grumbled.

"And you would not have had the pleasure of jabbing your confounded knife into my back! Still, I suppose you could be forgiven for not recognising me." Philip glanced at himself in the mirror. He was still wearing servant's clothes and a brown wig, which he tugged off. "Get me some brandy, Morgan. I've had a hard ride."

"Nonetheless I think the brandy had better wait, for you'll need a clear head this evening," Morgan warned.

Philip listened quietly as the Welshman told him of his meeting with Giles. His first reaction was relief that Theresa's possible whereabouts were known and that Giles was already on his way to her, but Thomas' situation was worrying and he knew there was no time to lose. His weariness left him with the need for action.

"Fetch me a sword, will you?"

He ran up the stairs to his bedroom to change his clothes and was stripping off his coarse linen shirt when Morgan returned.

"Did I hurt you?" Morgan said, for there was a smear of blood around the place where his knife blade had punctured Philip's skin.

"Yes of course you did, you vicious bastard, but it is nothing compared with what else has happened to me since I last saw you."

He turned to show Morgan the bullet wound in his shoulder. Morgan merely shrugged. "It was probably no more than you deserved."

"Oh, I knew you'd be concerned!"

Morgan hid a smile, not altogether successfully. "You've had worse!"

The Café Procope was situated on the other side of the river, not far from the Palais du Luxembourg. It was a fashionable coffee house and a gathering place for gentlemen and all those who wished to appear to be gentlemen.

"What led Thomas to the Procope?" Philip wondered as they passed the gardens of the Luxembourg.

"He discovered that one of the stable hands at the Palais Royale disappeared the day you were attacked and he thought it likely he was the one who informed your enemies of your intent to travel that day."

"I did make it known at the stables that I would be requiring a coach early in the morning," Philip recalled. "So Thomas thinks this fellow might have been in the pay of someone else?"

"He might well have been. At any rate he had been employed in Monsieur's household but a few days before the incident and he appears to be a man with few scruples. The other stable boys told Thomas that he boasted of knowing a great many important people through working at the stables of the Duc de Beauvilliers but when we enquired of the Duc's staff they had no recollection of a stable lad fitting his description. They did, however, recall a servant who had left somewhat abruptly, shortly before the loss of a silver dish was discovered, and his description fitted perfectly."

"And I suppose my Thomas then proceeded to dive into every den of thieves in Paris," Philip guessed.

"Exactly so."

Thomas had been brought up amongst the worst cut-throats and villains in London, so such places would have held no fear for him.

"What did he find out?" They were approaching the café now and both reined their horses, though there was nothing immediately apparent to cause them concern.

"He found who it was had sold the dish, for it was an exceptionally fine one, set all with precious stones and quite distinctive. The seller was neither servant nor stable boy but shady character called Lavisse, who made his living by assuming different identities so as to enter the houses of the nobility for whatever purposes suited him."

"Better and better. So is it this Lavisse who Thomas has come to meet tonight?"

"It is, my Lord."

Philip glanced at him sharply. He could read every intonation in the Welshman's voice. "Well tell me all, damn you."

"In order to gain Lavisse's confidence, Thomas had to first convince him that he was himself a thief."

"That should not have been too difficult for one who once thieved on the streets of London." A horrible suspicion suddenly crossed Philip's mind. "You don't mean he stole something to convince Lavisse?"

"In a way, but there was little fear of his being caught," Morgan assured him.

"And why was that?"

"Because he stole it from you. He simply took one of your silver candlesticks," the Welshman explained. "He reckoned you'd have little use for it now."

Philip burst out laughing. "And did it impress Lavisse?"

"Indeed it did. He got him a good price for it too."

"So I should hope!"

"As a result Lavisse, who thinks Thomas is already on the

run from the law in England, took him under his wing and promised to help him further. He was going to meet Thomas at eight o'clock and introduce him to two friends of his who would show him how to make a better living than he could from thieving, if he was not too particular who he worked for or what he did. Thomas is sure they are two of the men who waited for you on the Pont Neuf."

"We have to get him out of there now," Philip decided. "He is risking too much by this meeting. From what Giles told you, I fear Louvois' men are already watching him."

They tied their horses to a post across the street and approached cautiously. The last thing they wanted was to alert anyone before they themselves were ready. Philip could see Thomas clearly through the window pane. He was engrossed in earnest conversation with a man he took to be Lavisse.

Philip indicated a group of five men sitting at another table, also apparently engaged in conversation yet it was plain their hearts were not in it, for they glanced often around the room and were particularly attentive every time the door was opened.

"Louvois' men," Philip guessed. "If he's been watching Thomas as closely as I suspect then they are only awaiting the arrival of Lavisse's friends before they take them all, and Thomas too. Here's the plan. We will go straight to Thomas' table. Unless I miss my guess those men will move upon us immediately, taking us to be the ones Thomas is meeting. You grab Lavisse and get him outside whilst Thomas and I deal with them."

"Not one of your better plans," Morgan reckoned.

"I've not had too much time to come up with this one! Are you ready?"

"Whenever you are."

"There is just one more thing before we go in." Philip stayed his arm. "You say you never really thought that I was dead. So does Thomas think I'm dead?"

"Oh yes, my Lord."

"So would you say my appearance is going to come as somewhat of a surprise to him?"

"A considerable surprise, I'd say."

"Then let us hope to God he recovers his wits swiftly. Come on!"

The five men at the table turned to look at them as they entered the coffee house. Thomas was still intent upon his companion but he did glance up as they approached. He saw Morgan first and blinked in surprise, for he was not expecting him.

Then he saw who was with him.

There was no time to wait for his reaction. Five large men were bearing down upon them, their swords out of their scabbards.

At Philip's signal Morgan grabbed Lavisse from behind and, with his knife held to the Frenchman's throat, he started to drag him out the door.

"That leaves the two of us to settle with this scum of Louvois'" Philip told Thomas. "Are you able to fight."

Thomas, for once, was speechless, but he managed to nod.

"Then I suggest we start." Philip picked up a chair and threw it into the midst of the advancing men. Two went down, toppling a third, which evened the odds temporarily, and Philip and Thomas tackled one each of the two remaining. Thomas was not as strong as Philip, but he was nimble. He leapt upon the table and bore down furiously on his opponent, parrying the other man's, slower, jabs with ease.

Philip, meanwhile, had disabled his first assailant. As the man fell to the floor, bleeding profusely from a cut that had slashed his arm nearly to the bone, Philip kicked out at him. There was a sickening thud as his boot caught the man on the side of the head and he fell back, to be no more trouble during this fight.

Thomas had finished his man with a sword thrust to the shoulder, but the fellow had no sooner gone down than a second was ready to take his place. Philip's own shoulder wound was beginning to trouble him but he had no time to think about it, for another of Louvois' men was fast approaching him. Philip, at the last minute, turned his back on him, moving a little to the side. It was an old trick but it had worked many times for him. As his assailant went to seize this unexpected opportunity Philip spun around and, catching the man completely unawares, plunged his sword straight between the swordsman's ribs.

Thomas had nearly got the better of his second opponent. Taught by Philip himself, he was an agile fencer but he tired quicker than his master. Philip glanced toward him, but he still had one more of his own to deal with, who was bearing down on him rapidly.

A knife hummed through the air and the man screamed. He fell down, blood spurting from his mouth. Morgan's own silent messenger of death had done its work.

Now freed, Philip turned to help Thomas, but his man was already down and lying very still.

"Don't you ever fight upon the floor?" Philip asked him as Thomas jumped down from the table.

The servant grinned at him. "You did pretty well for a dead man, my Lord!"

"It will take more than a dip in the Seine to finish me, Thomas!" As he spoke Philip wrenched Morgan's knife out of the back of the man it had just killed. He bit upon his lip, for that effort had hurt him more than the swordfight, but he did not want Thomas to see it. The other customers of the coffee house had got out of the way and were watching them warily but none seemed inclined to interfere. "Let's go."

Outside they found Lavisse unconscious and tied over the saddle of Morgan's horse. "He didn't want to come with us," the Welshman explained.

"So I see! We could have managed without you in there, you know," Philip said, handing him his knife.

Morgan looked unimpressed. "Yes, a wonderful plan to be

sure, my Lord. Five against two, one of them nearly startled out of his wits by the appearance of a ghost and the other with a recent bullet wound in his sword arm!"

"You are injured?" Thomas cried.

"Barely a scratch," Philip said dismissively. "Let's ride or we may all receive much worse."

Thomas quickly collected his mount, which he had taken the precaution of leaving tethered in the street behind the coffee house, and they headed for the St., Michel quarter. Philip decided that, with Lavisse as he was, they should stick to the back streets. He and Thomas rode upon either side of Morgan to hide Lavisse from view, for they had no wish to draw undue attention to themselves. Fortunately St. Michel was almost deserted. Despite the efforts of La Reynie, the head of the Paris police, to make the streets safer, few law-abiding citizens ventured out after dark.

They arrived back home without incident. Lavisse was regaining consciousness but, with Morgan's cravat tied tightly across his mouth, there was little fear of his arousing their neighbours.

"I'll question him in the morning," Philip told Morgan. "Lock him in the cellar for tonight."

When Morgan had taken the Frenchman away Philip turned to Thomas and found the servant staring at him.

"What is it?"

"I never thought to see you again," Thomas said quietly.

"Of course you did!" Philip realised that the full import of his return had truly hit Thomas, now that all the activity was over. "Surely Morgan told you I wasn't dead."

"Many times, my Lord, but I didn't believe him."

"Then, in future, have more faith in his Celtic intuition!"

"I'll try, my Lord, but I hope I'll not be tested in this way too often."

"So do I! I am truly sorry to have put you through so much,

my poor Thomas," Philip said in a gentler tone. "I should not mock you, for I know you must have suffered."

"You can have no idea how much," Thomas said, "or how many times I have reproached myself that I did not insist upon accompanying you, even at the risk of incurring your wrath."

"Well here's another thought; if you had done so I might not have survived at all."

Thomas looked puzzled. "How so?"

"There is no saying that those three men on the Pont Neuf would not have got the better of us in any case, prepared as they were for murder. The only way I escaped them was to jump from the bridge."

"Are you saying that you wouldn't have been able to abandon me to save yourself?" Thomas said slowly.

"The last time I asked you to jump into water, if you recall, I had be there to catch you," Philip reminded him, for Thomas could not swim.

Thomas had been on many perilous adventures during his years in Philip's service but on that occasion he had needed to jump from a high window into the dark waters of the Thames. Philip knew it had been one of the most frightening moments of his young life.

"You wouldn't have saved yourself, would you?" he guessed. "You would have stayed by my side." Thomas looked shocked as he considered the implications of what Philip had said. "I might actually have been the cause of your death."

"Only if I had heeded you, which I rarely do," Philip reminded him.

"That's true." Thomas looked brighter already. "Let me see where they wounded you."

Philip removed his shirt. His shoulder was hurting more than he cared to admit, for he had torn the thin skin that was healing over the scar.

"You were scratched in the fighting as well, my Lord," Thomas told him, pointing to the mark on Philip's back.

"Oh, that! That is where my faithful Morgan attacked me with a knife," Philip said loudly as the Welshman came back into the room, having secured the prisoner.

Morgan looked unrepentant as he cast an expert eye over Philip's shoulder. His wife, Bet, was well versed in traditional cures of all kinds and Morgan had gleaned a little of her knowledge. "I can prepare a poultice for you if you wish."

"Not if it involves boiling dead cats in oil," Philip said with a shudder, for he knew Bet's remedies of old. He replaced his shirt quickly before Morgan got any ideas.

"It's a pity you two had to rescue me at that precise moment," Thomas said, "for I was about to learn the identity of Lavisse's friends."

"Little ingrate! Fear not, for we will learn tomorrow not only their names but who employed them," Philip said confidently.

"But what if Lavisse won't talk, my Lord?"

"Then I have a novel idea that will loosen his tongue."

"You're going to torture him?" Thomas asked uncertainly.

"Nothing so crude, but he will tell us all we want to know," Philip assured him.

Morgan groaned. "Another of his marvellous plans, I suppose."

"Just for that I shall not tell it to you until tomorrow," Philip decided.

"Will it work?" Thomas asked.

Before Philip had the chance to reply both servants pronounced as one the phrase they had so often heard upon his lips. "Trust me!"

FOURTEEN

❦

Giles entered the town of Versailles cautiously. It was late but there were still some soldiers in the streets.

"Wonderful," he muttered to himself. "Not only do I have to get her away from Santerre, I have to avoid the King's guards whilst I am doing it!"

He skirted behind the stables of the palace, keeping well clear of the main streets, and headed toward the church of Nôtre Dame.

He turned the corner and cursed as he came face to face with a company of the blue uniformed guards. Giles froze. Whilst nothing could be more natural than that he had joined the search for his missing sister, it would seem strange indeed if he was seen to discover her whereabouts straightaway when the King's guards had found nothing all day.

They were eyeing him suspiciously already. Giles knew his scar would make him easily recognisable, and if there was one thing he had learned in his twenty-six years it was that there are times not to be recognised. This was one of those times.

Spurring his horse, Giles rode straight through the middle of them and across the square.

They gave chase with a relish. Probably ready for a little excitement after such a fruitless day, Giles thought ruefully as they clattered after him down a narrow street.

Giles knew the town passably well but not as intimately as the soldiers and he knew he had no real hope of outrunning them. At any moment another troop could appear, drawn by the sounds of the chase, and he would be trapped.

His only chance was to throw them off the scent.

Giles slipped his feet from the stirrups. Whilst the horse was still going at full pelt he lowered himself skilfully and leapt from its back.

He rolled himself into a ball to take the impact, but was quickly on his feet and diving into an alleyway between two houses.

It was a daring trick he had taught himself when he was a captain in the army and he was delighted that he could still do it, for he led a less energetic life lately. The only damage he had sustained was a tear to his coat and, since Giles was no longer the dandy he had been before his face was scarred, he was not too troubled on that score.

A second later the soldiers rode by in hot pursuit of the riderless horse. With any luck, it would be a while before they discovered they were no longer chasing him and Giles congratulated himself on the success of his ploy.

His problems were far from over, however. He looked at the directions on the piece of paper d'Arsay had given him and realised he was still a long way from his destination. He could not move so quickly now that he was on foot but he was certainly safer. Dodging in and out of the shadows, he saw more guards passing by, obviously following the sounds of horses' hooves. They stopped but a few feet away from him and his heart pounded as he pressed hard against a wall, listening to their conversation. They decided to split up and started off in their separate directions.

Giles realised he was in more trouble than ever now.

He quickly weighed up his situation. His only hope was to hide out somewhere until they gave up on him, but the soldiers were obviously enjoying the chase and pursuing it noisily. It would not be long before the townsfolk of Versailles were out of their beds and peering from their windows, and Giles knew that would the end of it.

There was only one place he could think of which was close and where he would be likely to find sanctuary – Clagny.

He made it to the outskirts of town without encountering any more soldiers but he had open ground to cover before he reached the house.

He figured that his pursuers must have realised by now that they had been duped and would be looking for a man on foot, so there was no time to waste. He removed his hat, which might have made him too conspicuous in the moonlight, and threw it over a nearby garden gate. On consideration, he took off his cloak as well, in case it hampered his speed, and tossed that over after it.

Giles had never allowed excesses to mar his physical condition and his time in the desert had toughened him and taught him endurance. All this stood him in good stead as he ran, covering the distance between the town and the boundaries of Clagny with ease. He was barely even panting when he reached the house.

"I need to see Madame de Montespan without delay," he told her servant when he had announced himself.

"But she has retired to bed," the man protested.

"Then wake her, damn you!" Giles was in no mood to bandy words with Athénais' staff, not when a troop of Swiss Guards might catch up with him at any moment.

The servant obeyed and returned a few minutes later. "Madame de Montespan awaits you in her chamber," he said, somewhat grudgingly.

Athénais was in bed and looking incredibly lovely, with her long hair loose about her shoulders and wearing only a lacy shift.

Despite the urgency of his situation, Giles stood still for second, taking in the pleasing picture.

"You look absolutely delightful," he said honestly.

Athénais threw back her head and laughed, showing her white throat. It was a part of her that men liked to kiss and she knew exactly how to tempt them.

"You're sweet, Giles! But to what do I owe this pleasure? Do you have news of your sister to tell me?"

"Yes, I do," Giles said, "but first I need your help. I need you to hide me, should any have followed me here."

"Good gracious!" Athénais looked more excited than alarmed by his words. "Whatever have you done?"

"It's a long story but if you protect me then I promise I will tell you all, for I believe I can confide in you, if no-one else."

"I'm flattered. It's been so long since anyone involved me in their intrigues," Athénais said, a little wistfully. "Very well, Giles. I'll do whatever you say."

"Then tell your servants to swear I have not been here, should any ask after me."

"And who is likely to be asking after you?" she enquired, when she had rung the bell to summon her maid.

"The palace guards," he admitted.

"Really?"

Giles was relieved to see that Athénais did not seem in the least put out at this and, when her maid arrived, she gave orders that no-one was to admit to having seen her visitor arrive, at peril of their position.

"I have fulfilled my part of the bargain, now it's your turn," she said, when they were alone again. "You have to tell me everything." She patted the place on the bed besides her. "You've torn your coat," she noticed as he took it off.

"It's not important," he said.

"Of course it is. I will have it mended for you before you leave. We cannot have you looking less than perfect."

"Alas, Madame, there is no longer much perfection in my appearance," Giles told her regretfully, for he had once been very proud of his good looks. The loss of them had changed his nature considerably.

"What nonsense! You, Giles, will always be attractive," she informed him matter-of-factly.

Giles, with his fragile build, had a vulnerability about him that contrasted oddly with his powerful reputation. It was a combination that women found captivating and the scar, though ugly in itself, did nothing to detract from his allure but, if anything, added to his fascination. Giles did not see any of this, of course, and his total lack of pretension was enough to make a tender creature like Athénais long to reassure him.

"Now begin," she insisted, "before you drive me wild with suspense. What has happened to Theresa?"

"I have information that Luc Santerre is holding her here, in the town, but I cannot get to her whilst the streets are crawling with soldiers and the person who told me of her whereabouts is insistent that no-one else should know of it."

"Louvois," Athénais said knowingly.

"How did you guess?"

"Because of his connection with Santerre. It stands to reason he would not want this made public. What are you going to do?"

"I thought to wait until the town is quiet again and then see if I can find her."

"I pray you do. I've been so worried about the poor dear," Athénais said sincerely. "I suppose you did know that she was on her way back from visiting me when it happened?"

This was news to Giles. "No, I didn't. What was she doing here?"

Athénais told him of the proposition Theresa had come to discuss and Giles' regarded her gravely.

"You don't much like the idea of your niece marrying my son," Athénais said, seeing his expression.

"Frankly, no. Not that my opinion would make a scrap if difference, but I do have a position to uphold in England," he reminded her.

Athénais pouted prettily. "Are you saying it would be an embarrassment for such an important man as you to have your family linked with that of a woman who has been the King of France's mistress?"

"That's unkind," he protested.

She laughed. "I know it is, and I shouldn't make fun of you." She lifted one of his hands to her lips and kissed it, as if in penance. "You have delicate hands for a man."

"That's because I do very little work these days, since I have become so important," he replied, still a little huffy, for Giles hated to be teased.

"But you've hurt yourself, look." She had noticed a graze on his palm and licked it gently, as an animal might caress its young. There was a great deal of animal in Athénais and, in spite of himself, Giles felt a thrill go through him at the touch of her warm tongue.

"Is that better?" she asked him.

"Much."

"And am I forgiven?"

"Anything."

"Do you have any more grazes?" she said innocently.

"No, but I rather wish I did!"

Just then they heard a pounding upon the front door.

"Blast! They're here." He got to his feet but she pulled him down onto the bed again.

"Don't worry, you are safe with me – safe from the soldiers, anyway, she laughed. "Now, while my people are dealing with your pursuers you can tell me more. There is more, isn't there?"

Giles decided he would tell her everything about his relationship with Louvois, for it would be an insult to someone of Athénais' perception to do any less.

She listened sympathetically. "Poor Giles," she said when he had done. "How your past comes back to haunt you. What wrong did you do, after all, but save one of my countrywomen from a life of slavery?"

"I took her away with me as my wife," he reminded her.

"Well I think that is very romantic," Athénais decided. "Is she beautiful?"

Giles saw in his mind an image of Marianne, with her dark hair and her belly swollen with his child. "To me she is."

Athénais loved romance for its own sake, and did not seem jealous of the love he plainly bore his wife. "Giles, you are adorable, and because of that I am going to help you to free yourself from Louvois."

"How can you help me?" he said, mystified.

"By giving you a little dirt you can threaten to smear upon the mighty Minister of War."

"Louvois has a secret?" Giles asked eagerly.

"He does indeed, but I shouldn't really be telling it to an Englishman," she said mischievously, "not now we are at war."

"You are the most infuriating woman," Giles said, as she lay back on her pillows, watching him, "but you will tell me, won't you?"

"For a price, the price of a kiss. Is that too much to pay?"

It wasn't, and he paid it in full.

"Now shall you tell me?" Giles lay down beside her.

"Maréchal d'Humières is at the head of our fighting troops against your English army in Flanders, as you may know. What you may not know is that Louvois gave him that honour to keep him quiet."

"Go on," Giles urged as she paused, maddeningly, to toy with his auburn curls.

"You see the Maréchal discovered that Louvois was having an affair with his wife and threatened to expose him. Of course this would have been disastrous for, with Louis so much influenced by the pious Maintenon, every person in power must be seen now to be a man of virtue."

"Madame de Maintenon would have ruined him," Giles said.

"Without a second thought. She already hates him like the

plague and is only waiting for an opportunity to discredit him so that he falls from favour with the King."

"That is wondrous news," Giles said, scarcely believing his luck. This information was just what he needed to turn the tables on Louvois and break free of the hold the minister had on him.

"Isn't it though? And well worth another kiss, I'd say!"

"So would I!" To prove it he went to kiss her again, but this time they were interrupted by Athénais' maid returning.

"The soldiers have gone now," she reported. "They asked if they might search the grounds for you and when they found nothing they said they were returning to the palace."

"That's good," Giles said, relieved. "I had better be on my way then."

"Why don't you go in the morning?" Athénais said.

It was a tempting thought. Giles was tired and would have liked nothing better than to have spent the night in the arms of the enchanting woman who was nestling up to him, but he shook his head. "I have to leave whilst it is still dark."

Before he could stop her, Athénais handed his coat to the maid as she left, with instructions to repair it. "Well wait one hour at least. The streets will be safer for you by then and anyway," she added snuggling up to him, "you can't go yet for you do not have a coat to wear now!"

Giles knew when he was beaten. "One hour, then," he agreed as severely as he could, for it was hard to be resolute with Athénais undoing his shirt!

"And how would you like to spend the time?" she said, nibbling at his neck.

Giles appeared to be considering the matter. "I'm not sure," he said wickedly. "Do you have a billiard table, by any chance?"

A sharp bite on his shoulder warned him to be more respectful!

∽

The streets were empty by the time Giles left, in the early hours of the morning. The soldiers had, indeed, retired to their quarters and the good townspeople of Versailles were at last enjoying their sleep. Giles retrieved his hat and cloak as he passed by the garden where he had deposited them, for the air had grown chilly. He pressed on quickly. It would be light in a few hours and he guessed the search would be on again.

He found the place he was seeking, with the aid of Louvois' written directions. It was little more than a shack in a mean back street. From the age of it he suspected it might have been there since Louis' palace was no more than the hunting lodge used by his father.

Many of the older houses were being demolished now and the land bought up to be used to build the grand mansions of those who wished to reside near to the Court. The other houses in the street all appeared empty and the one Giles had been searching for looked to be completely deserted too. Birds had nested in the thatch of its roof and the window shutters had boards nailed across them.

Giles suspected the worst. He was convinced now that he had been sent on a wild goose chase by d'Arsay, but even if it was a trap he had no choice but to walk into it. He could not turn away, not whilst there was half a chance that Theresa was really inside the building, unlikely though that seemed.

He approached slowly and observed the door. There were footprints on the dirt path leading to it, indicating that it had been opened recently.

Giles drew out his pistol in readiness. He put a little pressure on the door and it began to give. He took a deep breath and kicked it open.

The scene in front of him stopped him in his tracks.

By the dim light of a single candle he could make out two

shapes. One was lying on the floor, covered with a blanket. The other leapt up from a chair as he entered.

"Giles, thank God! However did you find me?"

Theresa threw her arms around his neck and hugged him, crying tears of relief.

Giles held her for a minute until she calmed down. "Whatever happened here, Theresa?"

"Luc had a fit of some kind." She knelt beside the sleeping figure. "He foamed at the mouth and convulsed terribly. Oh, Giles, I thought he was going to die, and there was nothing I could do to help him."

"Help him?" Giles said, confused. "Did he not kidnap you?"

"Yes, he did do that," she admitted, shaking Luc gently.

"Then why did you not run away when you had the chance?"

"I thought of it but I couldn't leave him like that. I hid his horse behind the house so that no-one would see it and suspect where we were." Luc had stirred and she knelt by him attentively, speaking soothingly to him.

"Theresa, you haven't fallen in love with him, have you?" he asked her sternly. "Tell me truthfully."

Luc was younger than Theresa but he was a good-looking man.

She giggled. "No, of course not. Is that what you think?"

"What am I supposed to think? King Louis is disrupting the entire area searching for you. I rush from Paris to rescue you and I find you here, holed up with your abductor and more concerned for his welfare than your own."

"Don't be cross, Giles," she pleaded. "I do appreciate your coming to rescue me, really I do."

"Don't be cross?" he repeated in exasperation. "You know I am trying to take care of you, with Philip gone, and you have to help me. You were always so unruly."

Although Theresa was two years older than him, Giles had invariably been the more sensible one.

"I know, and I promise to be less worry to you in the future, but you will understand more when you hear what Luc has to say."

Luc woke at that moment and recognised him. "You," he gasped.

"Don't worry," Theresa said. "My brother will help us."

"I wouldn't be too sure of that," Giles warned him. "I am not so susceptible as my soft-hearted sister. Now what the devil is this all about, Santerre?"

"I wanted her to see the place where I lived as a child, before they tear it down," Luc said haltingly.

Giles glanced around the room. "Very nice! And you brought her here by force, I presume."

"I little thought she would come otherwise."

"I'm not so sure. Theresa has been known to do stranger things than that, as I have just witnessed!" Giles said sourly.

"I realise now that there is far more to her than I supposed," Luc admitted, getting slowly to his feet. "I thought she would be like the other ladies of the Court, with their grand ways and their spiteful natures."

"If you hate them so much why are you living amongst them?" Giles said.

"Because it is my birthright and because, that way, I had hoped to have the opportunity, one day, to avenge myself upon your brother-in-law."

"You killed Philip?" Giles leapt at him and grabbed him by the throat.

"No," Luc choked, as Theresa tried to pull upon Giles' arm.

"Let him go, I pray you, Giles. He had nothing to do with Philip's death."

Giles did release him, grudgingly. "How can you be sure?"

"He told me so."

"And you believed him?"

"You will believe him too when you learn who he is. Tell him Luc."

"Well," Giles prompted when Santerre hesitated, eyeing him

warily. "Tell me, then, before I kill you. What was Philip to you, Luc Santerre?"

"He was my father."

That was a shock.

Giles soon regained his composure. "Ridiculous!"

"No, it's true," Theresa said. "I am convinced of it. Hear him out."

"Go on, then. Giles straddled the only chair in the room and faced Santerre. "Convince *me*."

"My mother was an actress," Luc began. "She met Philip Devalle in Paris when he first joined the French army. "I was born when he was away fighting the Dutch and becoming a hero. When he returned he was too important a man to bother with the likes of us and she was left to bring me up alone. All he ever gave her was a lock of his hair and a small part in one of Jules Gaspard's plays. Shortly after that she caught the smallpox but Gaspard lay dying by then and, during his final illness, Devalle never left his side. No-one mattered to him except his crippled poet friend, not even the sick woman whose reputation he had ruined."

"Scarcely ruined, surely," Giles corrected him. "It is not unheard of, after all, for actresses to become pregnant by gentlemen of the Court."

"Nonetheless my mother felt she had been cheapened," Luc insisted. "After Gaspard was dead my father returned to England, leaving my mother and me paupers. She never recovered her looks nor trod upon the stage again, but she loved him until the day she died. She brought me up in this cottage." He indicated their humble surroundings. "Not much like the house in Paris, where we should have lived with him."

"You think he ought to have married her?" Giles said incredulously.

"He should have at least acknowledged me as his son and sent her money when she could no longer support herself," Luc maintained.

"Very probably he should but even if, and I stress the if, your story is true and you really are his son you should be aware that you are not the only bastard he has fathered in his time. He could not possibly have taken responsibility for all of them and your mother was, after all, only an actress. Why, actresses are not considered to be women of any particular virtue, are they? Indeed, I would have thought that, for women of her kind, the bearing of illegitimate brats was no more than an occupational hazard."

Giles was deliberately goading him, to see how much it would take to make him lose his self-control. Luc looked angry but Theresa was watching Giles knowingly, obviously guessing what he was doing.

"What makes you think he should have acknowledged you when he has deposited his wayward seed in women of far better breeding then your mother?"

That was too much. Luc's smooth façade fell from him like a mask. Giles had seen this transformation in his brother-in-law many times, for Philip could be savage when he lost control. Luc's tolerance was much lower than his, for Philip had taught himself a degree of restraint over the years, but the similarity in their reactions was marked. Luc's blue eyes flashed fire and the resemblance was complete.

Giles swiftly left the chair and held it out in front of him as Luc advanced menacingly. "Wait, you hothead," he said hastily, for he thought he may have pushed him too far. "I believe you."

Theresa, who had evidently been ready for this, stepped in between them. "He means it, Luc."

"He didn't believe me a minute ago," Luc said, still ruffled.

"Well I do now. I just saw your father in you as plain as though he stood before me and, damn you, it is all most inconvenient."

Luc started to protest but Giles silenced him with a gesture of his hand. "No, you have talked enough; now you will listen to me. Both of you," he emphasised, rounding on Theresa.

"Yes, Giles," she said meekly.

People often found themselves doing what Giles wanted, even King William, at times, and he had no intention of letting these two cause him any further aggravation. It was time to put the pair straight on a few facts.

"The reason I have found you here is because Louvois told me where you were."

They both reacted with astonishment to that.

"Did Louvois know who you claim to be?" Giles said to Luc.

"Yes. I introduced myself to him a year ago, after my mother died. He said I could be useful to him."

"As a spy in Monsieur's household?" Giles asked. "In return for Louvois' introduction to society I am guessing you were to report back on everything that happened inside the Palais Royale."

"Oh, Luc, how could you?" Theresa cried.

"He could because he is his father's son," Giles said dryly, "but you haven't heard the best part yet, has she, Luc?"

Luc hung his head but said nothing.

"I'll come to that in a moment. Back to Louvois, the noble Minister of War. He guessed that since you had lost the opportunity to reveal your identity to Philip himself you would probably not be able to resist revealing it to his wife, which is exactly what you have done, presumably in an attempt to receive some financial consideration by appealing to her guilt. With the entire Court out looking for you, Theresa, Louvois could not risk the embarrassment to himself if it was discovered that Luc had taken you, and that is why he dispatched me to deal with the matter. And here is the awkward part," he looked from one to the other, "he instructed me to kill you, Luc Santerre."

Theresa gasped in horror, but Luc shook his head. "No, he would never have ordered that. I'm useful to him."

"You fool! You have outlived your usefulness. Can you not

see that? This one irrational act was sufficient to convince him that you are more trouble than you are worth."

Luc looked so stunned that Giles almost felt sorry for him. "You don't know them very well, these people in high places, do you?" he said quietly. "Louvois will take no risks for you with his own reputation."

"What are we going to do?" Theresa said.

"What you are going to do is exactly what he told me you would do, which is to say nothing. He knew that if you did then it would only discredit Philip's memory. We will concoct a story of how you lost your way in the dark and fell from your horse, or some such thing."

"But what about Louvois' instruction, and why would he think you would cold-bloodedly kill Luc for him, particularly when you learned who he was?"

Giles looked into his sister's earnest grey eyes and knew he could not possibly tell the truth about himself and Marianne to her, as he had to Athénais. "I've really no idea."

"What do you intend to do about Luc, then?"

"Well I am not going to kill him," Giles reassured her. "In the first place, he may very well be, as he says, Philip's son. Secondly, and you're going to really like this, I know for a fact that he is King William's agent in France."

Theresa put her hand up to her mouth.

"This should further convince you of who he is," Giles pointed out, "for was not his father, also, a double agent at one time, spying for King Louis in England whilst actively working to put William on the English throne? This deviousness is obviously a family trait!"

"I feel myself to be part English," Luc explained to her. "I thought by working for England's interests I might endear myself to my father and also help your country."

"Very laudable, I'm sure," Giles said sarcastically. "Only a Devalle could apply such twisted reasoning to make an argument seem sound. Unlike your father, however, you are going to do exactly as I tell you and we may all get out of this unscathed. You will be able to continue working for William and you, Theresa, will still be able to take up Louis' magnanimous offer of a royal marriage for your daughter, if you so choose. Oh, yes, I know all about that," he assured her, seeing her look of surprise, "and I hardly think this to be a tactful time to remind the King of France that there is more than a taint of madness in the Devalle line. I very much doubt that he will be overjoyed to learn, for instance, that Philip's son has fits!"

"But how will you explain to Louvois why you let Luc live?" Theresa said.

Giles smiled. "Thanks to Athénais I have a little ammunition I can use against Louvois. You," he told Luc, "are to ride now to Clagny with a message to Madame de Montespan. You will have to be the one to go because you, the cause of all this, are the only one of the three of us who Louis' guards are not seeking," Giles reminded him tartly. "You are to tell her that Theresa is safe and ask her to have two horses brought here. One is for my sister, who can then ride to Clagny, where we can rely on Madame de Montespan to help her, and the other is for me, so that I can return to Paris. Do you think you can manage that without causing me any more trouble?"

"Yes, my Lord." Luc was looking at him now with respect. "What can I do to thank you?"

"You can return to the Palais Royale and attend assiduously upon Monsieur again, not to spy upon him this time but to please him and to give me an occasional respite. You are to particularly mention how much you would love to accompany him to the theatre!"

FIFTEEN

⤫

"You might at least tell us where we are going," Thomas said to Philip as they entered the forest of Fontainebleau.

"No. It's a surprise."

They had left Paris just before daybreak, taking Lavisse with them. The Frenchman was riding up in front of Morgan, who was watching him closely. He seemed more afraid of the stocky Welshman, who had dealt him such a mighty blow the previous evening, than he was of Philip, but it was obvious that he was more terrified of informing against those who had employed him than he was of either of them. Philip found this intriguing and not a little worrying but, one way or another, he was sure he could get Lavisse to talk.

"You get us up practically in the middle of the night and bring us out into the forest for a surprise?" Thomas was persisting. "Can't you even say how far it is?"

Philip sighed theatrically. "Dear God, it's worse than having a child with us! We are heading for Montereau, if you must know."

"Whatever for?"

Philip smiled at Thomas' impatience. "That's the other part of my surprise!"

He had told them nothing yet about his time upon the barge but, once out of the forest, he headed for the lock where he had left Françoise and her beau. The sun came up as they drew closer to it and Philip was pleased to see, through the rising river mist, that her father's boat had gone.

"Now, Françoise," he murmured to himself, "let us hope you took my advice."

Leaving his servants looking questioningly after him, Philip dismounted before the lock-keeper's cottage and knocked upon the door.

It was answered by the young lock-keeper, bleary-eyed and obviously roused from sleep. He stared at Philip, plainly not recognising him.

"How can I help you, sir?"

"Is Françoise here?"

"Why should you want to know?" the young man asked protectively.

"Not to do her harm," Philip assured him. "I'm a friend of hers."

The lock-keeper looked at him suspiciously. Philip was dressed as no friend of Françoise was ever likely to be dressed, but the lock-keeper must have figured that, since he was accompanied by men carrying arms, it would be better not to tell him a lie.

"She is here. I'll fetch her."

When Françoise herself came to the door she had no trouble whatever in recognising him.

"Guy!" she cried. "Why, how wonderful you look."

"Guy?" Thomas whispered to Morgan.

Philip turned to them. "This is a young lady to whom you owe a great deal, gentlemen, for it was she who saved your master's life."

Morgan doffed his hat to her and she smiled shyly before turning to Thomas.

"You are Thomas?"

"Indeed I am." Thomas jumped down from his horse and took her work worn hand and raised it to his lips as though she was the finest lady at Court. "It seems we are in your debt."

"No, no, rather I am in yours, Thomas," she insisted.

"How so?"

"May I tell him?" Françoise asked Philip.

"Please do," Philip said, delighted with Thomas for his courtesy to her. "He will not mind."

"I have had the smallpox," Françoise explained, "and I would not show my face to anyone, but then Guy told me about you and how you were also marked by the disease and yet you never pay it any mind."

"No more I do," Thomas assured her. "I contracted mine in the Bicêtre, and I would have died had a good friend not rescued me and nursed me back to health."

The good friend was Giles, who had found Thomas in the infamous Bicêtre, which was called a hospital but was, in reality, a prison that forcibly housed the scum of Paris. Thomas had reckoned himself fortunate to be alive and he would never forget the debt he owed to Giles. "Don't worry," he laughed, seeing her eyes open wide at the mention of the Bicêtre, "I am no criminal, at least not lately, but when one has been so close death what are a few pockmarks? As long as my master is not ashamed of me I will show my face to the King himself!"

"I show mine now too. André here is not ashamed of me either." She blushed. "We are going to be married next week."

"Bravo!" Philip shook the young man's hand.

"I know you now," he said, "but I'd scarce have recognised you."

"I always said he was a gentleman," Françoise reminded him.

Philip had already decided not to tell her quite how much of a gentleman he really was for, as matters stood, it may be that the less they knew about him the better, both for their own safety and for his.

"How is your shoulder?" she wanted to know.

"Healing nicely, thanks to you" he told her, "but I come here now seeking your help once again."

He drew her and André aside and spoke quietly to them,

after which the couple went back into their cottage and closed the door.

"What was that about?" Thomas said, ever curious.

"I simply asked them to pretend we were not here." Philip went over to the lock, which had been emptied when the last boat had gone through the previous day. One set of gates was already closed against the high water and he worked the lock's mechanism to close one of the second set of gates, motioning for Thomas to do the same upon the opposite bank. Standing on the narrow walkway over the gates, he beckoned Thomas to join him. "Now do exactly as I do," he told him.

Thomas copied him as he turned one of the wheels on top of the gates. "And what exactly is it I am doing?" he asked.

"You are putting down the paddle," Philip explained. "When they are both down the lock is sealed."

"I'm impressed, my Lord, but I doubt very much that you brought us all the way out here to demonstrate your skills as a lock-keeper!"

"Quite right! Morgan, bring Lavisse here."

"Do you propose to throw him in?" Thomas asked, looking down into the cavernous depths of the lock, its black waters reflecting their outlines against the early morning sun.

"Oh no, something far more subtle," Philip said with an icy smile.

"It is is pointless to kill me, for you will still not know who wanted to destroy you," Lavisse hissed, struggling, to no avail, in Morgan's fierce grip.

"That depends a good deal on how you are going to die," Philip told him pleasantly. "I propose to tie you to that ladder." He pointed to some iron rungs set in the side of the stone lock. The bargees used them to climb up in order to secure their ropes to the bollards above. "When I let the water in you will drown inch by inch."

Lavisse paled. "You're mad."

"Very probably, but you can save yourself this suffering if you will only tell me who it was that you informed of my proposed visit to Versailles that day. Who sent the men who were waiting for me on the bridge, Lavisse?"

Lavisse looked frantically around him, although he must have known he had no hope of escape. "If I tell you I'm a dead man," he cried.

"You're a dead man if you don't," Philip reminded him. "let's face it, Lavisse, you are damned whatever you do. You have even acquired Louvois as your enemy. If we had not abducted you when we did his men would have killed you at the Procope."

Lavisse glared at Thomas. "It was you Louvois was watching, not me. You led them straight to me. You'll pay for this."

"You would do better to consider your own danger, Lavisse," Philip told him. "There is only one way out of your dilemma. If you tell me what I want to know then we will let you go upon your way. You could be another twenty miles away from Paris before nightfall and they'll never find you."

"They'll find me wherever I go," Lavisse said. "You have an enemy so powerful there is no escape for either of us."

"Then tell me who it is," Philip said simply.

Frightened though he looked, Lavisse would not speak. There was evidently someone he feared more than Philip, even though the Frenchman was at his mercy.

Philip shrugged and turned to his servants. "Tie the fool to the steps."

Thomas and Morgan obeyed immediately. Despite the licence Philip allowed them on occasions, neither would have ever questioned his direct commands.

Thomas climbed down, for he was the more agile of the two. Morgan held on to Lavisse whilst Philip used a rope from his saddlebags to tie the Frenchman's his feet together. Then they suspended him, struggling for all he was worth, over the side of the lock. Thomas managed to grab his feet and secure them to one of the lower rungs.

"You do plan to wait for me to get out before you let the water in, I hope," Thomas said, for he was now trapped below Lavisse on the ladder.

Philip fastened a piece of rope to one of the bollards, laughing as he threw the end down to him. "Here, pull yourself up."

The side of the lock was covered with slimy mud but Thomas managed to scale it, with the aid of the rope and by grabbing hold of the rungs when he had climbed above the Frenchman's head.

"You're a dead man too if they learn who you are," Lavisse warned him.

If Thomas was perturbed at the threat he did not show it. "Tell him what he wants to know, Lavisse, and you can go free. It is a generous offer."

Lavisse looked frantic as Philip began to raise the paddles that were holding back the water on the other side of the lock, but he had still not divulged any names. Philip began to fear his plan might not work after all. He had no compunction about taking the life of one who had conspired to take his, but if that had been his only objective he could have just let Morgan kill Lavisse the previous night.

"I want their names, you bastard," he shouted to him over the sound of the rushing water filling the lock.

It had already reached Lavisse's feet and was rising rapidly. The Frenchman flinched at its cold touch.

Morgan squatted down beside him, watching him struggle. As the water reached his knees Lavisse finally cracked.

"I'll tell you. Just get me away from that madman."

"Tell me first!" Morgan said, "then all your troubles will be over."

If Lavisse had known Morgan better he would have found something more ominous than comforting in the Welshman's words. He spoke quickly, for the water was now up to his chest, and when he had done Morgan regarded him impassively.

167

"Help me, then" Lavisse screamed.

Morgan drew his knife. Lavisse had been party to an attempt on Philip's life and for that he would have to die. To Morgan it was that simple.

Philip joined Morgan and Thomas, watching as the waters closed over Lavisse's head.

"Why did you bother to cut his throat?" he asked. "He would have died in a few minutes anyway."

"But not by my hand."

Thomas was looking at Philip curiously. "You couldn't have stopped that contraption even if you'd wanted, could you, my Lord?"

"Of course not. Once the flood gates are opened the lock will fill. I thought you would realise that."

"Why would I know anything of country backwaters? I'm a city spark," Thomas told him proudly.

"Well you don't look much like one at the moment," Philip said, "or smell like one either!"

Thomas did, indeed, have a strong smell, for the walls of the lock were lined with all manner of filth and effluent.

"Whose fault is it that I am covered in stinking mud?" he demanded.

"Mine I guess, but since you could not smell much worse it does make you the logical choice to climb down and release Lavisse's body after I've drained the lock. Come, now, I can hardly leave him for Françoise and her sweetheart to deal with, can I?" Philip asked, seeing Thomas' expression. "We'd best be swift about it too," he added, "for the barges start moving early in these waters."

"What shall we do with Lavisse?" Morgan said.

"Bury him in the forest, I suppose, although he will be a little more difficult to handle, thanks to your final touch! No matter, I gather he told you what we wanted to hear."

"He told me," Morgan said grimly as they walked back to

empty the lock, "but I very much doubt you will want to hear it."

Thomas climbed down the ladder as the water went down, using the rope to help himself past Lavisse's body. The mud stuck to him worse than ever this time, for it was still wet and very slippery, but he was untying Lavisse's feet by the time Philip and Morgan returned.

"Not done yet?" Philip teased him.

"Why do I get all the best jobs," Thomas grumbled as Philip and Morgan hauled Lavisse up. "I shall stink like the very devil by the time we get to Paris."

"We're not returning to Paris," Philip said. "We're going to Versailles, at least I am. I doubt they'll let you in smelling like a duck pond!"

"But you can't calmly walk into the palace. Everyone thinks you're dead," Thomas reminded him, watching curiously as Philip took a handful of gold coins from his pocket and tied them up in his lace handkerchief.

"And they will have to think it for a little longer, especially in view of what Lavisse told Morgan, but I must find a way to see Theresa. I pray she is alright."

"Giles will have handled everything," Thomas reassured him.

"Ah, yes, the ever capable Giles! It will be good to see him again," Philip admitted, "although you are never to tell him that I said so!" He placed the coins by the door of the cottage. "It is for Françoise," he explained to them. "A wedding present!"

"Your mistress is safe," Armand informed Thomas and Morgan when they stood before him later that day, "but Giles has been arrested."

"Louvois?" both men guessed and Armand nodded.

"The soldiers took him when he was on the road to Paris.

They brought him back here this morning but I can't get near him, for they have orders that their prisoner is to speak to no-one until he has been seen by Louvois. Monsieur came hotfoot from Paris as soon as he heard and he is furious about it. Where is your master now?"

"He is by the Grand Canal," Thomas told him. We were supposed to ask the mistress to meet him there."

"She is in the gardens with Monsieur. Have you discovered anything about your master's attack?"

"We learned something today that is of great significance," Morgan informed him.

"We have all learned a few things of significance today," Armand said, for Theresa had confided everything to him, including the truth about Santerre, "but I will let your mistress tell you more about that. She will doubtless be back as soon as she has managed to calm Monsieur down."

Theresa was finding that difficult. She had never been quite at ease with Monsieur, the way Philip and Giles were, and, flattered though she was that he wanted her company, she little desired his at the moment.

When Armand had told her that Philip still lived she had wanted to laugh, to pray and even to cry, but she had been unable to do any of those things. Instead the news had left her strangely numb. After her despair at hearing of his death and the awful loneliness that had engulfed her, she had finally come to terms with the fact that he was truly dead. Now she could not bring herself to accept that he was not. Most of all she wanted to be alone and not listening to Monsieur complaining about Louvois.

The news of Giles' arrest had shaken her considerably too and she felt sure she was responsible. She could not even cheer Monsieur by telling him that Philip was alive. She felt guilty about that but she knew if she did every occupant of the palace would know within the hour. Then there was the little matter of Luc Santerre.

It was all too much.

They were sitting by the fountain of Enceladus and Theresa looked upon the agonised face of the giant, who strained to pull himself free of the rocks which were crushing him. She felt she understood his pain and that she, too, was being crushed. She sank her head into her hands.

Monsieur must have realised, at this point, that he was not absorbing his audience of one.

"Shall we go back?" he suggested.

"You go, by all means, Monsieur. I would like to stay here by myself for a while, if you don't mind."

Monsieur shrugged. "Suit yourself. Are you alright?" he asked, with a tinge of concern, which was unusual for him.

Theresa smiled at him. "Yes, perfectly, thank you, Monsieur," she lied. "It's Enceladus, I feel so sorry for him."

"Oh that," he said dismissively, obviously relieved that he did not have to press the matter any further. "Well, he shouldn't have tried to scale Olympus, dear!"

With that he teetered off on his high heels and Theresa was finally left to her own thoughts, but it did not help her much. It was nearly dusk and she knew she should be making her way back to the palace. She left the pond and walked slowly down the avenue of trees which led to the fountain of Apollo. In the half-light the sun god in his chariot, rising with his horses from the waters, looked quite real. She shuddered. It was definitely time to go back, she decided, before all the marble statues appeared to spring into life like ghosts of the antiquities they represented.

Before she turned to walk up the long lawn that would take her back to the palace, Theresa cast a last glimpse over toward the Grand Canal, which stretched out behind Apollo's pond. Two trees were silhouetted stark against the darkening sky at the very end of the canal and there were two other shapes her eyes could distinguish in the dim distance. She decided it was a man leading a horse along the bank. For some reason he caught her attention and she could not draw away.

She waited another five minutes, then ten. The lights burned brightly from the chandeliers of the palace and she knew she should be going back, for the evening was turning chilly, yet something compelled her to stay there until the figure came properly into view.

He looked familiar. He *was* familiar.

She started to run toward him.

Philip dropped his horse's reins and hastened to meet her, snatching her up in his arms. He kissed her until she was breathless.

"I saw you in the distance but I thought my eyes were playing tricks on me," she told him when they finally broke apart.

"Did Morgan and Thomas not tell you I would meet you here?" He kissed her forehead and the little wisps of hair that curled around her ears.

"Why no, I haven't seen them. I was in the gardens, talking with Monsieur. He is most upset because Giles has been arrested."

Philip frowned. That was unexpected. "What has he done, for God's sake?"

"Nothing I know of, save rescue me."

She started to tremble in his arms and then the tears began. It was as though the flood gates had been opened. Soon she was sobbing hysterically.

"Why did you have to come to France?" she cried. "You never listen to anyone, do you? So much has happened to us and it is all your fault."

Philip saw she was losing control. He guessed the nerves which had been stretched so taut had finally snapped. She began to hit him, beating her fists against his chest for all she was worth.

He pulled her closer to him so that she had to stop. "Hush, my darling, all is well. I am here now."

She still gulped for breath between the huge sobs which were shaking her whole body.

"You promised you wouldn't come here. You lied to me."

"I know, I know. It wasn't very fair." He stroked her hair to calm her down. "Stop crying now, Tess. You will make yourself sick."

"I do feel sick," she told him miserably, "and that is all your fault too."

He smiled at that. "Of course it is. Everything is my fault at the moment but you'll soon forgive me, for you always do."

"Not this time," she vowed, "not completely." Her hysteria had passed but she was still trembling.

"Yes, you will." he tilted her pale, damp face toward him and looked into her eyes.

He could see her anger slowly drain away.

"I love you such a lot," she said, when she was composed again. "I had no notion of what it would be like to be without you."

"Let us hope you do not have to find out again for a great many years." He kissed her damp eyelids tenderly. "Now tell me everything. Who ordered Giles' arrest?"

They sat down together by the side of the canal. It was practically dark now and there would be no-one left in the gardens to see them.

"Monsieur says that Louvois has him. I expect it's something to do with Luc. Talking of Luc, you might have told me about him, Philip," she said reproachfully.

"Told you what?"

"Who he is, of course."

"Who is he then?" Philip asked, mystified.

Theresa was looking at him suspiciously. "You really don't know?"

"No, why should I? I only met him on a few occasions, and I don't believe he liked me any more than I did him."

"In that case you are going to have a big surprise, my love. He claims to be your son!"

Philip lay back with a groan and closed his eyes. "This has been quite a day!"

"But is it possible? He says his mother was an actress."

"I don't know. How old is he? Eighteen?" Philip forced himself to do some mental arithmetic. "Yes, I suppose it's possible, but that is not to say it is a fact."

"Giles believes he is."

Philip pulled her down to lay beside him on the dampening grass. "Contrary to the views held by you and Thomas, my little sweetheart, Giles is not infallible, and shall I tell you something else about your precious brother? If Louvois has arrested him then my guess is that it is to do with some dirty little business of his own rather than with any illegitimate offspring of mine!" He rolled over to lie on top of her. "Dear God, Tess, but you are beautiful. I've a mind to take you here and now, out in the moonlight."

Theresa giggled. "Philip, please behave! What if Louvois won't let Giles go? He must be back in England before a month is out or William will be furious with him."

"Tess, I have been associated with Giles Fairfield for ten years and during that time I have learned that one never needs to worry over him," he reassured her. "Whatever trouble the man is in he always seems to have his own unique way of extricating himself!"

SIXTEEN

❦

Louis was about to enter Madame de Maintenon's apartments when the door opened and he was surprised to see Marie-Anne, one of his daughters, leaving in tears.

"Whatever is the matter?" he asked, concerned, for he loved all of his children very much.

"Madame de Maintenon has given me another lecture," Marie-Anne sniffed. "She says I am a wicked girl and that I will go to hell if I do not mend my ways."

"Not that wicked surely, not my Marie-Anne." Louis smiled at her, thinking how beautiful she was even now, dabbing at her eyes. Marie-Anne was the daughter of his first mistress, Louise de La Vallière, and whenever Louis looked at her he was reminded of her mother, a lovely, delicate creature, like some nymph from mythology. Louise had been a woman to meet by moonlight in the gardens or in a forest glade when others in his party were following the hunt. They had been happy then, in their Arcadian world, but he had spoiled it. He had loved her so much that he had declared his affections openly and forced her to be beside him, even when the Queen was there, but Louise was no Athénaïs, bold and sophisticated. Louise had shrivelled in the public glare and had retreated to a convent, from where she had never immerged.

Louis had been heartbroken, but in those days he had been young and inexperienced in such matters. He would have handled everything differently now. He suddenly thought of Theresa. She was not as beautiful as Louise and yet she had more than a touch of that same pastoral charm, with her love of gardens and solitude. He vowed he would not make the same mistake again. If Theresa would have him then he would ensure that their relationship never lost its delicacy. This time he would stay living forever in the sylvan glades with his secret shepherdess.

It was a pleasant dream, but Louis could not often allow himself to dream and he came abruptly back to reality. "Don't cry," he bade his daughter, for he hated to see her sad. "You have endured far worse than this."

She had indeed, for the young girl had but recently been widowed when her husband, the Prince de Conti, had caught the dreaded smallpox. Marie-Anne had suffered it too, but fortunately her looks were not impaired and he thought she might still make another good match. Louis had once offered her hand to William of Orange but he had turned her down to marry Mary Stuart saying, pompously, that his family only married the legitimate issue of kings. Another reason for Louis to dislike him!

Marie-Anne went on her way, endeavouring to put on a brave face to please him, and he entered Madame de Maintenon's chamber himself.

"Why was my daughter crying?" he demanded, opening the windows as he always did when he went into her room. Madame de Maintenon hated fresh air but Louis loved it, so when she was honoured by one of his visits she had to love it too.

"Marie-Anne upset the Dauphine." The Dauphine was the wife of Louis' legitimate son, the Dauphin, but she paid very little part in Court affairs for she was always ill and Louis had little sympathy for her.

"How has she upset her?" Louis wondered. "The woman is so dull I doubt she has the spirit to get upset."

Madame de Maintenon's lips pursed disapprovingly. "The Dauphine was lying on her bed and your daughter, thinking her to be sleeping, remarked that she was just as ugly asleep as she was when she was awake.'"

Louis hid a smile. "Is that all?"

"All? The poor woman heard it. She told Marie-Anne that if she was ugly it was probably because she did not have her advantage of being a love child."

"Then I would have thought the matter could have ended there."

"Do you wish me to be responsible for the care and discipline of your children or not?" Madame de Maintenon demanded. "It is bad enough that Madame de Montespan reverses every rule I make for her offspring."

"No, no, do as you please." Louis could not be bothered with the matter any further. "That was not what I came here to discuss with you. It is something far more serious. I am regretting the choice of Abbé Fénelon as tutor for my grandson."

"But the man is a saint," Madame de Maintenon protested.

"Whether he is or not, he is a good deal too free with his opinions for my liking." With that Louis produced a letter which he passed to her. "You will see from this impertinent missive that he accuses me of ruining the nation by this war with England and, further, he states that I love glory more than justice and reward those I ought to punish. I tell you now I am sorry I let you persuade me into appointing him, particularly since he may influence the Duc de Bourgogne, who is destined to rule France one day."

"It was ill-advised of the Abbé to write to you so," Madame de Maintenon agreed. "I shall reprimand him for his tactlessness, but it surely will not affect his appointment as tutor. He is excellently qualified for the post."

"Is he? What do you really know about Fénelon?" Louis said. "I have heard some disturbing rumours about him and I fear his religion has a little too much mysticism in it for my liking."

"He was recommended by my dear friend the Duc de

Beauvilliers," Madame de Maintenon reminded him. She had been instrumental in Beauvilliers also being appointed as Bourgogne's tutor. "I trust his judgement implicitly. Besides, what harm can Abbé Fénelon do? Your children and grandchildren have a Jesuit confessor do they not, at your absolute insistence?"

This was one of the points of religion on which they disagreed, but Louis had been unshakeable in his choice of a Jesuit.

"Indeed they do, for it is one thing to entrust a young mind to a person of dubious qualities, quite another to entrust a young soul."

"You would rather entrust it to such a person as Père La Chaise," she sniffed. Louis knew that she had always maintained that La Chaise, who was his own confessor, rated people by their political importance rather than upon their personal merits.

"I suppose you would sooner they came under the influence of Madame de Guyon, who goes into trances and is so filled with divine grace that she bursts her corsets," he flashed back. "You would do well, in my opinion, to be more discerning in your choice of those who come into contact with the girls in your care."

Louis was referring to St. Cyr, the school Madame de Maintenon had founded for the daughters of gentlefolk. He never interfered with its running and she rarely asked for advice, but he would give it anyway, especially when it enabled him to make a point. Since Madame de Guyon had herself been influenced by Fénelon, he considered his point well made. "What do you suppose your precious Abbé means when he says that I reward those I should punish?" he persisted, for he was not at all impressed by Madame de Maintenon's dismissal of Fénelon's criticism of him as mere tactlessness!

"How should I know?" She picked up some embroidery lying beside her and proceeded to busy herself with it.

Little escaped Louis. Her action certainly did not, and he

suspected it was prompted less by a desire to embroider than to save herself the necessity of looking him in the eye.

"Could he, perhaps, have been referring to Philip Devalle?" he said.

The needle moved furiously. "It hardly applies since Philip Devalle is dead."

"His wife, fortunately, is not dead, although I feared mightily for her safety. I can't think who would want to harm her, can you?"

"As I understand it no-one did harm her," Madame de Maintenon said, still concentrating fiercely on her needlework. "The word is that she merely lost her way in the dark and returned to Clagny the next morning."

"Yes, I know what she is saying, but it is a little curious, I'm sure you will agree, that she was lost over the other side of town and yet her horse was found the next day drinking from the Horse-Shoe."

The Horse-Shoe was one of the ponds in the gardens of the Trianon.

"Well you had better ask that woman, for I am sure she is in a position to know a great deal more about it than I, since they are apparently such friends," Madame de Maintenon said sourly.

"If by 'that woman' you mean Athénais, then I have already asked her but she knows no more than me."

"And did you also ask her how she felt about her son marrying a Devalle child?" Madame de Maintenon asked nastily.

"She is delighted at the prospect," Louis assured her.

"Even though the prospective bride has an uncle in the madhouse?" Madame de Maintenon no longer made any pretence at needlework. She was facing Louis angrily now. "What if a grandchild of yours is affected by this curse that I hear they call the 'Devalle sickness?' How pleased will you and the poor little Comte de Touraine's irresponsible mother be then?"

"The risk is small," Louis said. "Philip did not have this sickness, nor did his father before him."

"His grandfather had to be chained to his bed," she reminded him. "That is common knowledge."

"And is that why you hated Philip so?"

Madame de Maintenon picked up her needle once again. "I never said I hated him. If anything I pitied the poor wretch."

"No, you hated him," Louis corrected her. "You have never forgiven him for the way he treated you at his house all those years ago, just as you have never forgiven my brother for foiling your plans to deprive Philip of that same house."

"It was only fair and just that he should lose it, for was he not a Protestant at a time when French Protestants were being forced to sell their properties?" she asked. "There was no reason to treat him any differently from them."

"You managed to persuade me that such was the case," Louis said, "and I obeyed your wishes in the matter, even though I knew he would always bear me a grudge on account of it. When Monsieur offered to buy his beloved house and lease it back to him I considered the problem had been admirably solved. Philip no longer owned property in France and yet he was able to retain the place that held such precious memories for him, but that was not sufficient punishment for him in your opinion, was it?"

"He needed to be made an example of," she said.

"Did he? Why? He was no Huguenot, threatening my authority. Philip was a guest in my country, and one who, by his services to that country, had earned his privileges. Your grudge against him was a private one, if you could but bring yourself to admit it."

"I admit nothing, and it is impolite of you to rail against me so in my own chambers, particularly concerning events that happened such a long while ago," she said stiffly. "If you wish to speak to someone who hated Philip Devalle then why not visit

Louvois? He, too, was in favour of stripping him of his French assets, if you care to remember it."

Louvois was actually the next person Louis intended to call upon, but he wished to see him about a very different matter. He swept into the Minister's office without troubling to have himself announced.

"Why are you holding Giles Fairfield?" he demanded.

"He disobeyed my order to remain in Paris," Louvois said uneasily.

From his manner Louis guessed there was rather more to it.

"That is no good reason to arrest a man who holds such a high position of importance at the English Court. I like him no better than you but, for all that, he is entitled to be treated with the respect due to his rank. Besides, I will not have his sister upset any further. That unfortunate lady has suffered enough. When I saw her this morning she was in a dreadful state and now intends to return to Paris." This had not pleased Louis, but he did not feel he could put any pressure on Theresa at the moment, let alone ask for her decision upon his offer.

"You said you would not have Fairfield in the palace until the day of Devalle's ceremony," Louvois reminded him defensively.

"He was not in the palace," Louis pointed out, "nor do I believe he had the least intention of coming here. More likely he was endeavouring to help in the search for his sister. Now I have had to suffer the sight of her in tears on his behalf and Monsieur in a tantrum. You are to release him without delay."

"I was about to do exactly that, your Majesty."

"Good." Louis turned to go but then remembered something else. "I have been just now speaking with Madame de Maintenon who reminded me that you and Philip Devalle had an altercation some years ago. What was it about? I have forgotten."

"It was trivial matter," Louvois said. "I suspected him of participating in Passe Volants."

This was the name given to a practice which had been

common at one time amongst some of the army commanders. They would claim to have recruited more men than they actually had and draw their pay. When the troops were to be inspected they would borrow men from other regiments and some soldiers might be inspected in several different locations! It was one of the many corruptions rooted out by Louvois when he first became Minister of War.

"Not so trivial," Louis said. "If he had been found guilty he would have paid for it with a term in prison. What was the outcome?"

"I could never prove anything against him," Louvois admitted, "although that is not to say he might not have been guilty."

"There was one occasion, was there not, when you had him arrested?" Louis persisted.

"He was certainly guilty on that occasion," Louvois said. "Your Majesty might remember that he was caught aiding the Comte de Rennes' wife to flee to England before her conversion to the Catholic Faith. You released him, even though it was an offence for which a Frenchman might have been committed to the galleys."

"So he escaped you twice? You must have resented him for that."

"No, I had nothing but admiration for him, both as a soldier and as a man," Louvois protested.

Louis did not believe that for one moment. "About his murder…," he paused, looking hard at Louvois, "I trust his servants are not still carrying out investigations. I am holding you personally responsible should any problems arise from that affair. Any problems at all," he added, leaving him with that happy thought.

❦

"About time," Giles said testily when Louvois appeared. "What the devil do you mean by holding me here like a criminal?"

"I mean to teach you a lesson in obedience, my Lord. You were plainly told to kill Luc Santerre and yet today I saw him here, in this palace, speaking with Monsieur."

"Firstly," Giles said, affronted by his tone, "I am not an assassin and secondly I don't believe you are any longer in a position to give me orders. I obeyed your instructions to the letter as regards giving false information to King William's agent. You will have to get someone else to do your dirty work from now on, Louvois, for I have discharged my debt to you, as agreed."

"Oh, I don't think so, my Lord." Louvois smiled, as though he had been looking forward to this part. "You see I have your African servant held in a Marseilles prison. What do you say to that?"

What Giles said was a Moroccan word that was untranslatable into French.

Louvois looked smug. "I think I make my point, Lord Wimborne. You are in no position to be defiant with me, not when your servant has been charged with murder."

"Murder?" Giles tried to keep all expression from his face.

"Oh yes, my Lord. It seems your blackamoor completed the task you gave him." Louvois held up a piece of paper. "I have here a signed order for his release, which I will give to you once you have killed Santerre and properly completed your own task."

"If I was to do as you ask, would I then be free of all obligation to you?" Giles asked carefully.

"Completely free, my Lord, since, now that your countess is a widow, there is nothing to stop you marrying her, therefore my hold on you is broken."

"Quite. Well, Louvois, I believe I am in a position to make a trade for that document on my own terms."

"How so?"

"Let me say first that I have no intention of harming Santerre because he is Philip Devalle's son, as you are well aware. You did tell me the whereabouts of my sister, for which

I am grateful although, as matters stood, she was never in any real danger."

"I could not have known that," Louvois said defensively. "I suspected Santerre might be as mad as his forefathers."

"Be that as it may, your name has been kept out of the matter as you desired, for neither my sister nor myself will speak of the incident. I consider I have more than repaid that particular debt since, had the King's soldiers found them first, you, owing to your connection with Santerre, would have been under suspicion not only for her kidnap but, I suspect, my brother-in-law's death as well."

"Even so, you are in no position to bargain for Santerre's life, not if you wish to save your servant," Louvois reminded him.

"Oh, I think I am." It was Giles' turn to smile now and he thanked his stars for his friendship with Athénais. "You see there is one more piece of information that I can have King William's agent relate to Lord Marlborough. It concerns the Maréchal who is leading French troops against him in Flanders."

Louvois' face darkened. "D'Humières?"

"Exactly so. The unstable Maréchal d'Humières. How did such a man attain so high a position in your army?"

" D'Humières is an able soldier," Louvois insisted.

"He is an irritable individual, who will lead his troops into battle to appease his own whim," Giles said firmly. "He has been known to act rashly and without consideration for terrains or enemy capabilities. Such a man is scarcely the best choice to lead this particular campaign, I would have thought."

"How do you know so much about him," Louvois demanded.

"You forget that Philip knew him well. He once told me about him, including the fact that his failures in the past have been justified by official channels, but there is something of which my late brother-in-law was unaware, indeed I only discovered it myself quite recently. The Maréchal has a pretty wife does he not? She is your mistress."

For once Louvois seemed to have nothing to say.

"The Maréchal discovered you," Giles continued remorselessly, and to appease him you agreed to his recent appointment. You may have silenced him but you shall not silence me, Louvois. Now that morality and religion have become so fashionable at Versailles it will not look well, I fancy, if it is made known that the Minister of War seduces the wives of his officers!"

Louvois was beaten this time and he must have known it. Giles guessed that it was not a thing which happened to him very often for he did not take his defeat gracefully. He slung the order for Ahmed's release across the desk to Giles.

"This had better be valid," Giles warned him. "If I get to Marseilles and discover you have fooled me, or that my Ahmed is already executed, then I will have my revenge, depend upon it."

"It is valid." Louvois almost snarled the words. "Take it and be damned."

Giles pocketed the order, with almost as bad a grace as it had been given. He might have won this final round but Louvois had put him to a great deal of trouble and Giles would not forget that.

"It's Giles," Thomas cried joyously when he looked out of the window to see who was ringing the outside bell. "Louvois must have released him."

"I told you he would." Philip was actually more relieved than he wanted to show. He knew the amount of power wielded by Louvois and he knew, too, of his vindictiveness. "Giles won't yet know that I am alive," he guessed.

"No. No-one has had the chance to tell him."

"Good. Let him in and don't you dare say a word about it," Philip warned him as Thomas went to open the front door. "I'm going to surprise him."

"That's a bit mean, my Lord!"

"I know, but it is no more than he deserves for what he said to me on our last meeting."

It had been raining hard and Giles looked in a foul mood. He hurled his dripping hat and cloak onto the floor, cursing Louvois obscenely.

"Passionate little soul, isn't he?" Philip observed to Morgan as he watched him from behind the door.

Thomas listened sympathetically to Giles' tale. "Let me fetch you a cup of chocolate," he offered. "That will warm you up and make you feel better."

As Thomas stepped out of the room Philip slipped in and stood for a moment without speaking, watching as his brother-in-law took off his wet coat. Giles turned to hang it over the back of a chair and, for the first time, caught sight of who was in the room with him.

He let out an involuntary cry and clutched the chair for support.

"Did I startle you?" Philip asked innocently.

"You bastard!" Giles shook his head in wonderment. "You uncaring, thoughtless bastard! I can't believe you just did that to me."

"Come now," Philip laughed, putting an affectionate arm around him, "is that any way to greet a man back from the dead?"

SEVENTEEN

❦

Philip looked impatiently at the clock which stood in his entrance hall.

"Where is Giles? He's late." Philip could never abide to be kept waiting.

"You should count yourself fortunate if he turns up at all after what you did to him," Morgan muttered.

Philip laughed. "What? You taking Giles' part? Wonders will never cease!"

"He has his good points," Morgan admitted.

"Indeed he has." Thomas was always fiercely loyal to Giles. He had been engaged as his manservant when they had both been little more than boys and they had become good friends over the years. It was a friendship that had benefited them both, and which disregarded any differences of position or birth. Thomas always called Giles by his first name and Giles was fonder of Thomas than he was of his own brothers.

"Giles knows how I really feel about him," Philip said.

"It appears he does, for here he come now." Theresa looked out to see her brother approaching. "And he is not alone."

"Who has he brought? Not Monsieur, surely."

"No. It's Luc."

"What the devil does he think he's doing?" Philip said as Thomas rushed off to let the two men in.

"I think you'll like Luc when you get to know him," Theresa ventured.

"I already know him and I don't particularly want to get

to know him any better, my sweet," Philip said. "I really think I have all the trouble I can handle at the moment without dealing with someone pretending to be my son, although I can see he's touched your soft heart."

"I wish you would be friends with him. You will see him, won't you?" she pleaded.

"I don't seem to have too much choice, since your brother is evidently intent on foisting him upon me!"

Philip did not speak as they entered but he watched Santerre intently, noting how he moved and studying each line of his handsome features.

"Your Grace." Luc made him a deep bow. "I was delighted to learn from Lord Wimborne that you were alive."

"I thought I had better break the news to him myself, for such a shock as you gave me might well unhinge a delicately balanced Devalle mind," Giles informed Philip somewhat acidly.

"Quite likely, but the question is why have you told him anything at all?" Philip said.

"I thought he had a right to know, since he is your son."

"Don't you mean *if* he is my son?" Both you and your sister seem certain of it, but no-one has yet asked my opinion." Philip turned to Luc. "Why did you mention none of this to me when we first met at La Fresnaye?"

"I thought you would not believe me and, besides, you did not appear to like me too well," Luc said.

"And you think I shall like you any better for abducting my wife? I tell you this, Santerre, if you had harmed her in the least degree then, no matter who you were, I would have finished you myself."

"I had no wish to harm her," Luc said, "but I do not always have control over what I do. It sometimes seems that there are demons in my head and when they speak to me I commit acts of rage that I can scarcely remember afterwards."

Philip had his own demons, and only years of practice had

taught him to quiet their voices. "I do remember your mother," he admitted, in a slightly gentler tone, "but that does not make me your father."

"She had a lock of your hair, which she kept by her until her dying day." Luc produced a little wooden box from his waistcoat pocket. He opened it and showed him a lock of blonde hair.

Philip dismissed it with a gesture. "That proves nothing, for I tell you now I never gave her a lock of my hair."

"She never claimed you gave it to her," Luc said. "She cut it off one night whilst you were sleeping."

Philip raised an eyebrow at that. "Indeed!"

Theresa giggled and he looked at her sternly. "I am pleased you find this so amusing, madam."

"I'm sorry, my love, it's just that I would never have the nerve to cut off one of your curls."

"So I should hope but, in any case, what does it prove? It could just as likely be his own hair, for it is the self-same colour."

"No," Luc cried hotly, "it is yours. You knew about me, for my mother went to see you, begging you for money, but you abandoned us. You let her bring me up in poverty whilst you went back to England, to your riches and your fine estate."

Philip turned to Giles. "Thank you for bringing him here. This is certainly adding considerable pleasure to my day!"

Giles ignored his sarcasm. "I brought him here because he has a piece of information I thought relevant to our meeting and I believe you ought to listen to him. As for you, Santerre, you will not advance your position with Lord Southwick one jot if you adopt that tone."

"Quite right," Philip agreed.

"If there is one thing that he cannot bear," Giles said, "it is criticism." Philip threw him a warning glance but Giles continued. "We are to blame, I realise that," he told Philip. "Thomas, Morgan, my sister and myself. We have told you how wonderful you are for so long that now you can accept nothing but our admiration, not even when your refusal to heed our advice has lately caused you, and us, so many problems."

"Have you quite finished?" Philip asked him, annoyed that he was being attacked in front of all of them.

"Not yet. You are a person the like of which none of us have ever known. I was devastated when I thought you dead and neither King William nor my wife, nor even the prospect of my unborn child could lighten my darkness. I cannot speak for Morgan since, being closer to you, he sensed that you were still alive but as for Thomas, he went looking for your killers down amongst the most vicious inhabitants of Paris without a thought for his own safety, because he no longer cared if he lived or died. I will not even begin to describe how the news affected my sister for, despite how you treat her, she adores you."

"What is your point?" Philip asked, a little appeased by his words.

"My point is that you are the centre of our world, Philip. We worship you, but you must allow us to sometimes tell you that you are wrong."

"He doesn't worship me," Philip countered, pointing at Luc.

"Give him time," Giles said quietly. "None of us can resist you for long."

Philip made no reply but, after a moment, he indicated with his head that his brother-in-law was to follow him out of the room.

"Did you mean all that?" he asked him when they had closed the door on the others.

"Every word."

"Thank you." Philip was really quite touched at Giles' emotional outburst, and surprised too, for it was so unlike him. "I don't deserve you do I?"

"No, you don't," Giles agreed, smiling. "You can't imagine

how I suffered when I thought we had parted forever on such a sour note."

"We must never argue again," Philip said. "That way if anything should happen to either of us the other will have no regrets."

"I'll try if you will," Giles promised, "but that does not mean I am going to go along with everything you say and do!"

"You have never been compliant and I don't expect it of you," Philip said. "Now, talk to me about Santerre. Why have you really brought him here? If he has information you could have told it to us yourself, and don't give me this nonsense about feeling I should get to know my own son!"

"Why should you assume there is another reason?"

Philip sighed heavily. "Giles, I have known you since you were sixteen years of age. You intrigued me then and you beguile me still, but you have always been a devious little schemer. Tell me the truth, if you can still manage it."

Giles shrugged. "There is nothing more than you already know. I thought you might agree to take Luc back to England with us if you liked him."

"Why in heaven's name should I want to do that?" Philip said in amazement.

"To protect him. He is William's agent in France."

That was news to Philip. "Is he? I had no idea."

"Nor has Louvois, and hopefully he will not discover it, but he already wants him dead. I refused to be his instrument but he may well appoint another. That is all."

"You are still lying, Giles, and believe me I can tell."

"There is a little more to it than that," Giles admitted.

"Well of course there is. With you there is always a little more." Philip poured himself a glass of brandy and handed one to Giles. "Come, out with it. You know you'll have to tell me in the end."

Giles hesitated, but only for a minute, for Philip would have persisted until he got it out of him. "Very well, but you won't like it much," he warned him. "Louvois had a hold on me."

"I see." Philip had no intention of telling Giles that he had already learned about it from Armand, for he guessed Giles would prefer him not to know the truth about Marianne.

"I was forced to give Luc false information to pass on to Marlborough," Giles admitted.

Philip did not alter his expression. "And do you know the result of your action?"

"Yes, I'm afraid I do. For one thing it caused Marlborough to argue with the Prince of Waldeck. Because I sent word that the French troops were making straight for Charleroi, Marlborough insisted upon heading northwards to cross the River Sambre, whilst Waldeck was in favour of waiting. He planned to advance first upon the west bank of the Meuse to take Rocroi."

Rocroi was strategically placed near to the borders of Luxembourg. It had been taken from the Allies thirty-five years before by the French army under the command of Condé and to retake it now would have been a significant gesture.

"Without the English troops to back him he failed in his attempt," Giles admitted. "D'Humières had the place defended to the hilt, whilst Marlborough and his army were alone in the Forest of Mormal."

"Then it's just as well that it was Marlborough and not me leading the English troops," was all Philip said.

"You're not going to call me a miserable traitor?"

"Why no. You did what you had to do. Besides, Waldeck is an old soldier who engages in war as another might play a game of chess. The most damage you will have achieved is to upset the predictability of his game. What you will have done, however, is to lessen Marlborough's capabilities of judgement in Waldeck's eyes, and I don't mind that. I am more concerned with the hold Louvois has over you."

"I have dealt with it," Giles said simply.

"Good." Philip knew better than to ask how. "Then the important thing is not to let King William know about any of this and Luc is the only person who could give you away. I suspect that is why you promised we would take him back to England. You don't give a damn if he is my son or not, do you, just so long as he agrees to keep silent?"

"But you do own that he could be your child?"

"There are quite a few who could be my children. I was a very dissolute young man," Philip confessed.

"He has fits," Giles told him. "Your brother has fits, you told me so."

Philip shuddered. His older brother, Henry, was in Bedlam, the London mental hospital, and Philip rarely spoke of him. "If I have sired a son anything like Henry then I truly do not want him near me."

"He's not as bad as that, but when he gets upset or angry he foams at the mouth and thrashes about. Theresa told me he did it when she was with him so I thought he might be touched by the Devalle sickness."

"Insanity is not exclusive to the Devalles," Philip reminded him, a little pained, "but, since it will benefit you, I will consider taking him to England – only for you, mind."

"Thank you, Philip. I will not forget this," Giles promised.

"Yes of course you will." Philip poured them another drink and raised his glass. "A toast, Giles, to our friendship and our vow to be more tolerant toward one another."

Theresa was talking to Luc when they returned to the others. "He wants to travel back with us," she told Philip.

Philip cast a sidelong glance at his brother-in-law. "Yes, I know he does."

"Shall we take him then?"

"Giles seems to think we should and I am bowing to his decision, since he appears to know him rather better than the rest of us."

"Thank you, my Lord." Luc looked delighted. "I am sorry for my earlier outburst. It will not occur again."

"It had better not," Philip warned him, "and you may be sure that my decision in no way acknowledges you to be my son, nor shall I ever do so. I am taking you with us at the request of my brother-in-law and you will be in his care, not mine," he stressed.

Luc seized Giles' hand and kissed it. "I am yours to command, Lord Wimborne. I have already judged you to be a man I can admire and from this day forth I pledge to do your every bidding."

"That's all we need," Philip murmured to Theresa, "another willing slave for Giles, as if the two he brought from Morocco were not enough!"

"It was nice gesture on your part," she reckoned. "I am sure you won't regret it."

Philip was not so sure, but the deed was done now and since Giles had instigated it Philip was determined that he should be the one responsible for its outcome.

"You'll do pretty well with Giles," he told Luc, "only don't ever cross him, and that is good advice. Now perhaps we can get back to the reason why we are all here, which is to discuss the little matter of my death!" He indicated that they were all to be seated, although he himself remained standing. "Since it is claimed that I never heed the advice of those dearest to me, I will have the opinions of you all and I will act according to the wishes of the majority."

Theresa, Thomas and Morgan glanced at each other in astonishment. This was unheard of, for Philip always ruled his family and his household according to his own whim. Giles, he noticed, looked less impressed, but then Giles had seen him, in the past, turn an entire assembly of Whigs with what Lord Shaftesbury had called his 'silvered tongue' and Philip knew Giles had guessed that this was just a ruse to make himself appear more reasonable.

Whatever plan of action evolved from this meeting it would be the one that he had already set his mind upon!

"We will begin with you, Theresa." Philip turned to her. "What do you think we should do now?"

"Go home," she said unhesitatingly, "but the first thing we should do is to inform Louis that you are alive, for I am finding it nearly impossible to dissemble in front of him."

"I'll come to that. What say you, Giles? Are you in favour of returning home?"

"Yes, as soon as I am able."

"Now you, Morgan?"

"Punish your attackers as befits their crime and then openly accuse whoever employed them," the Welshman answered without hesitation.

Philip knew he could rely on him!

"Thomas?"

"I agree with Morgan, every bit," Thomas said staunchly.

"Well then," Philip turned his attention to Luc, "it appears this decision rests with the newest member of our assembly."

"Me, my Lord?" Luc stammered. He evidently had little thought that he would be included.

"Yes, certainly, for you must also have your say, since you are proposing to throw in your lot with ours." Philip looked into Luc's blue eyes, so like his own, and held his gaze. "Come now, and don't feel you have to agree with any to keep their favour, for this a free vote."

"Then I vote with Morgan and Thomas," Luc said. "When all is said and done, my family honour is at stake and I feel bound to avenge you, whether or not you own me as your issue."

"That was well said," Philip allowed. "It is decided then. I shall be avenged."

"Surprise, surprise," Giles muttered.

"The next point to discuss then is the suspects, and I will have your opinions on those as well."

"Louvois," Thomas said without hesitation. "To him you are now an enemy of France. He has never managed to best you and he could not bear to see you glorified by the offer King Louis made to you. Remember, too, that it was he who had me watched so closely."

"I, too, think it was Louvois," Theresa put in. "That is why he was so insistent that none knew Luc had kidnapped me, for he feared if suspicion rested on himself for that then it might rest on him for your fate also."

"Giles?"

"I have reason enough to hate Louvois, but I am not convinced that he is to blame for this," Giles said. "I think perhaps you should listen to what Luc has to say."

All eyes turned to Luc, who looked at Philip a little uncertainly, as though he was unsure as to how he would react to what he was about to relate.

"Monsieur returned from Versailles yesterday, having had an argument with King Louis. Apparently Monsieur was shedding a tear or two over you and the King grew very angry with him, saying he should be over his loss by now. Monsieur told him he would never get over it, especially since your murderers were still at large, whereupon the King flew into a fury. He said that Monsieur was not to mention the matter again and that he hoped he would get some peace now that you were dead, since he had known little whilst you lived."

Theresa gasped at that and Philip saw she had gone quite pale.

Thomas looked shocked too, but Morgan only nodded, as though Luc's words were no more than he expected to hear.

"There is more, I fear, my Lord," Luc continued, "for when Monsieur protested at his callousness, the King told him that he would do better to think less of fighting for justice in this instance and more of protecting the honour of their own household."

Philip frowned. "He actually said that?" It was one thing

to have suspicions, but quite another to have them apparently confirmed.

"I fear so, my Lord. I am sorry to be the bearer of such news."

"It is not entirely unforeseen," Philip admitted. "I think the time has come to tell you what Lavisse related to Morgan just before he died. Apparently he met Abbé Fénelon whilst he was still employed by the Duc de Beauvilliers. It was Fénelon who suggested he obtain employment at the Palais Royale and report my movements. It was Lavisse who told Fénelon's agents I was leaving for Versailles early in the morning and so I can only presume that the men who set upon me were acting upon the instructions of Fénelon.

"But the Abbé is a man of God," Theresa protested.

"He was recently appointed tutor to Louis' grandson, therefore we must assume that he is also a man of the King," Philip said grimly. What I do not understand, though, is how this man of God inspires fanaticism in a criminal like Lavisse, but you would have thought the Abbé was God Himself, so fearful was he of informing against him."

"It has been rumoured that Fénelon is connected with the Quietists," Luc said thoughtfully. "This Lavisse may have joined them.".

The name was new to the four English members of the gathering.

"What the devil are Quietists?" Philip asked, voicing the thoughts of the rest.

"Quietism is a mystic doctrine whose followers claim they have no need to pray because God communicates with them," Luc explained. "I don't know too much about them but I do know that its followers are mostly an odd bunch and quite fanatical about their beliefs. They go into trances to make themselves more receptive and believe that, since God is in them, whatever they do cannot be a sin as it is really God who is doing it."

"And Louis, the persecutor of Protestants for their nonconformity, allows a man like that to teach his grandchild?" Philip said in wonderment. "So, Luc Santerre, even suspecting that my enemy might be the King himself, do you still want to avenge me?"

"More than ever," Luc declared staunchly.

"That says something for your courage, if not for your intelligence! Where is Monsieur now?"

"At the Palais Royale. He was so upset when he got back from Versailles that he had to take to his bed. Indeed, it took me most of the night to calm him down."

"I'm sure it did!" Philip and Giles exchanged glances, for they both knew only too well how demanding Monsieur could be when he needed attention. "Well you had better get back to him and tell him, please, that you heard it rumoured in the Café Procope that I was still alive."

Luc looked confused. "But won't he tell everybody?"

"I am relying on it," Philip assured him. "The only person who will not believe it is my enemy, who is sure he had me killed! Trust me, Luc. Oh, and one more thing, I would like you find out everything there is to know about these Quietists."

When Luc had departed Philip turned to Thomas. "Are you still set upon your resolution to avenge me?"

"Of course."

"I will not even trouble to ask Morgan, but am I to assume, Giles, that you will wish to return home because the prospect of accusing a king of murder is too daunting for you?"

"You can assume what you damn well like, but the fact is I have something else I must do, and very little time to do it if I am to keep my promise to King William." Giles took out Louvois' order to show him. "This document will obtain Ahmed's release from a Marseilles prison," he explained. "Every minute that I linger in Paris is another minute that my faithful Ahmed languishes in captivity."

"And what has your faithful Ahmed done to find himself

incarcerated?" Philip asked, although he had his suspicions after what Armand had told him.

Giles was obviously not about to be drawn on the topic.

"Never mind that. Suffice it to say that I shall not have time to come back to Paris afterwards. I am sorry, Philip, but whatever incredible scheme you are planning I cannot, this time, be a part of it."

"That is all most inconvenient, for I particularly needed you here."

"Won't Armand or Luc do in my stead?"

Philip shook his head. "I'll not have Armand involved any further in this business. He, after all, must live out his life here when we've gone. As for Luc, I don't know him well enough to trust his nerve the way I do yours. When do you propose to leave?"

"Tomorrow at first light."

"Can't you even stay for my memorial service?" Philip asked him, piqued.

"Well I naturally presumed there would no longer be a service held for you."

"Not only will it be held but I fully intend to be there."

"You are proposing to attend your own memorial? Really, Philip! You have performed some preposterous acts before but I think this time you are going too far."

"It is not an action prompted by vanity," Philip assured him. "Well not entirely," he added a little sheepishly, catching Giles' expression, "although it will naturally be pleasing to hear myself spoken of in glowing terms, but the ceremony must go on, for it is there I thought to reveal my enemy."

"This is madness." Giles looked to the others for support but Morgan and Thomas were plainly taken with the idea, whilst Theresa, still white as a sheet, did not seem to be even listening.

She came out of her reverie when she realised he was addressing her. "I'm sorry, Giles, what were you saying?"

He sighed. "Never mind. I don't suppose it will make the

slightest bit of difference." He turned back to Philip. "What exactly are you planning?"

"A little bit of theatre, that's all. I thought we could pretend that I escaped unharmed from the Seine but had been seized by a fanatic loyal to France and held prisoner all this while. Seeing my memorial service as a fitting time for my execution, he will bring me to the upper part of the chapel at the point of his sword. Before he can carry out his dastardly plan, however, he will appear to have been shot by Morgan and Thomas, disguised as palace guards, and I will be saved." Philip paused for effect. "The audience below will be amazed and delighted at my sudden appearance, but one person present will know the truth of what happened on the Pont Neuf – the person who arranged to have me killed. I believe their reaction will plainly reveal their guilt for all to see."

"Ingenious," Giles allowed, "but who is to play the part of the villain in your little charade?"

"Surely it is of scant concern to you since you intend to abandon me," Philip retorted.

"When have I ever done so?" Giles flashed back. "How many times has my good sense prevailed against my regard for you?"

"Never, I am very pleased to say." Philip was delighted at his change of heart. "But what of Ahmed and your promise to King William?"

"I could ask Athénais if she will send someone to Marseilles with Ahmed's release, I suppose," Giles said. "As for William, I will have to take my chances on his disfavour. If I am truly essential to your plan then I'll not let you down."

"Essential? My dear Giles you are the very hub of it!"

"I suppose that means I am to be your kidnapper," Giles said resignedly.

"Who else?" Philip said. "Without you, my dear Giles, none of this can go ahead."

"And a very good thing that would probably be," Giles reckoned.

EIGHTEEN

❧

Theresa could not bring herself to accept that it was Louis who had ordered Philip's death and yet he had said to her plain enough. 'I killed him, Theresa'. They had been his very words. She remembered how kind he had been to her, how tender when he had given her the necklace. She wondered now whether that had been because he had been feeling guilty. She recalled, too, the plans he had made for the two of them, plans which could never have been made whilst Philip was alive.

She realised, suddenly, that she was hopelessly out of her depth. She had seen only Louis' good qualities. She had even allowed herself to be excited by his nearness and now she felt ashamed, and totally disloyal to her husband, as though she, too, had played a part in the plot against his life.

With these turbulent thoughts running in her head, she paid a visit to Athénais de Montespan that afternoon to ask if Athénais would arrange for Ahmed's release papers to be taken to Marseilles. She had offered to go to Clagny, since Giles was once more forbidden to leave Paris, but she was glad of the opportunity to speak with Athénais again.

"I would be pleased to help your little brother," Athénais told her. "He fascinates me, truly he does, although I find him most mysterious."

"Giles is a mystery to us all," Theresa said.

"So you have no idea what this nonsense is about?" Athénais pointed to the document Theresa had given her.

"Absolutely none. He was always secretive, even as a child.

The only person who could ever get anything out of him was Philip."

Theresa badly wanted to tell Athénais that Philip was still alive but she did not dare, at least not until she had the answer to a question she knew not quite how to ask.

Athénais rang for a servant and gave instructions for a messenger to start for Marseilles without delay.

"It is good of you to act so quickly," Theresa said gratefully. "I know Giles will be much relieved."

"To be honest with you I very much fear that if we do not act quickly then a pardon signed by Louvois may not be worth the paper it is written on, since he may soon find himself deprived of his position," Athénais said dryly.

"Louvois? Surely not!" Theresa cried in surprise, for she had always thought Louis relied utterly on his Minister of War.

"Well you may judge for yourself when I tell you that Louis has more or less accused him of Philip's murder."

"Do you think it was him?"

"I am sure it was not," Athénais said decidedly, "but how he proves it is another manner."

Theresa steeled herself to broach the subject that was uppermost on her mind. "Because Louis himself is the guilty one?" she ventured.

Now it was Athénais' turn to look surprised. "You believe Louis was responsible? How could you think such a thing?"

"I don't think so," Theresa admitted, "but there are some who do and I no longer know what to believe. After all, Philip has caused him a great deal of trouble in the past."

"Louis forgives those he cares about for the trouble they cause him," Athénais said quietly, "and if you doubt that only consider me. It is not too many years since I was accused of devil worship on account of my association with Catherine Monvoisin."

Theresa was familiar with the incident, which had caused a scandal in its day. Not only Athénais, but scores of other prominent people had been suspected of participating in black magic rituals and administering the poisons and love potions distributed by the woman known as La Voisin. She had called herself a simple fortune teller, and even Philip had visited her in that capacity, but there was a far more sinister side to Catherine Monvoisin.

La Reynie, the chief of police, had set up a committee to investigate the matter but, as soon as Athénais' name had been included in the list of suspects, Louis had closed the affair. It had meant that those already imprisoned were held there for the rest of their lives, but Athénais had remained untouched and the matter was never mentioned again.

"But that is surely a little different," Theresa said. She knew Louis could forgive women almost anything. "After all he was in love with you."

"And now he loves another who he will protect from scandal."

Theresa frowned. "Do you mean Madame de Maintenon?"

"Who else hated Philip enough to want him dead and Louvois enough to engineer his fall from favour?"

Theresa was silent for a moment as the full import of Athénais' words came home to her. "I can understand why she may have hated Philip," she said slowly, "especially in view of what you told me about his ordering her from his house, but why would Maintenon hate Louvois?"

Athénais seemed about to say something, and then changed her mind. "Who can say? Perhaps it is because, unlike all the other ministers, he refuses to consult with her on policy."

"There must be more to it than that," Theresa reckoned, looking at her closely.

"There is," Athénais confessed, "but it is a secret."

"Can't you tell me?" Theresa pleaded. "There is still so much I need to understand about all this. I'll tell you a secret in return," she added temptingly.

Athénais wavered, but only for a moment. "Very well. Louis and Maintenon are married."

Theresa blinked in astonishment. She had certainly not expected that to be Athénais' revelation. Whilst there had been talk of it for years, suspicions were very different from facts.

"It was a private ceremony of course," Athénais said, "and witnessed only by Louvois, but since that time it has been her driving ambition to have the marriage acknowledged. Each time she brings up the subject Louis refers the matter to Louvois and he always advises against it. She is a vengeful woman, make no mistake on that, and she will do anything to destroy him. She now claims to have information that he arranged Philip's death as an act of war against a potential enemy commander, but it isn't true."

"I thought she was supposed to be a religious person," Theresa said, still reeling from the news of Louis' marriage.

"Don't let her holy countenance fool you," Athénais snorted. "If you doubt her capabilities you need only consider how Armand's wife suffered in Brittany and Philip's relatives in Languedoc. It was Maintenon who persuaded Louis to destroy the Huguenots. It was on account of her that Louvois needed to employ his barbarous methods of obtaining converts. Nothing would satisfy her but the annihilation of every Protestant in France, even though she herself was brought up in that faith."

Athénais' high pitched voice quavered with emotion. Although a Catholic herself, she was a compassionate person and, unlike either Maintenon or Louis, had the imagination to put herself in the shoes of others and sympathise with their plight. Besides, she had seen many friends, like Armand and Philip, caught up in the troubles and imprisoned, and Athénais was loyal to her friends.

"But how could Louis allow himself to be influenced by such a person?" Theresa said.

"He will do anything that he considers will increase his country's glory in the eyes of the rest of the world," Athénais reminded her. "She managed to convince him that it lessened France's greatness to have some subjects worshipping in a different way from their king."

"Is she well acquainted with Abbé Fénelon?" Theresa asked her, recalling what had been said about him at Philip's meeting that morning.

"But of course. It was she who persuaded Louis to engage him as a tutor for his grandson. Louis can't stand the man, but why do you ask?"

Theresa smiled, her mind much eased. Everything was falling into place now and she could not wait to tell Philip what she had learned. "You will soon see," she promised.

"Now you are being as mysterious as your brother," Athénais said, "and you have not yet told me your secret. It had better be as good as mine," she warned.

"Oh, it is." Theresa took a deep breath, praying that her trust in Athénais was not misplaced, but she had committed herself now and that was that.

"Philip is alive!"

෴

"You have been a tower of strength to me," Theresa told Marguerite as they sat together in the chapel waiting for Philip's memorial service to begin. The pair had bonded from the first, for Armand's young Comtesse, like Theresa, was not of noble birth and had only acquired a title by marriage. "I don't believe I could go through with this if you were not beside me."

Marguerite pressed her hand. "Don't worry, Philip will manage everything, you'll see."

"I'm not too worried for him," Theresa admitted. "I am a little concerned for my brother, however. There is nothing he would not do for Philip and he has often got himself into trouble on account of it."

Theresa had another concern too, one she did not voice to Marguerite. She was still afraid that the charade Philip was planning would expose Louis as the guilty one, and she badly did not want it to be him.

The chapel was beginning to fill and Theresa was impressed at the number of important people who were arriving for the ceremony. Even the Dauphin was there, with his sickly-looking wife. Athénais swept in, looking her most glamorous in black lace and with a hundred ringlets crowning her lovely head, and she gave Theresa a knowing glance.

Ministers and courtiers were each escorted to their places and seated in order of their rank, according to the instructions laid down by Monsieur, who was the acknowledged expert on all matters of precedence, but when Monsieur himself entered all heads turned. It was fully expected that he would break down during the ceremony and, indeed, he already looked close to tears. Theresa watched him pityingly, for Monsieur had a great shock to come and she was not sure quite how he would take it. Madame was by his side, lending him moral support for once, and she looked over at Theresa with an encouraging smile. Theresa hoped very much that Madame would forgive her for not divulging to her that Philip was alive, but she had decided she could not give the outspoken woman so great a secret to keep from her talkative husband.

There were already rumours circulating that he had been seen about the city. The chance remark which Philip had instructed Luc to let slip to Monsieur had ensured that, and the result was an air of tense expectancy. It seemed the congregation were no sooner shown to their seats than they were deep in discussion with their neighbours and Theresa thought, not for the first time, how clever Philip was.

"The innocent are very plain to see," she observed to Marguerite, listening to the excited whispers all around them. Athénais knew the truth of course, but she was well able to dissemble and was discussing the rumour as interestedly as the rest.

Only Madame de Maintenon, it seemed, was her usual calm self. She entered with her hands folded piously, as was her wont, and her head bowed. To hide the gleam of triumph in her eyes, Theresa suspected, wishing she could slap her in front of everyone.

Armand joined Marguerite and Theresa then. "All is in readiness," he whispered, in answer to their silent questions.

Louis made his entrance a few minutes later, followed by the Bishop of Meaux, who was to conduct the ceremony, and the assembly rose.

There were other observers to his entrance. Well hidden from view, Philip peered down from the upper gallery. Normally this part of the chapel was reserved for the King, so that the congregation could observe their monarch at prayer, but today, since he had honoured Philip's memory with a bishop, Louis was to be with the rest of the gathering.

Armand, thanks to his rank, had been able to arrange for there to be no soldiers in the vicinity of the upper gallery of the chapel.

"The service is about to start," Philip said, fastening a rope around his own wrists, so as to give himself the appearance of being a captive. "Are we ready, gentlemen?"

"Ready." Luc took his place on the stairs.

"Ready." Morgan and Thomas, dressed as guards, pulled their hats down low over their eyes.

"Ready." Giles tied a black mask across his face and covered his distinctive auburn hair with a brown wig. He was rarely ruffled and, despite his misgivings at the start, he looked well prepared to carry out his part.

"Shall we wait to hear my praises sung for just a little while?" Philip said as Bossuet, the Bishop of Meaux, began to speak.

"If we must, though I still reckon Louis has chosen a strange person to sing your praises," Giles reckoned. "The words will probably stick in his throat!"

They all thought Bossuet an odd choice to preside over a memorial service for a Protestant, for he had been amongst those who had supported the abolition of the Huguenot faith. Philip wondered if Louis intended to demonstrate that, in spite of the inconvenient fact of Philip being a Protestant, he had not rebelled against the King, as had the Huguenots. He decided that, more likely, Louis had simply wanted the person he regarded as the best for the occasion, and he rated Bossuet so highly as to have once engaged him as a tutor for the Dauphin. Whatever way he had been chosen for the job, the Bishop launched into it with fitting enthusiasm, outlining Philip's glorious career with the French army. He mentioned his part in the crossing of the Rhine during the Dutch Wars and his almost legendary defence of the town of Woerden with only a single troop against the far greater numbers of the attacking Dutch army.

"Heard enough?" Giles said impatiently.

"Not quite." Philip was rather enjoying it.

"Some men are like mice," Bossuet intoned, "too timid to venture out into the world and some are sheep, so stupid they can only blindly follow others. Some are like bulls, which roar and snort and are feared but never trusted. Then there are the lions. These are the true leaders, for they are brave, intelligent and strong. Such a man was Philip Guy Devalle."

"Oh, I like that," Philip said.

"Now?" Giles suggested, his sword raised.

"Any time you like."

Philip stepped out in plain view of the congregation, his hands tied in front of him and apparently held at sword point by a masked man.

The chapel was instantly in uproar.

Louis' expression was one of unmistakeable relief. Monsieur, tears streaming down his cheeks, was applauding wildly. Athénais was staring fixedly at Madame de Maintenon so as not to miss a moment of her agony.

Her mouth was open, although no sound came out, and she was shaking her head. Then she reached out a trembling hand and pointed up at Philip, shouting out a single word that seemed to carry above all the noise around her.

"No!"

Louis turned to look at her, his expression unreadable, and she sank back into her chair, covering her face with her hands.

Everyone else was intent on observing the little drama being played out above them.

Two soldiers seemed to have entered the gallery, their swords drawn, and a furious fight began, but the mysterious masked man was holding his own against both of them.

"Where are my guards?" Louis demanded angrily, but, even as he spoke, several shots rang out in quick succession, echoing around the chapel and sounding alien in that most holy setting. They actually came from Giles' repeater pistol, being fired in the air by Luc, but it appeared as though several guards had reached the scene. The masked man let out a howl of pain and the onlookers gasped as he teetered perilously close to the edge before collapsing on the floor of the gallery.

The two soldiers pulled him to his feet and began to drag him away.

"Not so rough. I am supposed to be a wounded man, after all," Giles complained, in a whisper.

"Be gentle with him, for God's sake," Philip instructed them, "or I shall never hear the end of it."

Thomas grinned. "It was a fine performance though, my Lord, you must admit that."

Philip shrugged. "A little overacted, I thought! Theresa's

turn now. Good luck, Giles." Philip's eyes met his. "See you in England."

"I hope so."

At that moment Theresa screamed and appeared to swoon into Armand's arms. The attention of those down below was momentarily drawn from the drama taking place in the gallery and Giles took advantage of the distraction to make his getaway.

Once out of sight of his audience, he raced down the spiral stone staircase, pausing only to retrieve his repeater pistol from Luc. The most difficult part of his business was yet to come.

He cursed, for a guard, who had obviously heard the shots, was running towards the stairs. Giles stepped back into a small, circular recess at the bottom of the staircase. It was dark there and, being slim, he was able to press himself into it, hoping he would not be noticed.

He thought his quick thinking had saved him, for the guard ran straight by him and up the staircase. Then the man looked down.

Giles had been spotted through the treads of the stairs and he knew that there was little point in running now. The guard would only raise the alarm to alert others, and it was better for him to have to deal with only a single opponent. He drew his sword again, but this time the fight would be in earnest.

Their boot heels clattered on the marble floor as they moved around each other, Giles drawing the soldier away from the chapel as best he could, for he knew it was only a matter of minutes before folk recovered themselves sufficiently to rush out of the chapel doors to see what was occurring. Even Philip, expert as he was at holding an audience, could keep their attention for only so long.

Giles had not truly enjoyed swordplay since the accident which had robbed him of his good looks, but he had not lost his touch and he successfully kept his man at bay. Once outside in the courtyard the uneven cobbles made footwork difficult. His opponent caught him on the arm, but it was only a scratch and Giles paid it no heed.

He was not so well known as Philip but, even wearing the wig, he knew he might be recognised. Just the other side of the first set of gates he saw the coach Athénais had provided, waiting to take him to Calais, and the only object stopping him from reaching it was the wretched man whose sword, at that moment, sliced the air perilously close to his unscarred cheek.

Desperation gave Giles extra strength. He attacked furiously until the soldier, stumbling upon the cobblestones, overbalanced. He fell awkwardly but Giles did not wait for him to hit the ground before he started to run in the direction of the gates.

Fortunately, the courtyard was practically deserted. Nearly everyone, it seemed, was in the chapel and Giles made it through to the waiting vehicle without obstruction. The soldier was quickly up and after him, yelling at the top of his voice, but the driver was ready. He cracked his whip and was on the move before Giles had closed the carriage door behind him.

At the second set of gates a sentry, hearing the commotion raised his musket.

"Drive on," Giles shouted, replacing the bullets in his pistol. Giles had no more wish to hurt the sentry than he had the soldier in the courtyard, but he knew that if he was discovered it would be the end of Philip's little charade, and probably himself as well. Even as the sentry got him in his sights Giles fired – at his musket.

The weapon jerked from the sentry's hands and Giles' coach sped through the final gates to freedom.

"So help me, Philip, I shall never again be a party to your idiotic schemes," he panted, as he removed his mask and wig.

When they were safely upon their way, however, he began to laugh softly to himself. All in all, his visit to France had proved to be quite hectic. After this, he decided, life at King William's Court was going to seem just a trifle tame!

NINETEEN

❧

Madame de Maintenon did not leave her room for the remainder of that day and when Louis called upon her the following morning he was surprised to find she already had a visitor.

"Louvois!"

"I requested the Marquis de Louvois to attend upon me," she said, looking anxious and a little flushed. "He has been speaking to Lord Southwick and I wanted to discover the truth of what happened to him."

They both turned to Louvois. He knew exactly what had happened, because Philip had, that morning, told him everything. His moment for revenge had come, but retribution can take many forms and Louvois knew how to play this game to best advantage. Besides, to openly implicate Madame de Maintenon would only serve to incur Louis' wrath, whereas to appear to be covering for her would earn his gratitude.

"He claims to have been held a prisoner all this while by loyalist fanatics."

Louis was watching him steadily. "So this was a political kidnapping?"

Madame de Maintenon said nothing but the expression in her eyes begged Louvois to be generous and he smiled. He would always have ascendancy over her now.

"It would appear so, your Majesty. The idea was to publicly execute him as an enemy of France, and they chose his ceremony as a fitting place to do it."

Madame de Maintenon's relief was all too plain to see.

"I am bound to say that I find your reaction to this whole affair somewhat disconcerting," Louis told her sharply.

She fanned herself energetically. "A man returns from the dead and you are surprised that I suffered a shock?" How Philip had escaped death she would never truly know but if, by reappearing with his so-called kidnapper, he had intended to unnerve her then he had done a good job. "His wife fainted," she reminded him. "Did that surprise you?"

"Not in the least. Theresa loved him." Even so, Louis could not help but wonder if Theresa had been pretending for effect. Certainly the Comte and Comtesse de Rennes had whisked her away very speedily from the chapel before any could approach her. The more he thought about it the more he considered that the whole mysterious matter had Philip's conniving touch.

"What of the soldiers who shot at his kidnapper?" he asked Louvois for, like everyone else who had heard the six shots fired simultaneously, Louis had assumed that the masked man had been fired at by a troop of soldiers. "Did any of them recognise him?"

"No, your Majesty. No-one knows who he was, or even who the soldiers were who fired upon him, for they have not been found. It appears he was not too badly hurt, for he attacked a guard in the courtyard and shot at a sentry before escaping."

Louis weighed in his mind everything he had heard. A great deal was still unexplained and he guessed it would remain so. He would be speaking to Philip himself in a few moments, but he did not anticipate learning very much from his lips!

He did not doubt that Madame de Maintenon had been involved in the affair, but he had no intention of taking the matter any further. Some things, like Athénais' involvement in the black magic scandals nearly two decades ago, were best left undiscovered if Louis was to preserve his peace of mind. As before when internal troubles threatened them, the royal family would present a united front to the rest of the world. It was the only way to retain credibility, but Madame de Maintenon had damned forever the likelihood of persuading him to openly proclaim her as his wife, and he guessed she must have known it.

He turned back to Louvois. "This whole incident is to be forgotten."

"Yes, your Majesty." From his tone it was evident that Louvois had already anticipated that request!

"I did not see Philip's brother-in-law at the ceremony," Louis remarked to him casually as they left Madame de Maintenon's apartments, Louis on his way to meet Philip, Louvois already descending the marble staircase that would take him down to the courtyard.

Louvois paused upon the landing and looked up at him. "When I last spoke with Lord Wimborne he intended to travel down to Marseilles, your Majesty."

"And what would Lord Wimborne be doing in Marseilles?"

"Delivering a document that would release his servant from prison."

"What did his servant do?" Louis demanded.

"Lord Wimborne believed he committed murder."

"And did he?"

"No, your Majesty. The man Lord Wimborne sent him to kill had already died of the small pox last year, but it suited my purposes to have his servant imprisoned for a while, so I arranged for him to be arrested on a fictitious charge."

Louis regarded him over the balustrade. He had no idea what Louvois had been up to, nor did he intend to concern himself with it. "You are a clever man, Louvois," he told him. "Fouquet was a clever man too." Fouquet had once been Louis' Minister of Finance. He was now in prison. "Be careful you do not become too clever."

Louis could have been referring to the business with Giles, but he wasn't, and Louvois knew that.

"Yes, your Majesty."

❧

"Apparently Giles has already left France," Monsieur complained to Philip. "He didn't even say goodbye to me."

"You must not blame him too much, Monsieur. He had some problems to resolve," Philip told him.

They were trying to make their way to Louis' cabinet, but it wasn't easy. Although it was only ten o'clock in the morning, the palace was already full of people.

"Almost anyone can get into Versailles nowadays," Monsieur complained. "The only requirement is that they wear a sword, but there are men hiring out the damn things downstairs! It's getting much too crowded."

Philip felt inclined to agree with him. As well as those who had come hoping for a glimpse of the King, there were ministers bustling upon their business, soldiers swaggering down the corridors and, of course, courtiers. Some of these seemed to spend their entire day gossiping or simply showing themselves off. Philip had some sympathy for them, for most courtiers at Versailles were housed, like Armand and Marguerite, in tiny, dark apartments, so that they had little choice but to walk about.

He and Monsieur had reached the War Drawing Room and he looked at the life-size bas-relief of Louis on the wall before they pushed their way through to the Hall of Mirrors. The Hall was being decorated by the artist, Le Brun, as a tribute to Louis' military victories but it occurred to Philip that perhaps Louis' enemies were not the only people he trampled upon. Glorious though Versailles was, Philip would not have lived there for all the world, to have his life crushed beneath Louis' will, as was Monsieur's and that of so many others.

He saw Louis himself approaching them from the other end of the Hall. Beset upon all sides by those wishing him to notice them, he walked purposefully down the long gallery, nodding to one or two of those crowding in upon him, but stopping only to open a couple of the long windows that looked out onto the gardens. A great draught began to blow through almost immediately and several of the ladies looked as though they would prefer to scuttle for cover, but they dare not. At Louis' insistence all his courtiers shared his love of fresh air, or at least pretended that they did!

He spotted his brother and Philip, and beckoned them forward.

"Monsieur, permit to me to borrow your charming companion for a little while. Philip, you may walk me to my Cabinet."

It was the first time they had spoken properly since the drama in the chapel the previous day and Louis came straight to the point.

"So you were never shot?"

"No, your Majesty." Philip, like Louvois, had far more sense than to suggest that Madame de Maintenon had played any part in his attack. There were others upon whom he could have his revenge, however, and he fully intended to do just that, in his own way and in his own time.

"You never plunged from the Pont Neuf into the Seine?" Louis persisted, for Monsieur's coachmen had been persuaded by their master to change their story.

"Is it likely I would have survived such a fall, your Majesty?"

"Yes, I think it is, for you are tougher than you would have us believe, despite all your fancy clothes and little affectations."

Philip made a deliberate show of tossing back his curls and fluffing up the lace around his cuffs. "I really don't know what your Majesty means!"

"Very well, have it your own way. Give me your arm."

Philip was surprised at the request, but he obliged all the same. Louis was on his right side, so that he had no choice but to offer his wounded arm. Louis leaned upon it, lightly at first but then more heavily as they progressed.

Philip winced but said nothing. Louis' weight was beginning to hurt his shoulder, which was still not fully healed.

Louis, who had not taken his eyes from Philip's face, pressed down a little more and this time Philip could not hide the discomfort.

"Something the matter with you?" Louis said slyly.

"No, but I wish your Majesty would not rest upon me quite so hard."

"Hurts you, doesn't it?" Louis guessed, putting even more weight upon him until Philip could take it no longer.

"Yes, alright, it does," he admitted.

Louis released him. "You always have been a liar, Philip," he said amiably as they turned into his Cabinet. "In view of everything that has happened to you, whatever that was, I wondered if the offer I made you earlier had become less attractive."

"I believe it has, your Majesty," Philip said regretfully. "Honoured though I am by your suggestion of wedding my daughter into your own household I fear that she would find herself with a good many bitter enemies." He did not say 'within that household' but Louis must have known his meaning.

"Then perhaps my reward for your loyalty should take some other form. I assume I still have your loyalty," Louis asked him sharply.

"My feelings for your Majesty have never altered," Philip said, but it was not quite the truth. They had altered a good deal when he had thought Louis himself might be responsible for his attack!

"That's good. I have resolved upon something I believe will please you. I hope Theresa will not be too disappointed." Louis sounded wistful. "I would have liked to have kept her here."

Philip had always known how fond Louis was of Theresa, but the King's next words staggered him nonetheless.

"I expect she told you about the arrangement I had in mind for her, but you have to understand that I would never have approached her with such a proposition if I had been aware that you were still alive."

"Proposition?" Philip frowned. "What proposition?"

"Ah! She did not tell you then?" Louis looked a little uneasy, like one who had said more than he needed. "I felt quite certain that she would, for she is such an honest, open little thing."

"Not on this occasion, it would appear," Philip said crossly. "Am I to take it that your Majesty and my wife contracted an arrangement of your own?"

"It was merely a suggestion that I put to her," Louis said. "One which I would never have considered putting had I known the true situation, but surely, if she had indeed been a widow, you would hardly have expected her to remain celibate for the rest of her life."

"No, not for that long, but a month would have been nice," Philip said, somewhat sourly.

Louis' lips twitched. "If you are hoping for an apology from me then you waste your time, for absolutely nothing happened between Theresa and I. Surely I cannot be held to blame for my intentions. I am genuinely glad you are restored to me and, for proof of my affection, you have only to consider the grandeur of the ceremony I held for you."

"That was a mark of your Majesty's affection?" Philip said sceptically, for he knew better.

"Yes, of course, and here is another gesture that I hope will convince you. I propose to return to you and your issue the estate taken from your mother's family in Languedoc."

Philip was stunned. The Pasquiers, the French side of his family, had been Huguenots and, like many in the southern regions of France, had fought against Louis' efforts to convert them to Catholicism. As a result they had been virtually wiped out and their property forfeited to the crown. For it to be given back to a Protestant descendant of the family was unheard of, and Philip would never have expected it.

"Well?" Louis prompted, when he did not speak. "What do you think? Is that fair?"

"More than fair, your Majesty," Philip agreed. "I would even go so far as to say that it is probably more than I deserve," he added with a touch of irony, for he realised he was benefiting a little from Louis' sense of guilt over what had nearly happened to him, and at whose hands.

"There is, however, one condition," Louis told him.

"That condition had better not be my wife's body," Philip returned swiftly.

"Don't be ridiculous, although, mind you, I have bought the wives of other courtiers with much less than I offer you now," Louis reminded him. "What I am going to ask of you has nothing whatever to do with Theresa. It has rather to do with Monsieur. I confess I have been worried over him of late. He mourned you until he became quite ill."

"Yes. My servant told me that he fainted dead away when he thought I had been killed."

"He has been besotted with you for years, I fear." Louis was extremely fond of his brother and overlooked his unfortunate preference for his own sex. Sodomy was a crime punishable by the stake but Louis had ensured that the law would never be implemented all the time Monsieur was alive.

"I'll not become his lover," Philip warned, "not even for you, your Majesty."

Louis smiled faintly. "All I want is your promise that you will spend some time with him before you return home and also that you will come and visit with him regularly. It would make him happy."

"I shall find that no hardship," Philip assured him. I am very attached to Monsieur."

Louis nodded. "I know you are. Before you leave France I shall give you a document of safe conduct, signed by myself, enabling you to travel anywhere in France, whether or not our two nations are still at war. Furthermore, you may call upon me for assistance at any time. From this day on France is your country as much as England and I am your monarch."

Philip bowed low, kissing the hand that Louis offered him. As he left the King's Cabinet he felt that, all in all, things had probably turned out for the best.

"Well?" Monsieur asked excitedly. "What did he offer you?"

"The Pasquier estate, incredible as it may seem! Did you have a hand in this?" Philip said, for he knew that, upon certain matters, Louis would listen to the advice of his brother and would do a lot to please him.

Monsieur shrugged modestly. "A particle," he admitted, holding his finger and thumb an inch apart to signify a little. "I thought it would please you, especially since the Pasquiers refused to have anything to do with you when they were alive!"

Philip laughed out loud at that. "You're right. For some unaccountable reason they considered that my mother marrying into a family of English madmen was demeaning to their noble name! That doubles the pleasure of my acquisition, that and the knowledge that I now own something which was a part of my mother." Philip could not remember his mother but during his lonely childhood he had thought about her a great deal and longed for her to be there. "Once again I am indebted to you, Monsieur."

"You will still want to keep your Paris house?" Monsieur said worriedly.

"Yes, of course I will, but it is yours now, you know, so I only have it for as long as you are kind enough to let me live in it," Philip reminded him.

Monsieur beamed. Philip knew how much he liked the arrangement, for it made him beholden to Monsieur, a state of affairs the Frenchman enjoyed. "I suppose now, like Giles, you will be leaving me and returning to England," he sighed, his smile fading as he anticipated parting from Philip yet again.

"Not necessarily." Philip offered his arm, his left one this time, for his right was still sore from bearing Louis' weight. "I can remain here a little longer if you wish it."

Monsieur gave a shriek of joy that could be heard the whole length of the gallery, causing every head to turn. His antics generally made him the centre of attention.

"Well naturally I wish it. How long can you stay?"

"That rather depends on you, Monsieur. I am still your guest, after all.

Monsieur pouted. "I thought perhaps you accepted my invitation only so that you would have the opportunity of meeting with my brother again."

"Why ever would you think that?"

"People use me sometimes, you know. In fact I often wonder whether anyone ever wants me for myself at all."

Monsieur actually looked quite close to tears and Philip felt a stab of conscience.

"You must never think that of me," he said quietly. "I shall always be your true friend."

Monsieur leaned over and kissed him on the cheek. "Then I insist you are my guest for one whole month."

"Whatever you say."

Philip did not mind at all spending another month in France. Quite apart from pleasing Louis, he had a few affairs of his own to settle. Also it suited him rather well to be away from England for a while longer, for he did not doubt that William would dispatch him to Ireland as soon as he returned home, and it was not a duty he was relishing.

There was one person who would not be thrilled by the decision, though, and that was Theresa.

He did not go to find her immediately however. Philip was a bit disgruntled over what Louis had divulged to him and he needed a little more time to process it before he spoke with her. Instead he went to seek out Luc, who had travelled to Versailles with Monsieur.

"What did you manage to discover about these wretched Quietists?" he asked him.

"Their leader is a spiritualist called Madame Guyon. She is a strange person by all accounts but she has been converting people to her faith for years."

"In what way strange?" Philip said.

"She goes into trances and claims in one of them to have married Jesus Christ and that she wears his invisible ring upon her finger."

"Good Lord!" That sounded like heresy, even to someone who had such scant regard for religion as Philip.

"There is more. She takes off her clothes and rolls in nettles and, when she was a child, she sewed a piece of paper with 'Jesus' written on it to her chest with ribbon!"

"And they call the Devalles mad? What is this doctrine that she teaches?"

"It is love," Luc said simply.

"There must be more to it than that."

"Not really. She purports that if God is the centre of your life and love of God the only purpose in it then you cannot sin."

"Like a nun, you mean?"

"No, not quite, for they actively worship God and seek to lead good lives. Madame Guyon says one should do nothing but live in love. She does not believe in prayer or attending services. She claims to communicate directly with God and that His grace flows out to His followers through her body."

"Better and better," Philip decided. "She's obviously quite insane."

"Dangerously so, I'd say, but she has influenced a good many people all the same, including Madame de Maintenon, who even lets the woman teach the girls at St. Cyr."

"Does she indeed?" Philip smiled wickedly. "How wonderful! What is Abbé Fénelon's connection with all this?"

"He met Guyon through Beauvilliers, as did Madame de

Maintenon, and, according to Monsieur, he is having an affair with her, but I don't know whether to believe that," he added hastily, as Philip's face lit like the sun.

"Never underestimate Monsieur," Philip advised him. "I never do. When it comes to gossip he is rarely wrong. It is, after all, his speciality, indeed it's practically the only thing he ever turns his mind to these days. He has an army of informants and he gleans every scandalous scrap that he can. Very little escapes him and the stories that he manages to piece together often turn out to be uncannily accurate. You have done your research well," he told Luc.

"What do you propose to do with the information now that you have it?" Luc wondered.

"Have a little fun."

"But are you not returning home?"

"Not yet. If you wish to go to England right away you may accompany Theresa, but I am staying with Monsieur a while longer."

Luc did not reply but, at Philip's reference to Monsieur, his expression made his feelings very plain.

"You look as though you disapprove," he said.

"It is not my place to approve or disapprove your actions, my Lord," Luc said stiffly.

"Quite right, but if you are to disapprove of me then make it for something I have done, not something you believe me to have done."

"My Lord?"

"Monsieur, no matter what you may think of the man, has been loyal to me and I owe him a good deal, but I have never had an affair with him."

Luc looked embarrassed at his frankness. "Even so, I fear you are too careless with your reputation."

"To hell with my reputation! I care nothing for the opinions of those people who know me so little they would speak against me, and nor should you care. I have not been too much of a father to you, Luc, but if you wish me to behave as one now then I shall give you the benefit of my advice, and it is this; be true to your own standards and those of the people who you respect, not the standards set for you by mean-spirited folk inferior to yourself."

"I will be guided by your advice, my Lord," Luc said quietly, sounding ashamed. "As for going to England with Lady Southwick, if it is all the same with you I would much rather remain at your side here."

"Would you really?" Philip was pleasantly surprised. "Then stay by all means, but I warn you that I have a wondrous way of getting others into trouble!"

TWENTY

Theresa was in the gardens when Philip found her.

He spotted her sitting in one of her favourite places, on a stone bench by the Pond of Summer, in the middle of which the goddess Ceres lay upon sheaves of corn. Philip knew that she especially liked the statue because one of the little cherubs surrounding Ceres reminded her of Maudie. He had always found that to be rather endearing but he was still smarting after his interview with Louis and his thoughts of Theresa were anything but fond at that moment.

He had never had any reason to doubt Theresa's devotion to him. He knew he had not always been a perfect husband but, even so, it was hurtful in the extreme to him that she would have considered Louis' offer at all, let alone so soon after thinking herself a widow.

Although he had earned the reputation of a womaniser in his younger years, Philip had never loved any woman except Theresa, and he had certainly never been possessive about any of them. But this was different. Very different.

He sat down beside her, unsure of quite how to broach the subject. "I guessed where you would be," he told her.

"Did you see Louis?" she asked him.

"I did."

"What did he say?"

Philip decided to come straight out with it. "Did you truly intend to become his mistress?"

She did not answer but from the look of dismay upon her face he guessed she had not expected Louis to tell him

"Well?" he prompted impatiently. "Am I to take your silence as evidence of your intent?"

"I had not given him my answer," she said weakly.

"So you were at least considering it? How could you, Tess?" He turned to face her, unable to hide his anger. "You encouraged that lecherous bastard's advances when I was scarcely cold in my grave."

"But you weren't even dead," she protested.

"That hardly matters, for you thought I was," he countered. "I must really mean very little to you if you would fall so quickly into the arms of another."

"Oh, Philip, that's unfair. You mean the world to me."

"So, too, does Louis apparently," he said tartly. "What did he promise you?"

"Only his friendship."

"Don't lie, not to me. What do you truly think you could ever have meant to him? A furtive romance, carried out at his convenience whenever he could manage to spare you a few minutes of his precious time? Certainly he could not have given you more, not now he has married that bitch Maintenon. You know how Louis treats his mistresses," he continued remorselessly. "They are put through every imaginable discomfort and heartache before he discards them. Are you fond of him?"

He had put the question to her directly, and she must have known she had better answer it truthfully if she was not to make matters worse.

"I have always been fond of him," she admitted quietly. "You must know that, and he was so very kind and comforting to me in my loss."

"I can imagine! Did he kiss you?"

"Only as a friend," she assured him.

"And are you fond of him as a friend or as a lover?" Philip wanted to know, "because I tell you now that I would never force you to remain with me, even though you are my wife. If you want Louis and the life he will offer then you can stay with him."

"Now you're being ridiculous."

"Am I? You're still wearing the damned necklace he gave you, for God's sake."

Theresa had worn the jet beads every day, even though she was not now a widow, and it infuriated him.

She took the necklace off straight away and held it out to him. "Here take it. Give it back to him if you like or throw it in the pond if it upsets you. I just thought it was pretty."

"I don't want the wretched thing," Philip said sulkily. "I just don't want my wife wearing jewellery I did not give her."

"You're jealous aren't you?" Theresa said, sounding surprised.

It was the truth, of course, although he did not want to admit it. Theresa was the only one who had ever been able to stir that emotion in him. "Yes, I suppose I am," he muttered crossly.

She took both his hands in her own. "I am very flattered."

"So you should be."

"But you must know how much I love you, my darling. There is nothing I want more than to return with you to England right away. I am sick of all of this. It will be so good when we are at home with Maudie once again."

Looking into her eyes, Philip could tell she was speaking the truth. Unlike her devious brother, Theresa had always been completely transparent, and quite unable to hide her true feelings. As to Louis' intentions he had no doubt whatsoever, but he was prepared to believe that Theresa had been motivated mainly by a desire for friendship and comfort whilst she had felt so alone.

"I am prepared to put the incident behind us," he told her magnanimously. "But talking of Maudie, would you have agreed to Louis' plans for her to marry his son?".

"Yes, I would, for I thought it would be what you wanted. In any case, are you not always telling me I should think with my head and not my heart?"

"Perhaps I should have heeded my own advice."

Theresa stared at him, realisation of his meaning dawning upon her. "You turned it down?"

"I'm afraid I did."

"But why?"

"Why do you think? Do you imagine I am going risk losing you to Louis?" Philip saw little point in spoiling the moment by telling her the other factors that had weighed in his decision not to marry Maudie into the royal household. "Are you disappointed?"

"Why no. I am delighted." Theresa threw her arms around his neck, "but, Philip, what about your 'distant hills'?"

Philip smiled as he thought about the even more splendid offer Louis had just made to him. He decided not to tell Theresa about that just yet, not whilst he was benefiting so nicely from her pangs of guilt. She would be angry with him later, of course, when she found out that he had not told her everything, but he would deal with that when it happened. "There will be other opportunities," he assured her.

"I suppose so. When are we leaving for England?"

"You could leave tomorrow if you wished."

Theresa frowned. "On my own?"

"No. I thought Morgan could escort you. I must stay here for another month."

"Why must you?"

"Louis insisted I stay to please Monsieur. Apparently the poor man has suffered terribly on my account so I thought I would let him parade me around for a while."

"Whatever are you up to now, Philip?" she asked despairingly

"Why nothing," he protested. "You know what a triumph it will be for him to have everyone know that I am staying here just to please him."

"And that's it? You are staying for Monsieur? I don't believe it." Theresa declared, "and don't bother trying to look so innocent."

"I do have one or two entertaining little ideas in mind," Philip confessed.

"I suppose it is of little use to exhort you to be careful?"

"On the contrary, my sweet, I intend to be extremely careful. After all I shall be spending practically every waking hour with the brother of the King of France, and I can hardly risk endangering him, can I? Not unless I want to find myself back in the Bastille!"

❧

"I don't like it," Morgan said when Philip had explained his plan to him and Thomas. "It's too risky."

"If I never took risks where would we all be?" Philip said.

"You were very nearly at the bottom of the Seine the last time you risked your life," Morgan reminded him.

"But on account of it I am now the possessor of a sizeable piece of Languedoc," Philip reminded him, "so it seems to me it was a risk worth taking."

Morgan and Thomas exchanged glances that plainly said they did not think so.

"You do realise what the Pasquier estate is famous for?" Philip asked them.

The two servants shook their heads and Philip groaned.

"I might have expected that from a Welshman and a Londoner! It is a vineyard – vast, rolling acres of good land. What do you know about growing grapes?" he asked Morgan.

"Nothing at all," Morgan said. "I happen to be the steward of a Sussex estate."

"But there may come a time in the not too distant future when you will be the steward of a French vineyard, so I am counting on you to discover how to run one."

"You don't know either, then?" Morgan said.

"Of course not! Do I look like a son of the soil? I am relying on you, as ever, my dear Morgan!"

"Be that as it may, I still believe I should stay in France with you and Thomas." Morgan was not so easily distracted from his point.

"That really won't be necessary, besides, I particularly want Theresa to go home right away, and she cannot very well travel alone." Philip reckoned that the sooner she was away from Louis the better!

"Luc could escort her," Morgan suggested, but Philip shook his head.

"I need him here. I have a job for him to do."

"Can you trust Luc?" Thomas wondered, after Morgan had left them.

"I've really no idea," Philip admitted, "but, since he seems eager to impress me, I thought I would give him a chance. I have a tasks in mind for both him and Monsieur."

"A fine chance you and I will have if we need to rely upon Monsieur and an untried eighteen year old Frenchman who seeks to prove he is your son," Thomas reckoned.

Philip detected the passion in his servant's voice.

"So that is what this is all about," he said, suddenly comprehending.

"I don't even see why he has to come to England with us," Thomas persisted.

"Nor do I, frankly, but I have agreed to it now to please your mistress."

"And because you think he really is your son?"

Thomas was an uncomplicated young man, for which Philip was extremely grateful. Being usually wrapped up in his own affairs, the last thing he needed was a servant who needed understanding. That was not to say Philip could not show some consideration to him on occasions.

"Thomas," he said gently, "I took you from the streets when you were an unruly ruffian of a boy. Since then I have fed you, clothed you and protected you. I have taught you how to shoot, to wield a sword and to behave as a gentleman. Could I have done more for you if you yourself had been my son?"

"No, my Lord," Thomas said, his eyes downcast. "You have done more for me than anyone so lowly born had any right to expect and I am grateful."

"I did not do it for your gratitude, damn it! I did it because I have come to consider you almost *as* a son," Philip told him in an exasperated tone.

Thomas raised his eyes to him. "Truly?"

"Yes, of course truly. What do you think, that docile servants are not to be had, fully trained and subservient to their master's wishes? Do you imagine everyone takes such pains to acquire an impudent wretch who criticises his master's judgement and decisions?"

Thomas grinned at that. "I was a little outspoken just now, wasn't I?"

"Just a touch, but I would not have you any other way."

"So I am important to you, my Lord?" Thomas ventured.

"Yes, you numskull! How could you think that Luc, no matter who he claims to be, could ever supplant you in my affections?"

Thomas glowed with pride. "I did not realise how high I stood in your regard, my Lord. You have never said such things to me before."

"I would not have said them to you now, but I cannot have your resentment for Santerre ruing my little scheme, particularly since I intend to put you in charge of him."

Philip knew Thomas would like that notion, and he obviously did. "What happens to him after we go home, though," Thomas wondered.

"He will not be our concern," Philip said. "Giles wanted him, let Giles have him, I say. He will enjoy training him to his own strange ways and he will no doubt make of Luc whatever he intends him to be!"

Thomas smiled at that, for Giles had an uncanny knack of

moulding people to his wishes, including, to some degree, King William. "I am sure Ahmed will be able to keep him in his place, my Lord." Even Thomas was a little wary of the Negro, who still regarded himself as Giles' slave and who was always ready to attack any who gave offence to his precious master.

"Indeed. I would not like to be on the receiving end of Ahmed's blade myself," Philip admitted. "Perhaps what you should be feeling for Luc is pity, since he is to be at the mercy of those two!"

"I will prepare him for it," Thomas told him, looking happier, now that he no longer felt his own position to be threatened by the newcomer, "but I am still not sure about Monsieur. What use could he possibly be?"

"Monsieur may surprise you. Don't forget he was once a soldier."

"He fainted when I told him you had been murdered," Thomas reminded him.

"Even so, there is more to him than meets the eye," Philip reckoned. "Also he hates Maintenon like the plague and it is clearer to me now just why. I dare say he could have forgiven Louis for making her his mistress but as his wife she will have privileges, albeit it only in private, far above those to which her rank entitles her. You know how much store Monsieur sets upon such things. Besides, you may depend she disapproves of him and I doubt that my recent good fortune will help matters there, for it must be obvious he had a hand in it."

"What did the mistress think of the King's new offer?" Thomas said.

Philip coughed. "She doesn't actually know about it yet, but I imagine she will be delighted. Did she tell you anything about her meetings with Louis?" he wondered.

"Only that he talked about your likeness on the ceiling of the Marble Drawing Room!"

"Oh, that."

"Did you really persuade Coypel to make you part of the palace decorations, my Lord?" Thomas persisted, when Philip did not elaborate.

"Really, Thomas! It would take a very vain and ambitious man to go as far as that to ensure his own fame." Philip winked at him. "How could you ever think that of me?"

TWENTY ONE

❧

William Bentinck, the newly created Earl of Portland, greeted Giles warmly. "I'm glad you're back."

Giles didn't particularly like Portland, but then neither did anyone else. He had been nicknamed 'the wooden man' by the English at William's Court, because he could never bend to the will of others. They resented the fact that the King had given most of the best jobs to his own countrymen, but they resented Portland above all, for he had been given more than any and had given so little back.

"Have you missed me then?" Giles asked dryly, for he knew that Portland was none too fond of him either.

"No," the humourless Dutchman replied, "but, frankly, his Majesty has become so unpopular lately that it will be good for him to be seen in the company of a well-known Englishman."

"What has he done to upset them this time?" Giles said.

"Why, nothing," Portland insisted. "It is the English who are so ungrateful. I am told they are saying in the coffee houses that they have beheaded one king and thrown out another so they know how to deal with a third!"

Giles was not too perturbed by that. The coffee houses had always been a breeding ground for seditious talk and he had heard far worse during the previous two reigns. In any case, he knew that feelings did not run high against the King himself but rather because he showed his obvious preference for Dutchmen, and Portland in particular!

"There is not so much malice in the English as you would

suppose," he told Portland. "If he just gave his subjects some indication that he liked them they would like him in return. He can still win them round, if he cares to do it."

Therein, Giles knew, lay the real problem. William did *not* care to do it. He had been popular in his own country and expected to be so in England, but he had failed to take into account the differences in temperament between the lively English and the solid Dutch.

"It should not be necessary for one who has done so much for them to seek their acclaim," Portland said stiffly.

Giles knew that Portland could never see the least fault in William, his friend for many years.

"Nevertheless it *is* necessary." Giles was in a position to hear far more of the people's expectations. "The English like nothing better than a good show," he said, thinking back to his conversation with Philip on Coronation Day. "If King William gives them that from time to time they will be more content."

He had often thought that the wealthy Portland might be more popular if he was a little more ostentatious. The Earl dressed more like a servant than the holder of such an important post as Treasurer of the Privy Purse!

Giles had sent word to William the moment he had landed in England, but he had delayed his return to London by the few days it had taken him to travel to Sussex to see Marianne. The coldness of the King's greeting when he presented himself showed him that he had probably been wrong.

"You were meant to be absent from England for no longer than a month," William reminded him sharply. "Not only did you exceed that time by several days but you did not even come straight to see me directly you returned to these shores."

Giles had become accustomed to William's moods and he knew he must endure them. Those who sought to advance their careers upon royal favour must also expect to be subject to royal whim and Giles consoled himself with the thought that it might be worse – it might be King Louis' whim he needed to be dependent upon!

The French king was on William's mind also, it seemed. "And how did the most Christian barbarian treat you?"

"I did not even see King Louis." Giles said, recognising the sneering description.

William seemed somewhat appeased by that. "I was pleased to hear the good news about your brother-in-law," he told him, "but why has he not returned with you?"

"He is spending a month with Monsieur." There was no way to make that sound any better and Giles did not trouble to try.

"Is he indeed?" William's displeasure was plain to see. "Well when he does deign to return I have it in mind to dispatch him to Ireland to aid Schomberg."

"Yes, your Majesty," Giles said, anticipating Philip's joy at the news.

"We will see how enthusiastically he engages in a war against the troops of his precious French king in that savage land."

Giles knew that Ireland was a great source of annoyance to William, who feared he might have to go in person to settle the dispute. The only consolation for him was that it would have been difficult to justify England's interference in Europe had Louis not interfered in Ireland.

"Is King James causing much trouble?" Giles asked him, for he had not had a lot of chance to catch up on news of the war.

"Enough, but he is not too great a threat at present," William said. "It is Philip Devalle who I feel is more of a threat."

"Hardly," Giles protested.

"It is like you to defend him, and your loyalty does you credit, but I realise I shall never truly own the man. He has a restless spirit and he has intrigued for too many years to break the habit now. I fear if I do not keep him well employed he will grow bored and then I shall have the devil's own job to control him."

"Nonetheless I do wonder whether Ireland is the best place for him," Giles said carefully.

"Where then? Flanders? I couldn't rely on him there, loving the King of France as he evidently still does. I already suspect a traitor in our midst, for Marlborough received some information from one of my agents that nearly led him to disaster."

Giles did not want to discuss that, or the fact that Luc Santerre was due to return home with Philip. If William raised the subject later he felt sure he would be able to come up with some plausible explanation. "I was wondering if, perhaps, Philip wouldn't be better employed here, in London," he said. "He has a great many Whig supporters who will follow where he leads."

He knew that William was having considerable trouble with the Whig party at the moment. They had been chiefly responsible for placing him upon the throne and had assumed that they would benefit from his generosity, but William did not entirely trust them and had decided to rely, like his predecessors had done, upon the Tories, who traditionally supported the monarchy.

"I do have enough problems on my hands at the moment without them," William allowed. "My ministers would sooner quarrel amongst themselves than get on with any business."

He had been attempting to reconcile the Dissenters with the Church of England, but his Bill had failed in the Lower House, although he had managed to put through a Toleration Act, enabling them to worship as they pleased. He had even tried to help the Catholics, but with no success.

The one reform which he had passed into the law concerned the judges, who were now granted their commissions on condition that they behaved properly. To those, like Giles, who recalled the corrupt body who had once sat upon the Bench this was progress indeed, but he knew that William had a long way to go before he would be satisfied.

"With Philip's help you might win more of your subjects round," Giles persisted. "Despite all the devious things he has done in the past, the people still idolise him. Remember how they flocked to see him when we rode to London?"

William could not fail to remember that. When he had first landed in England the previous November and had travelled to the capital with his troops, few people had turned out to see them until Philip had joined him. After that folk had surrounded Philip everywhere he went. It seemed that more came hoping to catch sight of him than to see their future king.

"He does draw the crowds," William agreed, "and he seems to welcome their attentions." He shuddered at the thought of being pressed on all sides by so many people.

"Philip thrives on it," Giles assured him. "Admiration is as necessary to him as the air he breathes. Let Schomberg and Marlborough lead your troops. Fine soldier though Philip is, I'm certain he would be of more use to you here at the present. Let his showmanship work for you now as it did then. That is my advice."

William was plainly tempted by the idea. Not only could he benefit greatly from utilising someone who had all the charm and winning ways that he lacked but, Giles knew, it had the added advantage of the King being able to keep a close eye on Philip.

"I will give it thought," he promised, "if you believe that it will help my popularity. It does seem as though everywhere I turn I find criticism at the moment. As if things were not bad enough at Court, Lady Marlborough is now inflaming Princess Anne against the Queen."

"But I thought Queen Mary and her sister were as close as could be," Giles said in surprise.

"So they were, but now Anne has been persuaded that she should receive more money in exchange for relinquishing her claim to the throne. I already wonder how one person can spend so much! Marlborough is behind it all, I am quite sure, for you know he seeks to prepare for his future and if we cannot give

England an heir then the child that Anne is carrying might one day be King. Lady Marlborough has even canvassed the Tory party whilst her husband has been away and now the House of Commons are against me. I wish you would talk to Princess Anne, Giles."

"Can't your Majesty talk to her yourself?" Giles said, not relishing the job, but William shook his head.

"I never could. I swear that if I were married to her instead of to her sister I would be the most miserable man alive." Anne was a slow, dull person, quite unlike the quick-witted Mary. "Will you speak with her?"

Giles briefly closed his eyes, the weight of his responsibilities settling on him again. He had longed to be home yet, now that he was, he could not help remembering how good it had been to be free.

"I'll try, your Majesty, "but I doubt that it will be much use if the Marlboroughs have been working on her. Why should she listen to me and not to her own sister?"

"It's so unjust," William complained. "Is it not enough that Lord Marlborough has just received a most lucrative appointment as Colonel of the Royal Fusiliers? When will the man be satisfied?"

Giles had his own opinions of the Earl of Marlborough, and they were not flattering. Marlborough had been a favourite of King James but, after it was clear that James would lose his crown, Marlborough had deserted him to join William. A great many despised him for his disloyalty, including William himself, glad though he had been of his help. To Giles and Philip, the Earl would never be considered as a man to rely upon.

Giles studied William for a moment, wondering what was really the matter with him. He looked ill, certainly, and he was coughing but Giles barely noticed that anymore for William coughed constantly, sometimes so violently that he could scarcely draw breath. The King was a picture of despair and Giles realised that it was brought on by more than family squabbles or the infuriating Marlboroughs, more even than what was happening abroad, for William was a statesman and well used to dealing with such matters. "What else is troubling your Majesty?" he ventured softly. "I have never seen you quite like this."

William raised mournful eyes to his. "You are observant, as ever, my friend. The truth is, I suppose, that I am homesick. Horribly, dreadfully homesick."

Giles said nothing but waited for William to continue. He was a good listener and he knew that sometimes it was better just to let a person talk.

"It is this warm weather. It makes me so miss The Hague," William said wistfully. "How I long to be away from this foul, stinking city and walking in my palace gardens at Het Loo. I tell you, Giles, I would give a hundred thousand guilders to fly home like a bird through the sky."

Giles smiled pityingly. "You will be happier at Kensington House, I'm certain."

The Queen had persuaded William to buy a house at the nearby village of Kensington and was having it enlarged by Sir Christopher Wren, but as Wren was also working on plans for modernising Hampton Court the progress to both these alternatives to Whitehall seemed slow.

"I may well be happier but I fear it may make me even more unpopular if I move out of London."

Giles thought back to his earlier conversation with Portland. "If only you would let your people get to know you then I'm sure you could not fail to win them over." The trouble was, as Giles well knew, William disdained to court popularity for its own sake. "The English love to make merry," Giles reminded him. "They will like you well enough if you get drunk occasionally and lose some money on a horse! I'll tell you just the place to do it too – at Newmarket."

"You mean attend the races, like King Charles used to do?" William said doubtfully.

"Why not? You might actually enjoy it." Giles could remember the spirited days of Charles' reign, and so could many more. He thought privately that it was small wonder some people were dissatisfied with this pale and sickly foreigner with, apparently, no idea of how to have fun, even if he had delivered them from King James!

"Would you and Philip accompany me?" William asked.

"Yes, of course. The next meeting will be in the Autumn. We can discuss it when I get back."

William frowned. "Get back?"

"Your Majesty may recall that the Princess Anne is not the only one soon expecting a child," Giles reminded him. "Marianne is still at High Heatherton and I want to fetch her back before our baby is born."

"So you are going to leave me again?" William looked so distressed that Giles almost relented, but not quite.

"I will be away only for as long as it takes to travel back to Sussex and bring my wife here."

"Can't your sister do that? I assume she has not stayed with Monsieur also," William said, with more than a touch of sarcasm in his tone.

"Theresa is back in England," Giles told him evenly, "but I was hoping to escort Marianne myself. It is our first child, your Majesty."

William sighed. "Oh, very well, but you are to return to me as soon as ever you can. I trust your wife has been in good hands," he added, as though realising that he was being a little insensitive.

"She is in the very best of hands," Giles assured him. "My sister's maid is taking care of her and I would sooner entrust Marianne to her remedies than those of any medical man, even your own Doctor Radcliffe."

Giles was soon to have reason to be glad of Bet's capabilities.

When he arrived back at High Heatherton Theresa met him with an anxious face.

"Marianne is sick, Giles. She fell ill the day after you left. I was so afraid the King would delay you."

"He let me go on condition that I returned to Court in one week," Giles said. "I trust she will be well enough to travel before then or I shall have to return without her."

He made to go up to the room that was always given over to him and Marianne whenever they visited Heatherton, but Theresa stood in front of him.

"Giles, I don't believe you fully understand me. Marianne is ill, really ill. Not only will she not be ready to travel by then but I don't think you should leave her."

Giles stared at her aghast as the full import of Theresa's words hit home. Pushing past her he ran up the stairs.

Marianne was sleeping as he entered the room and Bet, sitting by the bed, beckoned him closer. Giles looked at his wife in disbelief.

A week before she had been a glowing picture of health when she had welcomed him back from France and teased him into feeling their child moving inside her. Now she was a pale shadow.

"She is very weak," Bet told him. "She can keep nothing down and her bones ache so much that she cannot stand." She shook her patient gently. "Marianne, wake up. Giles has come."

Marianne slowly opened her eyes and smiled up at him. "I've wanted to see you so badly."

Giles sat upon the bed and took her hand. "I'm here, my darling, and I shall not leave you."

"Oh, Giles, I never meant to be a nuisance to you," she said quietly. "I am so very sorry."

"Silly girl," he said, kissing her damp forehead.

"You're not angry with me?"

"No, of course not. Why would I be angry?"

"The King may be displeased with you if you are away for too long."

"To hell with the King! You are the most important thing now, you and our baby," he assured her.

"Bet says the baby is still strong."

"That's good." Giles patted the hump of bedclothes where they covered her swollen belly. "Now I want to see you strong."

"I will try, Giles," she promised, "but I feel so very tired."

"Then you must rest. Go to sleep now."

"Yes, Giles." Obedient as ever to his wishes, Marianne closed her heavy eyelids. "Will you be near?" she asked him.

"As near as ever you want me to be," he said, steadying his voice with a great effort.

He took Bet out onto the landing and closed the door behind them. "Do you know what ails her?" he asked.

"Yes. I have treated it before. One of the girls on the estate fell ill a week ago. The shivering has already begun and, if I am right, Marianne will be burning up with fever before the night is out."

"Did the girl live?" Giles almost feared to put the question.

Bet nodded. "She did, however she was not with child. I will not lie to you, Giles; it is unfortunate for this to happen now, so near her time."

Giles turned away, so as to hide his emotions, but Bet put her arms around him.

"Let it out, Giles. You will feel much better for it."

In her comforting arms Giles gave way to his feelings. He was not a person who did so easily but with Bet he had no need to hold back. He trusted her implicitly for she had seen the family through a good many tribulations. It was she who had dressed the dreadful scar that had altered Giles' life so much and it was she who had secretly treated his wounded arm when he was a rebel fugitive.

"Is she suffering much?" he asked, when he felt calmer.

"I believe she suffers mostly on account of you," Bet said honestly. "She fears to incur your displeasure by being ill."

"Am I such a monster then?" Giles cried, shocked. "I must be if she thinks the only purpose of her life is to please me."

"That is foolish talk," Bet scolded him. "You are an ambitious man, Giles, we all know that, and she doesn't want to inconvenience you too much, that is all."

Giles was stunned. It had never occurred to him that Marianne might feel that way.

Bet took his two hands in her own. "Giles, you are what you are. Marianne loves you very much and more than anything she wishes to be the sort of wife you want, that is all."

"She is a perfect wife. I love her too, Bet, but I hardly ever tell her so," Giles said wretchedly.

"Don't reproach yourself with such things," Bet begged him. "Besides, she knows it plain enough, just as I know Morgan loves me, though he has rarely said it, not even when he learned I was with child."

"You too? I did not know." Giles kissed her on the cheek. After six years of marriage Bet had almost given up hope of bearing children, so it was especially good news. "I trust it will not prove too much for you to nurse Marianne in your condition, though," he said anxiously.

"Lord, bless you, no. I'm as strong as an ox," she joked. "Of course if you would sooner send for a doctor I will understand," she added, becoming serious again.

"And have the poor creature bled and purged until she loses what little strength she has?" Giles shook his head.

Bet's skills were self-taught and her remedies brewed from recipes that had been handed down to her from her mother and grandmother. She had a cure for every ill and, since moving to Heatherton, she had treated not only the family but every person on the estate who needed her. Even those few who could afford to send for a doctor would as soon trust to Bet's homely cures than the uncertain methods employed by some of the medical profession.

So it was with Giles.

"My wife and baby are the most precious things in my life, Bet," he told her. "I give them both into your care, for I know you will do your best for them."

The days that followed were anxious ones for those at High Heatherton. Marianne appeared to be making little progress. She was burning to the touch, although Bet sponged her constantly with cool water, and she was often delirious. Sometimes she called for Giles, but mostly she spoke in French, the words fast and incoherent.

"The fever has reached her brain," Bet told Theresa early one morning. She had brought in some breakfast for Bet, who had been beside her patient all night, and Theresa was becoming concerned for the nurse, as well as the patient.

"What is it you are giving her?" Theresa said, turning her nose up at the syrup which Bet was pouring, drop by drop, into Marianne's mouth. She had suffered a few of Bet's remedies herself in the past.

"I am giving her rhubarb and damson juice mixed with liquorice and some cinnamon. That will take the heat from her body, and I have added some milk and honey. If she does not have nourishment the babe will not be able to grow inside her."

"Oh, Bet, what if the baby should die? What if he loses them both? It will destroy him."

"In answer Bet took her mistress' hand and put it upon Marianne's distended belly. "Feel how he kicks? This baby is a boy and he is as determined as his father! The question is not whether he will be fit for the world but rather whether she, poor soul, can bring him into the world."

Theresa withdrew her hand and looked worriedly into Bet's tired face. "What if she has not the strength when the time comes?"

"Then he may have to choose between them," Bet said grimly.

The outside bell jangled, mercifully interrupting Theresa's thoughts.

"Whoever can that be at this time of day? It's not even properly light outside," she complained as she bustled off to answer the door herself, really rather glad of something to occupy her troubled mind.

⌯

Giles was already dressed and standing by the window watching the pink and blue summer dawn rise over the downs. At any other time he would have been struck by the sight, for Giles had a deep appreciation of beauty, but he viewed it now only as the inevitability of another dismal day following yet another restless night.

He looked up expectantly as the door opened to admit Theresa.

"No changes yet, I'm afraid, Giles," she told him, "but this may cheer you all the same. You have a visitor."

Giles' brow puckered into a frown, for the only visitor he was anticipating was an envoy dispatched from King William. Theresa stepped quickly out of the room before he could protest.

The petulant words died on Giles' lips as he saw who actually stood there.

Dusty from his ride and near dropping from exhaustion, Ahmed fell down on one knee before his master.

Giles could not imagine a more welcome sight.

He stroked the Negro's woolly head affectionately. "My Ahmed! I was beginning to fear for your safety." Ahmed had taken so long to get home that Giles had been concerned and had reproached himself many times for not delivering his servant's release personally, as he had first intended.

"I had a little more business to complete before I left," Ahmed explained. "I am sorry if my delay has caused you worry, on top of your other problems."

"Never mind that, just so long as you are safe." Giles helped him to his feet. "You've heard about Marianne?"

"Yes, master."

"Oh, Ahmed, if she dies I shall never forgive myself. She might not have even caught this sickness if she and I had stayed in London, where we belonged. When you did not come I feared I had caused your death too."

"El Oued should never reproach himself on account of either of us," Ahmed told him earnestly. He still occasionally referred to Giles by his desert name. "But for your courage and your good heart we would both be already dead or suffering living death in bondage. When you rescued us from Suliman Bey you gave us both life, and we would count those lives well given if they were given for you."

Giles was touched. "What I intended to give you was your freedom, yet it seems I own you still."

"I belong to you," Ahmed insisted. "Nothing can change that, and it is the same for Marianne."

Ahmed and his mistress were very close. Such an experience as they had shared bound people together with threads that could never be broken.

"But does she know that I love her?" Giles wondered aloud.

"Yes, master, of course she does."

"And do you know how I feel about you?" Giles asked him quietly.

Ahmed grinned, his teeth showing white against his black skin. "Yes, master."

Giles nodded, content. "That's good. You had better clean yourself up now and rest, for we may have a long vigil to keep and I shall need you by my side. By the way," he asked, almost as an afterthought, as Ahmed started immediately to do his bidding, "what was this other business you had to attend to in Marseilles?"

"Ah, that." The Negro looked downcast. "I regret I failed you, master."

"Failed me? How? Louvois said that you had killed Marianne's husband."

"Alas, I was prevented from doing so. You see he was already dead. She has been a widow this past year."

"And that treacherous bastard knew it all along!" Giles, who occasionally displayed a similar temperament to his sister, kicked a footstool so violently that it careered across the room. "So why did he have you arrested?"

"A soldier accused me of robbing him. Although I protested my innocence they took from me all the money you had given me for travelling. The paper you sent from Paris gave me the right to return to England, but I had not the wherewithal to buy my passage."

"Blast!" It had not occurred to Giles that Ahmed might have been without money, for he had supplied him with ample funds. "What did you do?"

"I applied the remedy that the Marquis de Louvois himself put into my hands," Ahmed told him simply. "The fellow had obviously been offered my money as a reward for his false statement so I decided to take it back. I sought him out and robbed him, which was, after all, no more than they accused me of doing in the first place. I also left a reminder to show Louvois that no-one cheats my master." Ahmed patted the long knife at his belt.

"You did well," Giles said, "and I thank God you are restored to me."

Left alone, Giles again contemplated the Sussex downs. During the last half hour they seemed to have acquired a warming glow that had nothing to do with the brightening of the morning sky.

There was still another absent person whose company Giles craved.

In times of crisis Philip's very presence had a calming effect on those around him. "Where the devil are you when I need you, Philip?" Giles wondered. "In your bed and sleeping soundly, I've no doubt."

TWENTY TWO

Philip was actually on the Pont Neuf at that moment, looking down at the waters of the Seine. Thomas and Luc peered down with him.

"I jumped from this spot," Philip told them.

"Rather you than me," Luc decided.

"The alternatives were none too attractive," Philip said, sitting down upon the curved stone bench formed in the side of the bridge.

"But what exactly are we doing here at this unearthly hour of the morning?" Thomas wanted to know. "You drag me from my bed...,"

"*Your* bed?" Philip interrupted him. "I had to send Luc to find you!"

"Yes. I don't believe I properly thanked you for that favour, did I?" Thomas asked Luc, giving him a playful shove that all but sent the Frenchman off the top of the bridge himself!

Luc grinned. "She was rather pretty, my Lord."

"So I should hope! If any servant of mine is caught wenching when he ought to be attending to his master then she had better be worth the trouble," Philip said, with a wink. "But to answer your question, Thomas, what do you see over the side?"

"Water?" Thomas answered, with a slight shudder. Water was not his natural element. Philip guessed that Thomas would probably sooner have risked death at the hands of his attackers than leapt into the river.

"Before the water."

Thomas leaned further over. "There is nothing but a ledge."

"Exactly. A ledge. Would you say a small, nimble sort of person, who is not troubled by heights, could squat quite easily upon that ledge?"

Thomas turned slowly to look at him. Philip kept his expression bland, but Thomas obviously realised what was passing through his mind.

"No," he said decidedly.

"But Thomas…,"

"No," Thomas said again, shaking his head. "I can't swim, remember?"

"But you're not going to be *in* the water," Philip said patiently.

"I am if I fall."

"You never fall. You're as surefooted as a cat. I've seen you venture onto far more precarious places than that."

"Not with water underneath them you haven't."

Luc looked from one to the other and then sat down beside Philip on the bench. "He'll do it," he guessed.

"Of course he'll do it. I always have this trouble with him."

"That's because you always give me the worst jobs," Thomas complained.

"You don't even know what it is I want you to do."

"Nor do I wish to know."

Thomas joined them on the seat, on Philip's other side. The bridge was already beginning to come to life. Street pedlars and book sellers were setting out their wares and the policeman had positioned himself beneath the statue of Henri 1V, as he did every day, to watch for cutpurses amongst the crowds that would later be thronging the bridge. Philip reached over and drew out a silver watch from Thomas' waistcoat pocket. He had lost his own in the Seine and the rather fine silver one that Thomas always wore was one Philip had given him in gratitude for a great service he had done him in the past.

"The policeman comes on duty at seven," he murmured half to himself, as he checked the time.

"I was once arrested by one of those bastards not far from this spot," Thomas recalled cheerfully.

Luc's eyes opened wide. "What had you done?"

"Why nothing, as it happened, nothing at all, but they threw me into prison all the same."

"One of the few occasions he was actually innocent and he managed to get himself caught," Philip said, laughing. "There are a great many things you can learn from my Thomas, Luc, but honesty is not one of them. Tell him how you lost your finger, Thomas."

The little finger of Thomas' left hand was missing.

"A lady shut it in her carriage door."

"Well tell him the rest, then," Philip prompted.

Thomas pulled a face at him. "I was trying to steal her purse at the time," he admitted, "but I am quite reformed now."

A marionettist, setting up the puppets in his booth, looked curiously at them but Philip's eyes were fixed upon a cart, piled high with vegetables, which was trundling over the bridge on its way to the market at Notre Dames des Halles, as the church of St. Eustache was known to Parisians. "That's it!" he said. "Luc, could you drive a cart like that?"

Luc was caught off guard by the sudden change of subject. "I suppose I could, but where would I get one?"

Philip did not reply and Thomas laughed. "You'll quickly learn, Luc, that he only ever gives you the problems. The solutions you have to work out for yourself!"

Philip smiled at him. "Glad to find you in a happier frame of mind, Thomas. Now, perhaps, you are ready to hear your part. You I want to perch upon that ledge and leap out when our victims draw level. That doesn't sound so difficult, does it?"

"I suppose not," Thomas said grudgingly. "At least," he added, with a sidelong glance at Luc, "I shan't be driving a cartload of vegetables!"

"And why, exactly, will I be driving a cartload of vegetables?"

"So many questions," Philip complained. "Another thing you will learn, Luc, that you have to trust me!"

Thomas rolled his eyes heavenwards. "Here's another question for you, my Lord; how are you going to get the men to come here?"

"Leave that to me – and Monsieur."

Monsieur listened excitedly as Philip told him that he had a plan to bring his attackers to justice and would need his help.

"What part do I play in it?" he wanted to know.

"I want you to give me an introduction to the Duc de Bourgogne."

Monsieur's face fell. "Is that all?"

"It's very important," Philip said. For so it was. Although Louis' grandson resided at Versailles, he played no part in Court life. Bourgogne lived in the South Wing of the palace, away from everyone else. It would have been impossible for Philip to meet the seven-year-old Duc without an introduction, and who better to give him one than the boy's great uncle?

"I'll take you to him whenever you wish," Monsieur offered, "but I warn you he is not a pleasant child. He has a temper like the devil and will fly into a rage at the least thing. He broke a clock the other day just because it struck the hour for him to do something he did not want to do!"

Philip had heard plenty about the little Duc and had already formed a picture of him which was none too favourable. "How well does he agree with Abbé Fénelon and the Duc de Beauvilliers?"

"His tutors?" Monsieur shrugged. Plainly he had never given the matter any thought. "How should I know?"

"Think," Philip urged him. "I need to find out."

"I know that when the boy misbehaves all his books are taken away and no-one is allowed to speak to him until he apologises in writing to Fénelon," Monsieur recalled. "How can such means work upon a child like that?"

"It does seem strange," Philip agreed.

"It's not as bad for him as it was for his father," Monsieur said. "His tutors used to beat him."

"Beat the King's son? Surely not." Philip could scarcely believe that Louis would have allowed the Dauphin to be treated in such a way.

"Indeed they did! One day Bossuet broke the boy's arm."

"A fine man of God your brother chose for my ceremony," Philip muttered. "How did your tutors treat you?"

"They never really tried to teach me anything," Monsieur said blithely.

"Nor mine."

Philip had heard that Monsieur had, in fact, been a bright boy but, afraid that he would learn more than Louis, who must always be seen to be superior, it had been decided not to teach him anything at all. In Philip's own case the tutors that had been engaged for him were so afraid of his brother, Henry, that none had stayed for more than a few months. As a result, he and Monsieur shared a total lack of regard for education.

"Introduce me to him tomorrow, please," Philip said. "I will take my chances on his temperament. I have to find a way to confront Fénelon and Beauvilliers and this is the best one I can devise."

The south wing of the palace was Spartan compared with the sumptuous part occupied by the rest of the royal family. The rooms were so cheerless that, but for the view of the gardens and the two fountains that played outside the windows, it was difficult to remember they were in the same building.

No-one who was not connected with the upbringing of the Duc de Bourgogne was normally allowed in this part of the palace. Monsieur, of course, was allowed anywhere at any time and Philip had reason to be glad yet again to have him for a friend.

Bourgogne treated his great uncle respectfully. It was Louis' strict rule that everyone treated Monsieur with respect.

"I have someone here who would like to meet you," Monsieur said. Philip had no notion of how to treat any child except his own, but he did know how to treat royalty. As Monsieur introduced him he swept off his hat and made him as elaborate a bow as he would have made to Louis himself.

Bourgogne seemed to like that and offered him his little hand to kiss. "I know who you are. Everybody knows who you are. Why are you here?"

Philip was a little put out at his directness, although he took care not to show it. "I come to ask for your Grace's help to punish those who tried to kill me."

Bourgogne sat down on a small chair and regarded him coolly. "Why should I help you?"

Philip was at a bit of a loss as to how to answer that, but Monsieur came to his aid. "I imagine it will very likely annoy Abbé Fénelon."

That did the trick. The boy warmed visibly to Philip then.

"My grandfather says I must obey him in all things, but I don't," Bourgogne told him. "Fénelon says I am bad tempered."

"And are you?" Philip said.

The boy seemed surprised at the question. "If I rage and shout then people do what I want," he said simply.

Monsieur caught Philip's eye with an expression that plainly said 'I told you so'.

"If you do not rage and shout does he reward you?" Philip said.

"I do what I like," Bourgogne informed him haughtily, "but sometimes he will suggest a treat."

"And what does your Grace like to do?"

"I like to ride. I am better than anyone at that. If I have been what he considers good then he will let me ride around the park, sometimes as far as Trianon."

"And do your tutors accompany you on these rides?"

Bourgogne looked quite disgusted. "I hardly think that would be much fun, do you?"

Philip was not put out by his manner, for he had expected little better from this spoiled and passionate child. "It might be a great deal of fun if you agree to help me," he suggested. "I want you to request that you and Abbé Fénelon and the Duc de Beauvilliers go for a ride together to Trianon. I am sure you can persuade them."

"Of course I can."

"The three of you must be quite alone," Philip stressed, "for I intend to waylay you in the woods. You will be safe enough, for Monsieur will be with me."

"What?" The child hooted with laughter. "Monsieur does not ride."

"He certainly does, don't you, Monsieur?" Philip swung round to Monsieur, who looked surprised at being suddenly included in the conversation.

"Why, yes, when I want to."

"Monsieur can do a great deal more than most people suppose," Philip informed Bourgogne. "So, are you going to help me?"

"I have decided that I will," Bourgogne said magnanimously. The very prospect of seeing his effeminate and overdressed great uncle astride a horse was obviously very tempting! "Are you going to kill Abbé Fénelon?" he asked unconcernedly.

"No. Merely disturb his equanimity. His composure," Philip added, thinking he might have spoken over the boy's head, but he was wrong.

"I know what it means," Bourgogne told him scornfully. "I read, you know."

Philip and Monsieur exchanged another glance.

"Thank you, your Grace. I shall await your word," Philip said. "It only remains for me to request you to keep all this secret."

"That goes for you too," he warned Monsieur sternly as they

left. "And to think that child may one day rule France!" Philip knew he was not the only one to find that idea formidable.

Monsieur was too thrilled to think of anything but the part he was to play.

"What if he does tell anyone?" he wondered.

"Who would believe the word of a little boy against yours? You would lie for me, wouldn't you?" he asked Monsieur.

"Oh yes. I would do anything for you," Monsieur assured him, "but won't everyone think it strange for me to be out riding?"

"They'll think it is a whim to please me."

"I could be in disguise." Monsieur dearly loved theatricals. "Shall I dress up as a woman?"

"That won't be necessary," Philip said hastily. "If you really want to be unrecognisable you should try leaving off the disguise you always wear." He indicated the full beribboned wig and the ridiculously high heels, which gave Monsieur a mincing walk that was much imitated by the crueller wags of the Court.

"It's alright for you, you're tall," Monsieur protested. "Anyway, it is expected of me."

"Then surprise them all; be yourself for a change."

"My brother does not like me to be myself," Monsieur said quietly.

"Don't you ever get tired of playing the fop for his benefit?" Philip demanded. "You were a soldier once, damn it. You led troops into battle and now a child doubts if you can even ride."

Monsieur looked crestfallen and Philip cursed his own lack of tact.

"I'm sorry," he said quietly. "I didn't mean to sound unkind, but I'm fond of you and I can't bear to see you waste your life on organising ballets and advising courtiers on trifling points of etiquette that don't mean a thing outside of this palace."

"Are you really fond of me?" Monsieur said, picking up on the one part of Philip's remarks that he liked.

"Extremely fond," Philip assured him.

"Then I am content."

All the same Monsieur did have the good sense to exchange his high heeled shoes for riding boots when they set out a few days later to meet Bourgogne and his tutors. The young Duke had been as good as his promise and had managed to persuade both Fénelon and Beauvilliers to accompany him. It was all arranged that they should meet in the woods that led from the Grand Canal to the Trianon. Few passed that way in the early part of the morning and, if any did, who would have thought anything untoward? The Duc de Bourgogne would be, after all, in the company of a member of his own family. Monsieur was the key that could open any door for Philip.

He and Monsieur rode side by side along the Ride with Thomas and Luc behind them and Monsieur turned around to look at Santerre. "Luc tells me you are taking him to England. I do wish you wouldn't. He is such a pleasant boy."

"That one is not for you, I'm afraid," Philip said firmly. "One day I will tell you why. Ah! Here comes our party now."

As they drew level, Beauvilliers cursed as he realised they had been duped. Philip doffed his hat to Bourgogne, who went to join Monsieur, whilst Thomas and Luc skirted around the back of his tutors, lest they should try to leave.

Philip had never met Fénelon before and he looked with interest upon the dignified man who held a position of such importance. With his flowing hair and kindly expression, the Abbé was a picture of benign grace, but Philip was not so easily fooled. He harboured no belief in the innate goodness of his fellow men, particularly members of the clergy. During his involvement in the plot against the English Papists, ten years before, his association with Titus Oates, a minister of the cloth who had lied outrageously as a prosecution witness, had taught him harsher views than that. What Philip saw was not an angel but an ambitious, scheming man who fancied himself a second Cardinal Richelieu with a future King of France in his manipulative hands.

Beauvilliers, who Philip had encountered in the past, was less composed than Fénelon.

"You have ambushed us," he said angrily. "I demand that you allow us to continue without delay."

Philip ignored him completely.

"I have decided, Abbé, that the time has come for us to meet," he said to Fénelon.

"There are more conventional ways to meet me, your Grace," Fénelon said mildly.

"Yes, but you would have avoided taking them, and I have very little time left in France to accomplish what I wish to do."

"And what is that, pray?"

"Bring my enemies to justice."

Fénelon's expression hardened. The change was barely perceptible but Philip was observant and little escaped him.

"I have heard enough of this," Beauvilliers declared. "I intend to ride to the palace right now and summon the guards."

"You will stay exactly where you are, Beauvilliers," Philip said quietly, indicating with his head where Thomas and Luc watched them with their hands on the hilts of their swords.

"This is insufferable. The man is threatening us."

"I think, perhaps, we should talk to him," Fénelon said. "He has evidently taken a great deal of trouble to arrange this meeting and I believe Lord Southwick is a person one should not lightly disregard."

"The same might be said of you, Abbé," Philip returned. "Indeed, you have become a very influential man, thanks to the favour of Madame de Maintenon."

"The lady has been gracious enough to advance my cause with his Majesty," Fénelon said evenly.

"She has indeed. I would even go so far as to say that, without her help, you would never have acquired the position of tutor to his grandson."

"Abbé Fénelon is much respected by his Majesty," Beauvilliers interrupted.

Philip silenced him with a look. "You know better than that, don't you?" he enquired of Fénelon.

"I understand he was a little doubtful of my suitability for the post," he admitted.

"He can't stand the sight of you!"

"I suppose the King informed you of this himself," Beauvilliers sneered.

"Lord Southwick has his sources of information," Fénelon reminded him, looking down the Ride to where Monsieur was racing with the little duke and, Philip was pleased to see, doing rather well.

"Monsieur?" Beauvilliers retorted. "Southwick may control the King's brother but he does not control his Majesty and King Louis shall soon hear of how he dared to place the King's grandson in danger."

"I shall not tell you again to be quiet, Beauvilliers," Philip said with a sigh. "The next time you speak out of turn I swear I shall knock you from your horse."

"I think he means it," Fénelon warned. "It might be wiser not to try any further the patience of someone of such uncertain temperament. Besides, the Duc de Bourgogne is hardly in any danger since our captor had the foresight to bring along another member of the royal family. You are a very clever man, Philip Devalle. What else do your sources tell you, other than that I do not have the favour of the King, who seems to love you so well?"

This time there was a more than a trace of pettishness in Fénelon's tone. Philip smiled to see a wrinkle disturbing the Abbé's smooth facade.

"Unfortunately, it was Louis' favour which brought me the enmity of Madame de Maintenon. She was furious when the

King offered to marry my daughter to his son, as you no doubt know."

"How should I know anything about that?" Fénelon said stiffly.

"You certainly must know that she discussed it with Madame Guyon, the spiritualist, for I understand you are Madame Guyon's lover."

Now Fénelon's composure was truly shattered.

Philip glanced at Beauvilliers who, this time, was shocked into silence. "It's the truth," Philip assured him. "She claims it was God Himself who united them so intimately. She calls the Abbé 'Bibi', by the way."

Fénelon looked like a man for whom the sun just left the heavens.

"You see what a creature you have nurtured?" Philip asked Beauvilliers.

"This has nothing to do with me," Beauvilliers insisted crossly.

"But it has everything to do with you, Beauvilliers," Philip contradicted him. "You are the very key to the whole matter, and I refer now not to some tasteless affair between the tutor of the King's grandson and a mad mystic who also claims to be the wife of Jesus, scandalous though that will appear to the rest of France when it is broadcast. I am referring to something which concerns me much more personally."

Now that Philip's attention was turned upon him Beauvilliers looked as though he no longer wished to participate in the conversation. "I had nothing to do with the attempt upon your life, if that is what you are implying."

"Not directly, perhaps, but it was you who introduced Madame Guyon to Fénelon. It was also through you she met Madame de Maintenon. Madame Guyon claimed to have seen my death in one of her so-called visions, did she not?"

Philip was guessing now, but Beauvilliers' expression showed him that he had hit the mark.

"She did say that," he agreed, "but only to comfort Madame de Maintenon."

"Very probably, but it did not end with her prophesy, did it, Fénelon? I suspect Madame Guyon thought of a way to further endear herself with her influential patroness by suggesting that she could arrange for such a turn of events to be brought about if Madame de Maintenon desired it."

"Have a care, your Grace, when you speak of Madame de Maintenon, for you are speaking of a very pious woman," Fénelon protested.

"I am speaking of a very gullible woman if she allowed herself to be susceptible to the likes of Madame Guyon," Philip flashed back. "What happened next, Abbé? Did your lover come to you and ask for your help in engineering my downfall?"

Fénelon attempted to look indignant. "Why would you suppose me to be connected in any way…?"

"I captured Lavisse," Philip said, cutting him short. "Before he died he told me everything."

"You fool!" Beauvilliers turned on Fénelon. "You used Lavisse? You knew the nature of the fellow. He stole from me."

"Who should I employ to do such work?" Fénelon demanded. "An honest man? I wanted nothing to do with this. Everything was down to Madame de Maintenon, though she now denies all knowledge of it."

"Trouble amongst the Holy Set?" Philip enquired sweetly, for so Maintenon, Fénelon and Beauvilliers were known amongst the more irreverent at Versailles.

"What exactly do you want?" Beauvilliers asked him.

"Well what do you think I want? Retribution, of course." Philip viewed them both coldly. "I cannot directly attack Maintenon, I realise that, but Madame Guyon is another matter. What does the King actually know about this woman, I wonder? How much favour do you imagine you would both retain if the full extent of her evil was known, especially since he already hates religious nonconformity with a passion?"

"Madame Guyon is to be made the scapegoat? That is unjust," Fénelon cried.

"Protect her at your peril," Philip warned him. "You," he pointed at Beauvilliers, "will bring her down, as a reward for which I will allow you to go free of my vengeance."

"I shall put pressure on Madame de Maintenon to remove the woman from St. Cyr," Beauvilliers said. "What about the Abbé?"

"Fénelon I intend to leave alone, for I have sufficient faith in human nature to believe that he will engineer his own downfall in the end," Philip said. "My price for not hastening that end is the three men who were unwise enough to try to take my life. I want them delivered, unsuspectingly, into my hands, for they will not escape my justice, even if I am forced to let the guiltier parties go free."

"You're going to kill them?" Fénelon asked.

"I'm going to execute them," Philip corrected him.

Beauvilliers looked uncomfortable. "He will get us all into trouble."

"On the contrary, Beauvilliers, I am offering to sell you my silence, and I think it is a fair price. You have but little choice in any case, for you surely don't imagine Madame de Maintenon will protect you? You must know she would abandon you as swiftly as she will Madame Guyon," Philip said, for Maintenon was known to be fickle to her friends and most certainly would not be loyal to any who might endanger her position with the King.

Both Beauvilliers and Fénelon had advanced on her recommendation and must have known that she would cast them off if there was the slightest risk that they could prove to be her undoing.

"What guarantee do we have that you will keep your word?" was all Fénelon said.

"Why, none whatever but, be assured, should either of you not keep yours the King will learn of all this, and from a source he trusts implicitly." Philip looked meaningfully toward Monsieur, who was returning down the Ride with the little duke.

"You've told Monsieur about this?" Beauvilliers gasped. "But we will never be sure that he may not one day give us away."

"I know." Philip smiled disarmingly. In fact he had told Monsieur very little, for he had always found that to be the best way, but he had no intention of relieving their anxiety. "That, gentlemen, is the truly delightful part!"

TWENTY-THREE

✑

Louis studied his brother long and hard over dinner later that day. Monsieur was talking nineteen to the dozen, but there was nothing unusual in that, for he was always talkative, and yet there was a kind of glow illuminating him on this occasion.

It seemed that Louis was not the only one to have noticed. The ladies around the table were making a special fuss of him. They always did fuss him, of course. They always had. Monsieur had been blessed with delicate good looks and an endearing capacity for amusing chatter that had made him a favourite amongst the hardened females of the Court ever since he was a child.

Louis almost envied him at times like this, for he had no opportunity to be frivolous like his younger brother but, as ever, he dismissed such feelings as unworthy, for he loved Monsieur. Besides, he consoled himself, the admiration of the Court beauties was wasted on a man who, though he had sired four children and had been known to take a mistress or two, was generally unmoved by their attentions.

This time, however, even that was different. His brother was positively flirting; so much so that he was forgetting to eat!

"Are you not enjoying the turkey, Monsieur?" he asked him. Louis himself was very fond of turkey and had them bred upon his own farm

Monsieur, subservient to his older brother as usual, obligingly took another piece. In fact he was not quite so fond of it, but that was one of the dishes in front of him and it was considered bad manners to request something from a dish you could not reach. He ate the meat dutifully enough, still managing to amuse his audience between mouthfuls, but it was obvious that his mind was not upon the food and when the fruit appeared he did not trouble to pocket some, as he was accustomed to doing, to eat later. This was an unfortunate habit of his, for fruit was always peeled and then replaced in its skin before it reached Louis' table. This meant it was quite unappetising by the time Monsieur came to eat it out of his pocket, although that never particularly troubled him.

"Are you having fun with your visitor?" Louis asked him after dinner, when they met in the Diana drawing room, which had been laid out as a games room ready for the evening's entertainment.

"Oh yes," Monsieur said happily.

"I thought you were particularly witty today," Louis said. "Evidently exercise is good for you. I hear you were out riding in the park this morning with Philip."

"Indeed I was. We met with your grandson and I raced him. I won too!"

"He is only seven!" Louis could not help laughing at the thought of Monsieur, ringlets, ruffles and all, cantering down the Ride with the determined little Bourgogne in hot pursuit. "I'd like to have seen that," he said with a slight wistfulness in his voice that did not escape his brother.

"I wish you could have some fun too," Monsieur said impulsively. "You seem to have so few diversions these days."

Louis nodded sadly. He had been sad since Theresa had left France. Nothing more had been said about the tentative plans he had made for them, but their parting had been poignant for him, for it reminded him of the lack of passion left in his life. His relationship with Madame de Maintenon was comfortable but not exciting. He had chosen a companion who would help him lead a more god-fearing life, for he was very much afraid of suffering eternal damnation on account of the wild pursuits of his youth. She was the one who had convinced him of that, yet now a disquieting doubt had been cast over her own probity.

Philip had seen the royal brothers enter the salon and he crossed the room to speak to them. Louis did not stand on ceremony on 'Appartement' evenings, as they were called, whilst Monsieur never required any particular deference from him and he greeted them with a combination of familiarity and respect that was all his own.

Monsieur, still bubbling over with his new found enthusiasm for life, was soon in demand to play at Lansquenet, so much so that an argument broke out as to who he should play with, much to Philip's amusement!

"Monsieur tells me you took him riding," Louis said conversationally.

"I trust your Majesty approves of that?"

"I approve of anything you do to make him happy, but I caution you not to misuse the power you have over him." Louis was smiling but the lightness had left his voice.

"I would do nothing to hurt Monsieur," Philip assured him.

"What about me?"

"I would give my life for you." The words came straight from Philip's heart. Louis may have had failings as a man but, so far as Philip was concerned, there had never been any to compare with him as a monarch.

"I really believe you would," Louis said, looking pleased, "but let us hope no such sacrifice is ever required of you for my sake. All I ask of you now is that you give me a little peace."

"Monsieur and I intend leaving for Paris in the morning," Philip said innocently.

"As if that was what I meant! And what are the pair of you proposing to do in Paris?"

"I have one or two things in mind."

"I'd wager on that! Shall you be returning to Versailles before you go back to England?"

Philip looked over to where Madame de Maintenon was sitting, a little away from the rest, conspicuous by her sober clothing. She glared at him.

"I think not, your Majesty. Not if you want some peace."

Louis followed his gaze. "Perhaps you are right. I look forward to seeing you when you next manage to return to France."

"Which I hope will not be too long, for I have a property to inspect, thanks to your Majesty's graciousness."

"It has been an eventful visit for you, one way and another," Louis remarked.

"To say the very least," Philip thought as they parted, Louis to play at billiards whilst he himself went over to speak with Armand and Marguerite.

"Whatever have you done to Monsieur?" Marguerite said. "He is positively radiant this evening."

"I finally succumbed to his advances," Philip teased her.

"Don't talk like that, you dreadful man!" She tapped him on the arm with her fan. "Armand, make him behave!"

Armand laughed, for he knew how Philip delighted in trying to shock her, but his face soon grew serious again. "Alas my friend, the time has come for us to say goodbye once more. It seems we are all three leaving Versailles in the morning."

"You are going home?"

Armand shook his head regretfully. "Would that I was. Marguerite will be returning to La Fresnaye but I am about to begin another tour of duty. I fear Louis will keep me working until I drop."

"The bastard," Philip muttered with feeling. He knew it was Louis' way of punishing Armand for daring to defy him by marrying a Huguenot at a time when such unions had been forbidden. It mattered nothing that Marguerite had eventually changed her faith, and even less that Armand's illustrious military career had benefited France so much in the past. Louis was simply not a forgiving man.

It was late before Philip returned to the tiny apartment allotted to him for his visit. It faced one of the inner courtyards and looked out upon nothing save a drainpipe fastened to the opposite wall. He'd had enough of Versailles for one visit, he decided, closing the curtains and looking around the dingy little room. More like a cupboard really.

Thomas came in not long after. Despite his own cramped situation, Philip had offered to let Thomas share the accommodation with him, for the servants' quarters were even more abominable. Thomas would have had to share a cupboard there with three or four others!

"Said your goodbyes?" Philip asked him.

"Yes, and do you know I won't be sorry to be leaving," Thomas admitted, taking up the silver hairbrush, without which Philip would never have travelled anywhere.

"Just what I was thinking." Philip closed his eyes as Thomas commenced to brush his hair for him. He was a good servant and looked after him very well. "Do you suppose that means I am growing old?"

Thomas laughed at that. "Not you, my Lord. You'll never be old!"

"Bless you for that, but I used to say I would never tire of Versailles. Has it changed or have I?" he wondered.

"Both," Thomas said, sagely. "Versailles for the worse and you for the better."

"Infernal cheek! Just for that I've a good mind not to tell you the rest of my plan."

"I'm not even sure I wish to hear it."

"Of course you do! Fénelon has agreed to send a message to the three men who attacked me. He is to tell them that a lady of his acquaintance has come to him for help upon a most delicate matter and that he would consider it a great favour if they would assist her. In order to protect her reputation, the meeting must be held in secret and she has suggested meeting them at dawn upon the Pont Neuf, by the statue."

"What lady?" Thomas interrupted him.

"I'm coming to that. When they arrive she will be alone in her carriage, so that they approach her unawares. As they advance toward the vehicle Luc, driving a cart as though to market, will start to cross the bridge. They should take no notice of him until he draws level. You will be hiding upon the ledge below the parapet. They will not even see you until it is too late.

"And where will you be all this while? "

"Driving the coach, of course. Whilst you and Luc are tackling the others I propose to unmask their leader. We will take them totally by surprise. What do you think?"

"Not bad," Thomas allowed, "but who is the woman going to be?"

"That's the problem, for frankly I don't know one who I can ask to do this. That is why I thought to use a man dressed as a woman."

Thomas almost dropped the hairbrush. "Not Monsieur!"

"Why not? He'd love it."

"But he might get hurt, and then you'd have to answer to the King of France."

"Well we'll have to make sure he doesn't get hurt, won't we? Anyway, he may not agree to it."

"Oh, he'll agree alright. He would do anything for you, particularly if it involved dressing up! Morgan would never have let you do this, my Lord. You know that, don't you?"

Philip smiled. "Well naturally I know it! Why do you think I made him go home with your mistress?"

෴

Theresa woke Giles from a fitful sleep.

"You had better come," she told him. "The babe is on its way and Marianne is calling for you."

Giles dressed hurriedly and a few minutes later joined his sister and Bet at Marianne's bedside.

"Him too?" Bet asked, seeing Ahmed enter with him.

"Marianne would want him to be there," Giles said.

Bet shrugged. She had been involved with this family for so long that nothing would ever surprise her. "As you wish."

Marianne had fought her illness valiantly. With Bet's care and Giles' constant encouragement she had beaten it, but she had been left very weak and in no good condition to give birth to a child, particularly one who had decided to come a month ahead of its time.

"Bet fears Marianne may not have the strength to push," Theresa said, taking him aside.

"What if she cannot?"

"Then the baby will suffocate. There is one thing Bet can do," she added, a little hesitantly, "but it is only as a last resort."

"What is that?"

"She can cut Marianne and release the muscles, but it is a risky thing to do. Bet does not claim to be a surgeon and such a wound might become infected and kill her."

Giles looked at her in horror as he considered this, but a howl of agony from Marianne cut through his thoughts. He flew to her side and gave her the hand she instinctively reached out for.

"Must she suffer so?" he asked Bet.

"All women suffer in childbirth," she said. "If you doubt that ask your sister, who was fit and well when she gave birth. And she did not have the benefit of her husband to comfort her," Bet added. "He was such a nuisance that I made Morgan keep him out of the way until it was all over!"

Giles smiled, in spite of himself, at the thought of Philip, of all people, being ordered around by the determined Bet.

There was something soothing, too, about Bet's matter-of-fact manner.

"Is there anything I can do?" he asked her. "That is if you intend allowing me to stay!"

"You can stay, so long as you don't get under my feet," Bet said crisply. "Here, give her some of this."

Giles sniffed the contents of the glass she held out to him. It smelled quite palatable for one of Bet's potions.

"You need not look like that," she retorted. "It is nothing but cinnamon and wine, into which I have ground a little penny royal. It will ease her labour and help to clear away what comes after the baby."

Giles held it up to Marianne, who obligingly drank a little of the concoction.

"Did your sister explain everything to you?" Bet asked, looking him hard in the eye.

"Yes she did."

Marianne was gripped in another spasm of pain, which the medicine Giles was administering seemed to have done little to ease.

"You know the decision must be yours if it comes to a choice between them," Bet said quietly.

Giles nodded, his thoughts in turmoil.

"And that you may need to make it soon," Bet prompted, "for the pains are coming fast now. If the moment of choice arrives I must know which I am supposed to try to save."

Giles saw the concern on her face and he knew she needed him to make the decision, but he also knew it was a decision he was not prepared to make. His determination had never allowed anything to stand in the way of what he wanted in the past and this situation, he vowed, was going to be no different.

"The moment will not arrive," he said firmly. Going back to the bedside he took his wife by the shoulders. "Marianne, look at me."

She opened her eyes, a little bleary from the wine which Bet had been forcing down her for an hour. "Yes, Giles?"

"Do you wish to please me, Marianne?

"More than anything."

"Then you must obey me."

"I always obey you, Giles," she said.

"I know you do, but it has never been more important to me than now. You are not to lose the baby and you are not to die. I love you Marianne, and if you leave me I shall not want to live."

"You will, Giles, for you will have our child to console you," she said tearfully, but he shook his head.

"I shall not want it, not if it was the cause of my losing the person I love more than my life."

He saw Bet and Theresa exchange glances.

However mystifying Giles' tactics were to the onlookers, they worked on Marianne.

"I will bear our baby, Giles, and I will live," she promised, gasping as her body was once more racked with pain, "but, oh, it hurts so that I don't know how I shall be able to stand it."

Ahmed stepped forward then, untying one of the leather straps he always wore around his wrists. He put it between her teeth. "Bite on that. It may help you."

Giles looked at him gratefully. "Ahmed and I will give you all the strength you need," he assured Marianne as they stood on either side of the bed, each holding one of her hands whilst she gripped onto them tightly. "Together the three of us will always be strong because we are each other's strength."

TWENTY FOUR

❦

Despite his earlier misgivings, Thomas had to admit that Monsieur was convincing.

Wearing an elaborately styled wig, with carmine on his lips and paint upon his long, dark lashes, Monsieur tossed his head so that his long earrings danced.

"You've put on some weight since you last wore this," Philip complained, struggling to fasten the bodice of Monsieur's dress. "Perhaps we should lace your stays a little tighter."

"Any tighter and he won't breathe," Thomas muttered. "I can't believe I am watching my master fit the First Gentleman of France into a silk dress!"

At last Philip was satisfied. Monsieur not only looked like a woman but a very beautiful one.

Philip viewed the transformation with pride. "Keep the hood of your cloak up," he instructed, "and don't forget to hide your face a little with your fan. You look perfect."

Monsieur beamed.

"Well?" Philip asked Thomas, as Monsieur surveyed himself in the mirror. "Did I do a good job?"

"I have to admit it, but I still wonder at the wisdom of letting him carry that," Thomas said as he saw Monsieur lift his skirts and tuck a small pistol into the top of his garter.

"He is only to use it to defend himself, should he be in any danger."

"You had just better hope he doesn't faint," Thomas retorted.

It was only just after four o'clock in the morning when they left the Palais Royale, for Philip was taking no chances on the men being at the bridge first. He stopped the coach by the side of the statue of Monsieur's grandfather and Thomas slipped from the vehicle and climbed over the side of the bridge to perch upon the ledge just below them

"Good luck," Philip whispered.

"Can you see Luc yet?"

Philip looked and picked out a dim figure on the Les Augustins quai, ready to cross with his cart as soon as the three men started upon the bridge.

"He's there."

There was nothing to do now but wait. This was the part Philip knew Thomas had dreaded most of all. Although the ledge was wide enough for him to lie upon, he would be able to look down and remember that there was a great deal of water just below him.

Fortunately, he was not to have too long to think about it. At a little after five o'clock horses' hooves could be heard approaching them, but not from across the bridge, as Philip had anticipated. The riders came, instead, from the direction of the Place Dauphine opposite, for the Pont Neuf not only spanned the Seine; it also joined, in its centre, with the Ile de la Cité.

Philip cursed. The men were obviously being cautious and had crossed the river at the Pont Saint-Michel. Luc might not see them until it was too late and he would not be able to risk hastening with the cart, for the least untoward action would alert their suspicions.

"You will have to delay them for as long as you can," he whispered to Monsieur through the communicating panel of the coach.

The three men approaching, suspicious though they might have been at the start, could have seen nothing now to trouble them. The coach contained no-one save its female occupant, who beckoned them urgently.

"Over here, and hurry please," he begged them in a high, wavering voice. "I must return before my husband wakes or I am undone."

"Now, Luc, now," Philip murmured to himself as he sat, head bowed so as to hide his face, appearing to take no interest in the proceedings.

Luc must have seen the three men silhouetted against the streaks of the dawn sky. Even as Philip willed him to appear, he urged his horse onto the bridge.

"Who's that?" the leader of the men swung round at the sound. His face was masked, as it had been on the fateful morning when they had taken Philip.

"It's only a market cart," one of the others reassured him, watching Luc's plodding progress.

"Surely you don't suspect me of mischief?" Monsieur protested. "I am only a poor woman, half-dead from fright."

"Your pardon, my Lady, but we suspect everyone. Even as he spoke the leader walked around to the other side of the coach and peered in through the window.

"What do you think, that I have a man hidden in here?" Monsieur cried. "I beg you, gentlemen, deal kindly with me, for I have suffered enough. Indeed, I feel quite faint."

So saying he took a vinaigrette from around his neck and inhaled from it, keeping the men waiting a minute longer, long enough for Luc to have arrived at the third arch of the bridge.

"Good, good," Philip said to himself. The lumbering cart, piled high with cabbages, would draw level with them in a very short while now. Despite his hunched appearance, Philip was poised and ready to spring, and he could almost feel Thomas' readiness a few feet below him.

Abbé Fénelon said you were in trouble," the leader prompted Monsieur, who was fluttering his fan, as though very agitated.

"Not half as much as you," Monsieur laughed, for at that moment Philip gave his signal.

Luc jumped down from the cart, his sword in his hand, and set upon the man nearest to him. At the same instant Thomas vaulted over the parapet onto the bridge and intercepted a second, whilst Philip threw himself from the driver's seat to land squarely on the leader of the three men, bringing him crashing to the floor.

Philip held him down, kneeling upon his chest. He ripped off the black mask and finally discovered the identity of the man who had tried to murder him.

"D'Arsay!"

Philip was strong, even with his injured shoulder, and the Marquis struggled against him in vain.

"Why did *you* want to kill me?" Philip demanded.

"I care not if you live or die, Southwick. What I did was done to spite Louvois. Fénelon said Louvois would be blamed for it and I would never have had to take orders from him again."

"How long have you belonged to Fénelon?"

"Since I realised Louvois' days in power are numbered." D'Arsay was finding it difficult to get the words out, for Philip's weight was crushing his chest. "Fénelon will be the most powerful man in France when the Duc de Bourgogne becomes King."

Philip regarded him disgustedly. "D'Arsay, you truly are a fool. You have betrayed those of your own Huguenot faith and you have betrayed the man who rewarded you for doing it. Now you have hazarded everything for Fénelon, who is an even greater fool than you if he thinks he can ever beat King Louis. Worst of all, you now have me for an enemy, and you must know I am very vengeful man."

"Go on, then. Kill me if you're going to do it." The Frenchman's tone was still defiant but there was fear in his eyes.

"Your men will die quickly but for you, d'Arsay, I have reserved a special fate." Philip stood up and yanked him roughly to his feet, holding him in an iron grip as he turned to see how Thomas and Luc were faring.

Thomas' man was fighting furiously but Thomas was more than a match for him, trained as he was by Philip himself. It was no honourable fight. His opponent kicked out at him and brought him to the ground but, whilst he was down, Thomas brought his boot up sharply into the man's groin and he staggered back in agony. Thomas would have leapt up and finished him there and then but a quick glance over to Luc showed him that the young man was in trouble. Luc was an agile swordsman but he was less experienced and, although he was holding his own well, he appeared to be tiring.

Thomas, taking advantage of his own opponent's momentary weakness, rolled over toward them and grabbed the ankle of Luc's adversary, bringing him crashing down.

"Thanks Thomas!" It was all the edge Luc needed.

Thomas sprung to his feet and turned back to his own man, who had recovered and was advancing dangerously fast.

"I know you now." The man fairly spat the words. "You are Thomas Sullivan. You tricked Lavisse."

"That wasn't difficult," Thomas panted, returning blow for blow, but he was beginning to flag.

The knowledge of who Thomas was seemed to have given his adversary fresh strength. "If it were not for you we would never have been discovered."

This time Thomas lost the upper hand. His opponent lunged at him, bringing his weapon up so quickly that Thomas' sword slipped from his grasp.

He had always relied upon his speed and agility to get him out of trouble and he did so now. Jumping upon the wheel of the coach he swiftly pulled himself up onto the domed roof, crying out to Luc, who had finished his fight, to help him.

Luc came straight to his aid, but not before the swordsman, furious at his opponent's escape, had pulled a knife from his belt and hurled it at Thomas' chest.

Thomas dodged the blade without too much effort but,

distracted for an instant, he missed his footing on the roof's smooth surface.

Philip, holding d'Arsay, was powerless to help him from so far away.

Thomas slipped down from the top of the coach and landed heavily upon the parapet. He was winded and hurt, and quite unable to steady himself.

Philip watched helplessly as his beloved servant rolled toward the edge of the bridge.

With a howl like a wild animal, Luc hurled himself at the parapet and grabbed Thomas' arm, just as he was about to plummet down to his death in the murky waters of the Seine.

Thomas' assailant laughed triumphantly as Luc strained to haul Thomas back onto the bridge. "Now I have the both of you."

A gunshot pierced the early morning stillness. Monsieur had fired, and with deadly accuracy. The man fell at Luc's feet, a bullet through his head.

Philip breathed again. It had all happened so quickly and yet it had seemed that time had stood still whilst Thomas was in danger.

Luc helped the stunned Thomas into the coach and Philip, his pistol in his hand, turned back to d'Arsay. "Now it's your turn. Over the side."

"No." Panic was rising in d'Arsay's voice. "I'll not do it."

"There is to be no discussion on the matter," Philip said pleasantly. "I'm giving you the same chance as you gave me. You are going to jump into the water and then I shall shoot you. I have sometimes been known to miss, of course. Not often though," he added with a disarming smile, prodding d'Arsay with the muzzle of his pistol, so that he had no option but to climb on top of the parapet of the bridge.

"Mind the ledge beneath you," Philip warned him as he prepared to jump.

"Can't I at least take off my boots?"

Philip considered the matter for as long as it took him to recall d'Arsay pointing a gun at him and gloating before he pulled the trigger.

"No."

D'Arsay jumped, screaming, from the bridge. Philip took aim and fired. He did not miss.

He wasted no time, for the shots fired by himself and Monsieur had been loud enough to wake every sleeping resident of the Ile de la Cité.

With Luc's help, he hoisted the bodies of d'Arsay's friends over the side of the bridge and then searched for the knife which had so narrowly missed Thomas. He found that in the gutter and tossed it over after them.

Luc swiftly got into the coach and, before climbing back into the driver's seat, Philip quickly turned the cabbage cart around and slapped the old horse on the rump, sending it trotting back home in the direction it had come.

The city of Paris was beginning to stir as he drove off. Shutters were opening in the nearby Place Dauphine. In an hour the policeman would take his place. In two hours the alchemists and lace sellers would be plying their trades.

Philip looked back and smiled. There was little to indicate that anything untoward had even taken place there. Only a bloodstain, which would soon be dispersed by the wheels of a hundred vehicles.

And a cabbage, which had rolled against the railings at the base of King Henri's statue!

Philip had one more thing he wanted to do before he left for England the following day. Late in the afternoon he went with Monsieur to the Cimitière des Innocents, where his friend, Jules Gaspard, was buried.

He stood alone at the graveside for a long time and remembered the writer who had affected his life so deeply.

Philip had encountered little kindness in his early life and met few who had genuinely cared for him beyond his usefulness. Through Jules' eyes he had learned to see a different, better side to the world. They had not been destined to enjoy their friendship for long but Jules was a part of Philip still and always would be.

Monsieur alighted from the coach and joined him when he obviously considered Philip had dwelt upon his memories for long enough.

"You have to let Gaspard go," he said in a soft voice, far removed from his usual high tones.

"I know." Philip turned from the headstone, which bore the simple French inscription, 'Jules Gaspard. Un Poète et un ami plus bien-aimé'. Poet and most beloved friend.

The buildings of Paris were showing dark against the fading sky as they made their way back in the coach.

"I wasn't thinking only of Jules," Philip confessed, "but of myself too. So much has happened to me since he died. I was young and knew so little of the world. I wonder sometimes how different my life might have been had Jules lived, for I might then have stayed in the French army and never gone back to England."

"It does not do to dwell upon such things," Monsieur said, a little bitterly. "I do it on occasions, and it only makes me sad. I often wonder what my life would have been like if I had stayed in the army myself."

Philip looked at him in surprise. "I have never heard you say that before."

"I would not say it now except to you," Monsieur confided.

Philip had already noticed that quite a remarkable change had come over Monsieur during the last month. With other matters than the trivialities of the Court to occupy him, the First Gentleman of France had seemed aware, suddenly, of the petty limitations of his life.

"There is still time for you to change," Philip suggested, for Monsieur was only in his forties.

"Louis would never allow me to change."

"You can't let him do this to you," Philip cried in exasperation. "You are intelligent and brave. Why should you always be subservient to his wishes?"

"I have no choice," Monsieur told him flatly. "I cannot fight him. I never could, not even when we were children. My mother always said I should give in to him. That was why she made me wear dresses and play at being a girl, so that he would always be the stronger one."

Philip was of the opinion that their mother, Queen Anne of Austria, was a stupid and unfair woman, but he would never have said that to Monsieur. In any case there was little point. Monsieur was what he was, the product of a warped upbringing and a suppressed manhood. There was nothing Philip or anyone else could do to help him now. Monsieur's one chance of asserting himself had been after the Siege of Mons, when he had proved himself a hero, but he had let that chance be wrested from him by his brother's insecurities.

Philip put his hand on the Frenchman's shoulder. "I understand, I truly do." And so he did. Monsieur was an actor playing a part, a part that was all the more abhorrent to him when he stopped to think about it. "It is unkind of me to urge you to change. You are very dear to me just as you are."

"I'm going to miss you," Monsieur sighed as they turned into the grounds of the Palais Royale.

"I shall miss you too, for I don't know when I have enjoyed a month in anyone's company more," Philip told him truthfully, "but I can stay no longer."

"You will come back soon, though, won't you?" Monsieur said anxiously.

"As soon as ever I can, but I fear King William may be planning to dispatch me to Ireland to fight against your cousin James."

"You are to refuse to go to Ireland," Monsieur insisted. "You might be killed."

"I was nearly killed in Paris, if it comes to that," Philip reminded him. "Besides, since it is prophesied that I shall die in prison then I imagine that an Irish battlefield will be as safe for me as anywhere else!"

Monsieur shuddered. "Don't joke about such things!" He was very superstitious.

There was another part of La Voisin's prediction, a part known only to Philip and Athénais de Montespan, who had taken him to see the fortune teller. It was that his death would be caused by a royal personage. Philip had told no-one else of that, not even Theresa or Morgan, although it was a thought that haunted his more troubled moments. He had suspected his end would come when King Charles had held him in the Tower accused of treason and, after his acquittal, he had sometimes wondered if La Voisin had been wrong, but he would never be certain. He knew William didn't trust him and James could still be a threat. After what had happened, he wondered if he could ever be completely sure of Louis again. Then there was Monsieur.

Philip banished that last thought as unworthy. There was nothing but honest concern upon the Frenchman's face. He was sure Monsieur would never do him any harm. Not intentionally, at least.

"William is still my sovereign," was all he said. "I must obey him or lose everything I have worked so hard for in England."

"You don't need him anymore." Monsieur dismissed the Dutchman with a careless wave of his hand. "You can live in France, near to me."

Philip smiled as he helped him down from the coach, thinking how well advice about how he should spend his life came from a man whose own destiny had been shaped for him. "Ah, Monsieur, if only my life was that simple!"

Thomas was packing Philip's trunk, ready for the journey,

when he got back to his house. He straightened up as Philip entered and let out an involuntary groan.

"Does your back still hurt you?" Philip asked him worriedly. Thomas had been badly shaken by his fall and Philip was racked with guilt. "Lie down on the bed and I will rub it for you," he offered. "We must have you fit to travel in the morning."

Thomas groaned afresh as he lay down upon his stomach, for the effort hurt him, but he soon relaxed as Philip skillfully massaged the sore muscles of his back.

"It is good of you to do this for me, my Lord."

"I know it is, but you've done the same for me sufficient times and I don't forget these things."

"I'll warrant I never get the opportunity to forget this!" Thomas said.

Philip laughed. "How well you know me! However I do not propose to have to tend to your aches and pains too often, my impertinent one. You are to be more careful from now on."

"That's rich, coming from you," Thomas declared, wincing as Philip's probing fingers found a particularly sore spot. "When were you ever careful?"

"We're not talking about me. Is that better?" Philip asked his patient.

Thomas stood up gingerly. "Yes, much. Thank you."

"It is the least I can do. After all," he added quietly, "I very nearly got you killed this time."

Philip's spirits were already low that afternoon. He had been pondering upon Jules' death and the futility of Monsieur's life, but he suddenly thought about Thomas and how close he had come to losing him.

Thomas glanced at him. "What's wrong, my Lord?"

"I have seen you attempt some daredevil feats in the past, Thomas, but I have never before seen you fall. I suppose I always thought of you as indestructible and I was wrong."

"Does that mean I no longer get the worst jobs?"

Thomas knew exactly how to lighten Philip's darker moods.

"No, of course it doesn't!" His good humour restored, Philip regarded his own pleasing reflection in the glass." I just want you to consider my position in the future, if you please. I would never hear the end of it from your mistress if I returned home without you."

Thomas smiled and closed the lid of the trunk he had been packing.

"Yes, my Lord."

TWENTY FIVE

∽

High Heatherton had been blessed with a good harvest. Whilst Philip had been away everyone had toiled hard under the leadership of John Bone, the estate manager.

"You have done well, John," Philip told him, as indeed he had. With Morgan also absent from his duties, Bone had needed to supervise the tree cutting as well, for Heatherton's timber was sold to the boatyards at Shoreham harbour and was an important part of the estate's revenue.

John flushed with pride at the praise. "I am just thankful you are alive to see the results of my labours, Lord Philip."

"I doubt I would be still alive had I not learned to dive and swim with you when we were ruffian boys," he told him. Theirs was a special relationship, for Philip would never forget how much John's companionship had meant to him during his lonely childhood. "Now away to your festivities, John, for you have earned a holiday."

It was the day traditionally set aside at High Heatherton to celebrate the harvest. From early morning the estate workers and their families had been setting out the harvest fare. There were breads and cakes, made from their own flour, fruit from their trees and jugs of cream, home-cured hams, pies and neat's tongues, as well as home brewed ales and many other treats, all provided from the land they tended.

When they had enjoyed their fill of Heatherton's bounty there would be country games played and then music and dancing far into the night. It was a day to remember and to warm their hearts when the cold Winter winds swept the Sussex downs. Philip was pleased for them to celebrate and had revived the old custom, which had been discontinued in the days when his father had wanted to keep Philip's unpredictable brother, Henry, away from the rest of the world.

The members of his household were preparing for their own celebrations. Giles and Marianne had been blessed with a fine, healthy son, whom they had named William, and the family were taking this opportunity to welcome him properly into their midst. As Philip neared the house he could see the long, wooden table being carried from the kitchen by the maids, under Bet's noisy supervision. She had trained some of the labourers' daughters as servants in the house and they were well used to her sharp London tongue. They loved her nonetheless for Mistress Bet, though prickly on the outside, had a soft heart and was mother, sister and friend to every troubled soul who needed her.

When it was placed to her satisfaction, beneath some shady branches, she dismissed the girls to join their families and looked around for other hands to help her bring out the fare to lay upon it. She spotted Thomas lounging against a tree, enthralling John Bone's pretty daughter with tales of his recent adventures in France.

Thomas' worldliness did not impress Bet one bit, for she had practically raised him. "Come over here you lazy slubberdegullion," she hailed him, "or do you think these preparations take care of themselves? And you needn't look so cocky," she warned Luc, catching him grinning at Thomas' plight. "You can help too." She repeated the instruction in French, lest he had failed to grasp her meaning, and the two young men trotted meekly after her.

Philip smiled, that is until she turned to him!

"Don't you dare," he warned and grabbed Giles' arm. "I think we should absent ourselves for a little while, or she will have the two of us fetching and carrying as well."

"Bet has always had a soft spot for me," Giles said smugly.

"Well you are fortunate. She has tried to bully me since I first met her! I wanted a chance to speak with you alone in any case."

They walked along in companionable silence until they came to a deep pond, hidden amongst the trees. The water was always dark and cold, for the sun rarely penetrated that far into the woods, but it was the very place where Philip had swum with John so many years before. He looked up at a tall tree, from whose overhanging branch they had dived so many times.

"It seemed much higher to me when I was a child," he reflected.

"It still seems high enough to me," Giles said, "although it is certainly not as high as the Pont Neuf. You really are a lucky bastard, aren't you?"

"Yes, I suppose I am," Philip agreed, "but who would have thought that by surviving a fall into the Seine I would have become the master of a chateau in Languedoc? It is, in fact, my plans for the Pasquier estate that I wish to discuss with you."

"If you had any sense you'd sell it," Giles said.

"That's what you said about Heatherton once," Philip reminded him. "We are talking about my birthright and my daughter's inheritance."

"Some of us have to manage without an inheritance," Giles replied, somewhat sourly, for he was unlikely to receive a penny piece from his father. With five other younger children to provide for out of his modest means, Squire Fairfield considered that his eldest two had done quite well enough for themselves.

Philip found that amusing. "But you are likely to end up richer than the lot of us!" Giles had always been shrewd with money and even Theresa had no idea of how much her acquisitive brother was really worth. "You don't have time to enjoy yourself, you never gamble and you spend but a fraction of the amount I do on clothes."

"You say that, but I gamble every time I allow myself to get caught up in one of your elaborate schemes," Giles reckoned, "and

I risk more than a few guineas, for I put my very future at stake each time I ally myself to you. As for the clothes, well they are a little wasted on me now, I fear." Giles touched the scar upon his cheek.

"And what about enjoying yourself?" Philip never let him dwell upon his injury.

"You have me there," Giles admitted, "but William appreciates all I do for him."

"So he should, even more of late since he has learned how hard it is to manage without you," Philip said, "but, God knows, such a sickly creature will never make old bones. How do you think you will fare should Princess Anne ever reign?"

"None too well," Giles admitted, "particularly since William has decided to involve me in this dispute over her income."

"Quite. So before you exhort me to dispose of my new property perhaps you should consider rather how it might, one day, be the salvation of us all."

"All?" Giles said.

"Surely, my dear Giles, you don't think that, if affairs in England went badly for us, I would leave you to your fate?"

"I am never sure, 'my dear Philip', of quite what you would do," Giles said frankly. "You have never been exactly reliable!"

"Maybe not, but one thing I will never do is abandon you," Philip promised, "not after all we have been to each other. Our lives have run together, Giles, even though there have been times when we would rather they had not. You have shared often enough in my misfortunes and I fully intend you to share in my good luck. Unless, of course, you would prefer to return to herding slaves across the desert!" He looked over at his brother-in-law. "What I am trying to say, without becoming too sentimental, is that should the day ever come when your future looks uncertain then I will be your refuge."

"Let us hope it never comes to that," Giles said, sounding surprised and touched by his offer, "but if it should then I shall be delighted to help you grow grapes in Languedoc!"

He began to laugh, a thing Giles rarely did, for he was essentially a serious person.

"What is it?" Philip asked, struck by this unusual phenomenon.

"Why, just the vision of us as two old men, peacefully surveying their vineyard!"

Philip could not help but laugh at that thought himself. "It does not seem too likely a way for you and I to end our days," he admitted. "We will probably die of boredom! But then again," he added, thinking of the fortune teller's prediction, "there are many worse ways for a man to die."

Giles glanced at him, guessing what was passing through his mind. "These mystics are sometimes wrong, you know," he said quietly.

"I know." The moment had quickly passed and Philip brightened to see Theresa approaching them through the trees.

"I have come to fetch you for the harvest meal," she said, impulsively linking arms with her brother and her husband as they walked back to the house together. "I'm so happy, for we are all together again and everything turned out alright."

"But of course it did, my darling! When will you ever learn to trust me?" Philip demanded.

He was saved from a reply because, at that moment, they rounded a corner and came upon a tableau that affected all three.

The whole household was grouped about the garden in the sunshine. Thomas was crawling across the lawn on all fours with a laughing Madeleine riding him like a horse. Luc was fanning Marianne and chatting to her in French, whilst Ahmed cradled Giles' son in his strong arms. To complete the picture, Morgan and Bet, the mainstays of them all, were sitting close together in an attitude of unaccustomed tenderness, Bet's swollen figure showing plainly how soon she, too, was to become a mother.

"Heatherton's bounty," Theresa murmured, taking in the pretty scene, and Philip knew she was not referring just to the harvest table, heavy laden with farm produce.

She and Giles went on, soon becoming a part of the picture themselves, but Philip lingered for a moment, watching them all.

The assorted band of people in front of him meant more to Philip than they would ever know. They were his family and he was dependent upon them, just as everyone there was dependent upon him and upon each other. It was a good feeling.

As he joined the others Philip vowed that, no matter what might befall them in the uncertain years ahead, he would do his utmost to keep them together and to keep them safe.

Whether in the sunlit plains or in the distant hills beyond.

EPILOGUE

Louvois lived for only two more years but managed to remain in power to the end of his days, despite the best efforts of his enemies to destroy him.

Quietism was abolished in France within the next ten years.

Madame de Maintenon abandoned everyone connected with it.

Abbé Fénelon was made Archbishop of Cambrai and banished forever to his diocese, from where he continued to exert influence, in secret, upon the Duc de Bourgogne.

Bourgogne died of small pox at the age of thirty and never did become King of France.

Louis survived to the age of seventy-seven, having outlived both his son and grandson.

Monsieur remained handsome, outrageous and amusing. Despite his preference for his own sex, he fathered eleven children and was the 'grandfather of Europe', as most royal families could trace their ancestry back to him! His son, the Duc de Chartres, became Regent of France after Louis' death. Monsieur died, suddenly, of a stroke, when he was 61 years old.

Queen Mary did not bear William an heir. The English throne eventually passed to Mary's younger sister, Anne.

A new era had begun!

ALSO BY THE AUTHOR

Designs of a Gentleman: The Early Years

Designs of a Gentleman: The Darker Years

High Heatherton

The Orange Autumn